D0792352

GREEK MYTHS
ULYSSES AND THE TROJAN WAR

Retold by

Anna Claybourne and Kamini Khanduri

Illustrated by Jeff Anderson

Designed by Kathy Ward and Zoe Wray

Edited by Anna Claybourne

Series Editor: Felicity Brooks

CONTENTS

PART ONE: THE TROJAN WAR

PART TWO: THE ADVENTURES OF ULYSSES

CHAPTER ONE

THE BEAUTY CONTEST

"Welcome, everybody. A warm welcome to you all!" called Nereus, the sea god. He was busy greeting the last few guests to the wedding of his daughter, Thetis. The celebrations in the vast banqueting hall were already in full flow, and everybody was having a wonderful time. Thetis was marrying King Peleus, so it was quite an occasion. Hundreds of well-known people had been invited, and so had all the important gods and goddesses. All, that is, except one.

Thetis and Peleus had decided that Eris, the unpopular goddess of spite, might cause trouble and spoil their wedding day, so they had purposely left her off the guest list. But that didn't stop Eris. She turned up anyway, in a terrible rage, and stormed her way through the mingling guests.

"How dare you!" she screamed in fury, wagging a bony finger at the bride and bridegroom. "How dare you insult me like this! I suppose you thought you'd get away with it, didn't you? Well, you underestimated me, you fools! I'll make you pay for this ~ just you wait and see!"

As she spoke, she reached inside her long, black cloak and pulled out a gleaming golden apple. She hesitated briefly, looking around with a hideous scowl on her face. Then, with a shrill cackle, she flung the apple onto the floor, and flounced out of the hall.

For a moment, everyone stood there in shocked silence. Then Nereus bent down and picked up the apple. He turned it over in his hand.

"There's writing on it!" he exclaimed. " 'For the fairest'," he read aloud. "That's what it says. 'For the fairest'." He looked up. "So, who is it for then? Who's going to claim this golden apple?"

Again, there was silence. Then the deep voice of Hera, queen of the gods, rang out through the hall.

"Well, it's for me, of course! There's no doubt about it. I'm the most beautiful, so the golden apple is mine."

"Yours!" said Athene, the goddess of wisdom and war, her grey eyes flashing. "Why should it be yours? Anyone can see that the apple is meant for me."

Aphrodite, the goddess of love, was not going to stand for this. "Ladies, ladies," she purred sweetly. "What can you be thinking of? Everyone knows that when it comes to beauty, no one can compete with me. The apple is mine and that's all there is to it." And she laughed a tinkly little laugh and fluttered her unusually long eyelashes.

Feeling rather confused, all the guests turned to face Zeus. He was the king of the gods, and also Hera's husband. Whenever there was a decision to be made, he could generally be relied upon to make it.

This time, though, Zeus was in a tricky position. If he agreed that Hera was the fairest, people would accuse him of putting his own wife first. But if he chose another goddess, Hera would be wild with jealousy. So, after a few moments thought, he came up with a crafty plan.

"Why is it always me who has to make the decisions?" he grumbled. "Why not let someone else have a try? What about. . . hmmm. . . let me see. . . What's the name of that handsome shepherd who lives on Mount Ida? Paris, isn't it? Yes, Paris ~ a fine young man with impeccable taste, I'm sure. I hereby decree that Paris shall be the judge of this contest. Now, enough of this squabbling. On with the party!"

And, apart from Hera, Athene and Aphrodite exchanging the occasional hostile glance, the wedding celebrations continued without further ado.

One day, not long after the wedding, Paris was sitting on a grassy knoll on Mount Ida watching his sheep, when Hermes, the messenger of the gods, suddenly appeared. With him were Hera, Athene and Aphrodite. All three were dressed in their finest robes and looked radiantly lovely, standing there in the dazzling sunlight. Paris was speechless with fear and amazement.

"Paris," announced Hermes, "don't be afraid. Zeus has decided that you are to be the judge of a very important contest. You must give this apple to whoever you think is the most beautiful of these three goddesses."

He handed Paris the golden apple, but before the shepherd could open his mouth, Hera spoke.

"Young man," she proclaimed, in her most queenly tones, "if you choose me, as I'm sure you will, I will give you all the power and wealth you could ever ask for."

Not to be outdone, Athene chimed in, "And if you choose me, as I know you will, I will give you success in war."

Aphrodite just smiled sweetly at Paris and whispered softly in his ear, "When you choose me, I will give you the most beautiful woman in the world as your wife."

"Now make your choice," said Hermes.

Paris stood stock-still, hardly daring to breathe. He glanced nervously at the three powerful goddesses in front of him. Then,

after what seemed like a lifetime, he passed the apple to Aphrodite.

Hera and Athene were beside themselves with rage and disappointment. Hera pointed resentfully at Paris.

"A beautiful wife won't get you anywhere, you silly boy. Just you wait and see!" she fumed.

"You'll regret this," Athene added. "One day you'll wish you had me to help you. But it's your choice, I suppose!"

Then, as suddenly as they had appeared, Hera and Athene vanished, along with Hermes.

Aphrodite held the apple up to the sun and sighed happily. Then she spoke to the bewildered young shepherd.

"The most beautiful woman in the world is Helen," she told him. "She lives in Greece, at the court of Menelaus, the king of Sparta. In due course, you will go there and she will fall in love with you, just as I have promised. But now I must leave you."

With that, the goddess disappeared.

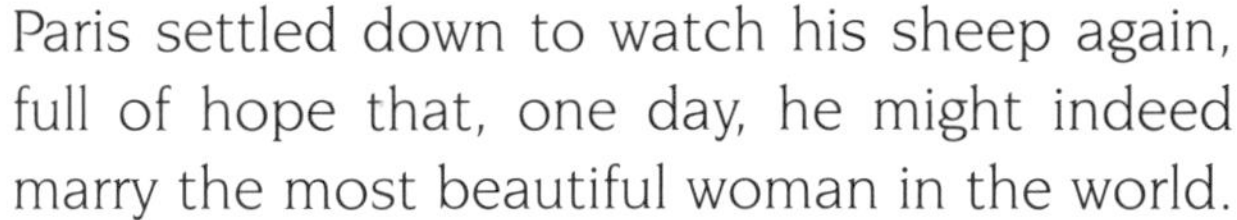

Paris settled down to watch his sheep again, full of hope that, one day, he might indeed marry the most beautiful woman in the world.

Several years passed, and Paris began to doubt that anything would come of the goddess's promise. He was becoming a little bored with his quiet shepherd's lifestyle, and yearned for some excitement, so in the end he decided to go down the mountain and visit the nearby city of Troy. He'd heard that King Priam was holding a games contest there, and Paris thought he'd like to enter.

When he arrived in the city, he followed the crowds until he reached the huge field where the games were about to begin. Paris entered as many events as he could and, to his amazement, he won nearly all of them. Years of scrambling up and down the mountainside had made his legs immensely strong, and he also discovered that he was a very fast runner. He even managed to beat Priam's own son, Hector.

"What a fine young man!" said King Priam. "I wonder who he is?"

"He looks strangely familiar," said his daughter, Cassandra. "I have a peculiar feeling that I've seen him before."

King Priam and Queen Hecuba looked at each other. Cassandra had special powers and could see things other people couldn't.

"Well, let's call him over and find out," suggested Priam.

As Paris approached, Cassandra kept her eyes fixed on his face. Then she suddenly let out a shriek, ran forward and flung her arms around his neck.

"Cassandra!" cried Hecuba, looking shocked. "What are you doing?"

"Mother, don't you recognize him? Can't you see who it is?"

"No," said Hecuba. "I've never seen him before in my life. You really are behaving very oddly, dear."

"But it's *Paris!*" said Cassandra in exasperation.

Paris was very surprised at this. How on earth did she know his name?

Meanwhile, Priam and Hecuba were staring at the swarthy youth in front of them. Many years ago, they had had a baby son, named Paris. When he was born, the gods had predicted that he would bring destruction to his own city. The king and queen loved their baby, but knew they could not risk such disaster, so they reluctantly gave orders for Paris to be taken to the nearby mountainside and left to die. Surely this boy couldn't be. . .

"Tell me, young man," said King Priam, "where are you from?"

"Mount Ida, sir," replied Paris.

"And what do you do there?"

"I'm a shepherd."

"Who are your parents?"

"My parents are dead, sir, but they were shepherds, too."

"And your name. . ?"

Paris began to feel uneasy. He had always known that the shepherds who brought him up were not his real parents. They'd explained to him that they'd found him on the hillside as a baby, and assumed he must be a gift from the gods. When Demeter, the goddess of crops and children, visited his mother in a dream to tell her the child's name, they were even more convinced.

"Well. . . " said Paris finally, "my name's Paris."

Hecuba gasped. "He must have been rescued by the shepherds," she whispered. "Oh, Priam ~ he's alive after all these years!"

The king and queen were so thrilled to be reunited with their long lost son that they put the gods' prediction out of their minds. Paris was welcomed with open arms.

The young prince spent the following few months getting to know his family. Priam was very anxious that his son shouldn't feel like an outsider, so one day, he summoned Paris to his chamber.

"My dear son," he said. "I want you to know how happy you've made us. To show you how much we love and trust you, I'm sending you on a very important mission. Many years ago, my sister, Hesione, was captured by the Greeks. Now I want you to sail to Greece and bring her back here to Troy."

Paris's heart was filled with excitement and pride. "Really?" he asked, amazed. "Are you sure you want me to go ~ not Hector?"

"Of course!" replied Priam, smiling indulgently. "It'll be your chance to prove yourself."

Paris kneeled down in front of the king. "Thank you, Father!" he beamed. "I'll do the best I can ~ I won't let you down, I promise. Just tell me when you want me to leave."

When Cassandra heard about this plan, she begged her father not to let Paris go. She said she was sure the trip would bring disaster to Troy. But now that Paris had been promised the mission, Priam didn't feel he could let him down, so he ignored Cassandra. Several days later, after a great deal of preparation, Paris set off for Greece, with a group of Priam's bravest soldiers as companions.

So much time had gone by, that Paris had almost forgotten Aphrodite's promise that he would eventually marry the most beautiful woman in the world. But the goddess herself had not forgotten. She watched over Paris very carefully, and when she saw his ship approaching the shore, she blew gently into the sail so that it veered off course and had to make an unexpected stop near Sparta, the city of King Menelaus, one of the great leaders of Greece.

When the king heard that a Trojan prince was in the area, he sent a message inviting him and his friends to visit the palace. The Trojans accepted, and on their arrival, they were met by Menelaus and his wife ~ Helen.

She truly was the most beautiful woman Paris had ever seen. Her face was perfect in every way, with a full, curvy mouth and sparkling eyes. Her thick, shiny hair flowed around her head in ringlets and curls.

But beauty had not brought Helen happiness. She did love Menelaus, but he was older than her, and sometimes she found him a little boring. She longed for some excitement and adventure.

As soon as Helen laid eyes upon the handsome young Trojan prince, she decided he was much more exciting than her husband. And when Paris saw how beautiful she was, he forgot all about rescuing Hesione. All he could think of was Helen.

Over the following ten days, Menelaus entertained the Trojans most generously. No host could have been kinder or more attentive to his guests' needs. They feasted on delicious food, and drank cup after cup of fine wine. All the time, Helen and Paris were exchanging furtive glances, longing to speak to each other in private. And before long, they got the chance.

On the tenth day of their stay, Menelaus summoned his guests.

"My friends," he said. "I have an announcement to make. An urgent message has arrived from Crete and I have to go there at once. However, there's no reason for you to leave. My dear wife is here to take care of you and see that you have all you need. I leave you in her capable hands."

That afternoon, Menelaus left for Crete. As soon as the palace gates had closed behind him, Paris sneaked away from his companions and tiptoed along the corridors to Helen's room. He found her sitting alone, combing her lovely hair. For a moment he lingered in the doorway, watching in silence. Then he coughed quietly. Helen jumped.

"Sir!" she gasped, flushing red with embarrassment. "You mustn't come to my room! It's not right. Please go back to your friends and your feasting."

Paris ignored her. He took a few steps into the room.

"Helen. . . " he said, desperately. "Helen, you must realize I'm completely in love with you. How can I possibly enjoy myself while you belong to another man?"

Helen opened her mouth to speak, but Paris went on. "I'm eaten up with jealousy every time I even think about Menelaus," he said, rushing across the room and taking Helen's hands. "Let me take you away from here, across the sea to Troy."

"Oh Paris," wailed Helen, her eyes filling up with tears. "Don't ask me to do such a thing!" She pulled away from him. "It would be terribly wrong to leave my husband and my home ~ what would people say? But. . . " she let out a strangled sob, "I can't bear the thought of you leaving. I want to be with you, Paris. Oh, what shall I do?" Tears began to roll down her cheeks, and she hid her face with her hands.

"We'll go to my father," said Paris decisively. "I'm sure he'll help us. Trust me ~ everything will be all right."

Helen felt as if she were being torn in two. She couldn't bear to think of poor Menelaus's reaction when he found out she'd gone. She knew how much he loved her, and she didn't want to hurt him.

But how often did she get the chance to be swept off her feet by such a gorgeous stranger? How could she resist Paris's good looks, and the offer of an escape from Sparta? The choice seemed impossible to make.

Paris wouldn't give up. He stayed in her room until late into the evening, begging her to go with him.

In the end, she agreed.

That night, while everyone else was asleep, Paris summoned his companions, and, along with Helen, they crept from the palace and boarded the Trojan ship. They raised the sail as quickly as they could, then, softly and silently, they sailed away over the dark blue sea.

When Menelaus returned a few days later, he strode around the palace in search of his wife and guests.

"Helen!" he called. "Where are you?"

The palace servants looked at each other nervously as they went about their work.

"Has anybody seen my wife?" Menelaus asked. No one answered.

"Well, speak up. Where is she?"

Still not one of the servants dared to say anything.

"Will somebody please tell me what is going on?" the king shouted.

At last, an old servant woman mumbled, "She's gone, sir."

"Gone? Gone where?"

"She went just after you left for Crete, sir. In the night. With the Trojan prince."

"With the Trojan prince? What are you talking about, woman?"

They crept from the palace and boarded the Trojan ship.

For a moment, Menelaus was confused. Then his confusion turned to anger as the awful truth dawned.

"Is this the same Trojan prince I welcomed into my home?" he snarled through clenched teeth. "The same Trojan prince I entertained with fine food and drink? The young, charming, handsome, well-dressed Trojan prince?" His voice rose to a bellow.

"*Traitor!*" Menelaus roared, storming through the empty hall. "So this is how he repays me! By sneaking away in the night, and taking my wife with him! Cowardly thief! He'll be sorry for this! I'll make him wish he'd never set foot in my palace!"

A faithful old servant came up and reached out kindly to the king, as if to touch his arm, but Menelaus turned away violently. There were tears in his eyes.

"Helen," he whispered to himself. "How *could* you? How could you leave me?"

He pulled himself upright and clenched his fists. When he turned back to face the servant, his features were set in a furious, determined scowl.

"THIS MEANS WAR!" he yelled suddenly. He spotted a young messenger trembling in a nearby doorway.

"You!" he ordered. "Take an urgent message to my brother, Agamemnon. Tell him to gather together all the Greek leaders. We'll raise an army ~ a huge, unbeatable army ~ the biggest army ever! And we'll sail to Troy and wage war on those Trojans until they give me back my wife. No one treats Menelaus like this. I'll get my revenge!"

And he stormed out of the palace.

Meanwhile, Paris and Helen were sailing away happily across the wide Aegean Sea. Spiteful Eris looked down on them from Mount Olympus, and gave an evil laugh.

"My plan worked!" she shrieked. "This will be the longest and bloodiest war that's ever been fought. Those puny mortals, those smug gods and goddesses ~ they'll be *very* sorry that they insulted me. Very sorry indeed."

Then, wrapping her long, black cloak tightly around her, the goddess scurried away to her cave.

CHAPTER TWO

PREPARING FOR WAR

King Agamemnon stood gazing around the army camp at Aulis, on the coast of the kingdom of Boeotia. As soon as he'd heard what had happened to Helen, he'd promised to do everything he could to help his brother Menelaus get her back.

Agamemnon was the leader of all the nations of Greece, and it was natural that he should be commander of the Greek army. Messages had been sent to all the different kingdoms, and most of the leaders had arrived at Aulis with their troops. Nestor, king of Pylos, was there, as were Diomedes and Ajax, Greek leaders famous for their bravery; and of course, Menelaus himself and his soldiers. Thousands of the strongest, fittest men in the land were camped by the shore, ready to set off for Troy.

But Agamemnon knew well that the war couldn't be won by numbers alone. He needed the strategic skills of King Ulysses of Ithaca. And he had heard the prophecy of Chiron the centaur. Chiron had foretold that the Greeks could never beat the Trojans without Achilles, the half-god, half-human son of Thetis and Peleus.

At this very moment, in fact, Agamemnon was waiting for news from his messengers. They'd been sent to get Ulysses and Achilles, and they certainly seemed to be taking their time over it.

Meanwhile, in the kingdom of Ithaca, Ulysses and his wife Penelope were having supper. They'd finished their main course of roast boar, and were starting on some fruit, when there was a loud banging on the palace gates.

"Whoever can that be?" exclaimed Penelope. "I hope they haven't woken Telemachus."

Just then a servant appeared in the doorway.

"Sir," he said, "there's a soldier here with an urgent message for you. He's come all the way from Aulis."

"Very well," said Ulysses. "Show him in."

The soldier marched into the hall, took a deep breath and recited this message:

"King Ulysses! Come to Aulis at once with your army. The Trojans have stolen Menelaus's wife. We are sailing to Troy to wage war on them. Remember your oath. From King Agamemnon of Mycenae."

As the news sank in, Ulysses sat up, looking shocked. He glanced at Penelope.

"Oh, Ulysses," his wife whispered. "You *can't* go ~ you might be away for years."

"But the oath. . . " he said.

Before Helen had married Menelaus, many of the other Greek leaders, including Ulysses, had wanted to marry her because she was so beautiful. Helen's father had chosen Menelaus as her husband, and to make sure the marriage lasted he had made all her other admirers take an oath. They had to vow to leave Helen alone, and to help Menelaus to get her back if anyone ever kidnapped her. A few years later, Ulysses had fallen in love with Penelope, and since then, he hadn't given Helen another thought. Until now.

"I can't break my oath," he whispered to his wife. "But it seems ridiculous to go to war over this. It'll blow over soon anyway. I mean," he added, reassuring himself, "they can't really need me, can they?"

He turned to the messenger. "Tell King Agamemnon I'll. . . send him my reply very soon," he said.

As soon as the messenger had left, he set to work on a plan.

Several months later, there was another loud knock on the gate. When Penelope was called, she found a group of soldiers standing there.

"Queen Penelope?" said their leader.

"Yes," she replied.

"My name is Palamedes, my lady, and I've been sent by Menelaus. We're here to collect your husband."

"Ah yes," answered the queen in an odd voice. "Just wait a minute ~ I'll go and get him."

She slipped back into the palace, leaving the soldiers waiting outside. After some time, they became impatient, and were about to knock again when Penelope reappeared with her baby son, Telemachus, in her arms.

"I'm so sorry," she said, smiling awkwardly. "My husband's in rather a strange mood. . . he seems to have

decided to go and work in the fields. Come with me."

She led them around the palace to the fields at the back. In the distance, they saw Ulysses steering a pair of oxen. He was walking along behind them, sowing seeds in the furrows they made. The soldiers watched curiously as he came closer. Then Palamedes turned to Penelope. "Is your husband quite all right, my lady?" he asked.

Penelope shrugged.

"I mean," Palamedes went on, "what's he doing sowing the fields? Surely that's servants' work?"

"Wait a minute," said another soldier, peering at the king. "He's not even sowing grain! It looks like some kind of white powder instead."

Penelope sighed.

"Yes," she said wearily. "I think it's salt. I'm afraid he's not been himself over the last few months. His mind is. . . well. . ." Her eyes filled with tears and she lowered her voice. "The physicians say he's insane. You won't make him go to war, will you? I really don't think he's up to it. He certainly couldn't be relied upon to make any sensible decisions."

Palamedes scratched his head. He hadn't heard anything about Ulysses losing his mind. Surely the news would have spread if it were true? He gazed out over the field. As he did so, Ulysses glanced up and their eyes met. Something about the other man's expression made Palamedes suspicious.

"Madam," he said to Penelope. "Could I hold your baby for a minute?"

Penelope looked surprised, but passed Telemachus to the soldier.

Palamedes began to walk across the field. When he was standing in Ulysses's path, a little way in front of him, he bent down and gently laid the baby on the ground. Then he stepped aside.

Ulysses drove the oxen closer and closer to the spot where the child was lying. The two huge creatures lurched nearer, their hooves spiking the earth. The baby kicked his legs and gurgled happily.

When the oxen were inches from the baby's head, Penelope screamed "*Ulysses*!" Palamedes winced and looked away.

Then, at the very last second, just before the beasts trampled right over the tiny child, Ulysses let out a dreadful roar, and frantically hit the animals with his stick, forcing them to swerve to one side.

There was a moment of silence. Then the baby began to wail loudly. As Ulysses ran to comfort him, Palamedes trudged slowly back to the edge of the field.

"Your husband's a very clever madman," he said to Penelope. The soldiers smiled, and Penelope looked at the ground.

Now Ulysses had no choice. A few days later, he said a tearful farewell to his son, and to his parents, Laertes and Anticleia, who had only recently handed over the throne to him.

Hardest of all, though, was saying goodbye to his beloved wife. Hugging her tightly, he promised to return as soon as he possibly could.

"You will be careful, won't you?" Penelope sobbed.

"I will," he promised, kissing her a final time. "Try not to worry."

As a leaving present, Penelope gave him a golden brooch, showing a hunting scene with a hound and a deer. Then, with it pinned to his cloak, Ulysses finally boarded his ship, and left for Aulis with an army of men.

In another part of Greece, the goddess Thetis was soaring through the air on her way to the island of Skyros, clinging tightly to her son, Achilles.

"Where are we going?" he shouted, the wind whipping his face. "Can't we slow down?"

"No," snapped Thetis. Then, when she saw his annoyed expression, she added, "I'm sorry, but there's no time to lose. The Greeks have been planning this war for some time. They'll come looking for you soon."

"Do they want me because I'm such a good soldier?" asked Achilles. Although he was still young, Achilles had a high opinion of himself, especially when it came to using weapons. His teacher, Chiron, the old centaur, had trained him to be a deadly fighter.

"Probably," said Thetis kindly. She couldn't tell Achilles the real reason she had to hide him away ~ Chiron's prediction. The centaur had not only said that the Greek army would need Achilles if they were going to capture the city of Troy; he'd also foretold that Achilles would die fighting there.

At first, Thetis wasn't too worried. After all, Achilles was no ordinary boy. When he was a baby, she'd taken him to the magical River Styx. She'd kneeled down on the riverbank and, holding him carefully by his tiny heel, had dipped his body in the swirling water.

"There!" she'd whispered, pulling him out and wrapping him in a warm blanket. "Now you'll live forever ~ just like me."

Thetis had never told her husband, Peleus, what she'd done. He was just a human being, and didn't understand the importance of these things. But it made Thetis feel much happier knowing that she'd made her precious son immortal.

Now, though, with all this talk of a war, she couldn't afford to take any chances ~ even though she was sure Achilles couldn't be killed. She had to hide him.

"Are we nearly at Skyros yet?" asked Achilles impatiently.

"Yes, dear," said Thetis, kissing his cheek. "We're nearly there. And I'm going to make sure no one will find you."

One hot afternoon at Aulis, Ulysses burst into Agamemnon's tent.

"Sir!" he said. "Sorry to disturb you, but there's something you should know."

Agamemnon looked up. Here was someone he was always pleased to see. From the moment he'd reached Aulis, Ulysses had thrown himself into the preparations with great enthusiasm. Agamemnon relied on his intelligence and bright ideas. If only they could find Achilles, Agamemnon thought, they could get going and set off for Troy.

"What is it, Ulysses?" he asked.

"There's a story going around that Achilles might be on Skyros, at the court of King Lycomedes. I wondered if you wanted me to go there to try to track him down?"

Agamemnon's eyes lit up. "You must go at once," he said.

Ulysses soon arrived at Skyros, laden with gifts for King Lycomedes and his daughters. After laying these out on a long wooden table, he began to question his host.

"Is there a young man named Achilles at your court?" he asked.

"No," replied Lycomedes, pouring his guest a cup of wine. "I've never met him. But his sister's here. She's one of the young ladies over there with my daughters."

He pointed to the group of girls who were clustered around the table, shrieking with

"Where are we going?" he shouted

delight as they examined the glittering jewels and fine embroidered fabrics.

"Which one is she?" asked Ulysses.

"The one at the back ~ the tall one," said Lycomedes, wondering why his guest was so curious about this particular young lady.

Ulysses looked across the room and saw the girl at once. She was taller than the others, and didn't seem interested in the gifts. In fact, she looked bored. She gazed out of the window as if she would rather be outside.

When she glanced at her companions, something seemed to catch her eye. She moved nearer to the table, and, watched closely by Ulysses, stretched out her hand. From under the folds of a sumptuous red cloak, she pulled out a sword with a gleaming bronze blade and a hilt studded with jewels.

Ulysses waited. The girl lifted the weapon up from the table, raised it above her head and, for a moment, held it motionless. Then, suddenly, she sliced the blade through the air, in one graceful sweep.

"Achilles!" Ulysses called out.

The girl spun around, the sword still in her hand. The expression of boredom had disappeared, and now her eyes shone with excitement. Ulysses knew his suspicion had been right. The 'girl' was Achilles himself in disguise. Thetis had put a spell on him so that no one would recognize him. But the spell had been broken the moment Achilles had heard his own name, and soon everyone wondered how they had ever mistaken this tall, handsome young man for a girl.

In the midst of the confusion, Ulysses managed to guide Achilles into a quiet corner of the room. He explained to the boy that he was needed in the war against Troy. Achilles was more than willing. He had hated pretending to be a girl, and longed for some action. The idea of a war thrilled him. Without a moment's hesitation, he agreed to go.

At last, Agamemnon was ready to leave for Troy. A thousand large ships loaded with supplies were lined up along the shore at Aulis, and over a hundred thousand men were gathered at the camp. They'd come from all corners of Greece, tramping for months across rough ground, over steep mountains, and through thick forests.

Most had started out full of energy and keen to fight. But as the weeks had turned to months and the months to years, they'd grown bored and frustrated. Rumbles of discontent had spread around the camp, and Agamemnon knew that if the war didn't start soon, there'd be trouble.

But there was still one problem ~ there was no wind. And without wind, the ships couldn't sail. Dreading the idea of more delays, Agamemnon had summoned old Calchas, the soothsayer, in the hope that he'd be able to explain.

"Where in Zeus's name is he?" muttered Agamemnon, drumming his fingers impatiently on the table.

Menelaus went to look outside.

"He's on his way," he said, as he came back in. "He's shuffling across the field, mumbling some nonsense to himself."

A few minutes later, there was a rustling in the doorway.

"Ah, Calchas," Agamemnon said. "Here you are at last. Come in, come in. Now, you probably know why we've called you here. It's this wind ~ it just won't start blowing. Any idea what the problem is?"

"Er. . . yes. . . but, to be honest, sir, it's not very good news," said Calchas.

"Not good news? What are you talking about?" the king demanded.

"Well. . . it's Artemis," Calchas said, nervously.

"Artemis? The goddess of hunting? What's she got to do with it?"

"She's angry with you," said Calchas.

"Angry? With me? What on earth for?"

"You've killed one of her sacred deer. Apparently," Calchas added hurriedly.

Agamemnon laughed loudly. "More likely she's jealous because I'm a better hunter than her!" he snorted.

"Sir!" gasped Calchas. "If she hears you saying that, there's no telling what she'll do. You know what a temper she has."

"All right, all right, I'll try to make amends. What does she want? An old goat sacrificed to her and a lot of weeping and praying?" Agamemnon smiled to himself ~ gods and goddesses were so predictable. "I'm right, aren't I?"

"Well, not exactly, sir," mumbled Calchas.

"Not exactly? Not exactly? Then what exactly, you old fool? Come on, I haven't got all day. Get to the point."

"Agamemnon. . ." Menelaus began. "Let's not argue. Do whatever Artemis wants, so we can set off."

"Absolutely," said Agamemnon. "Come on Calchas, I do have a war to fight, you know. Just tell me how to please Artemis, so she'll make the wind blow. Then we all can get on with the job in hand!"

Calchas took a deep breath.

"She *does* want you to make a sacrifice," he began.

"There! I knew it!" crowed the king.

"But she won't be satisfied with a goat," continued Calchas.

"All right, two goats, ten goats, a cow, a flock of sheep ~ what, in the name of the gods, does she want?"

"Your daughter," blurted Calchas.

Agamemnon stared at him.

"What?"

"She wants your daughter, Iphigenia," Calchas repeated.

"Iphigenia?" Agamemnon asked. He was almost whispering. "Iphigenia?"

He looked confused, frightened and suddenly much older. He gazed around the tent, as if he hoped the other leaders might be able to help.

"I. . . I. . . there must be some mistake," he pleaded, turning to Calchas.

The soothsayer raised his head and looked Agamemnon in the eye.

"No, sir," he said sadly. "There's no mistake. Artemis will only forgive you if you sacrifice your daughter."

"But ~ how can I? I mean ~ she's just a young girl. She's never harmed anyone in her life. She won't understand. What will I say to her? How will I explain?" Then a look of absolute horror flickered across his face. "What will I tell her *mother*?"

No one said anything. There wasn't anything they could say. Agamemnon just stared vacantly into space for a few seconds. Then he stood up, and with a last, desperate glance at Calchas, he gathered his cloak around his shoulders, picked up his helmet and walked slowly and unsteadily out of the tent.

The news spread like wildfire, from man to man and from tent to tent. Soon, the whole camp buzzed with snatches of gossip:

"Have you heard? Agamemnon has to sacrifice his daughter."

"They say he's trying to get out of it, but the others are insisting it's the only way we'll get to Troy. . ."

"But his own daughter. . . "

"He's sent for the girl ~ told her mother he's found her a husband!"

"Imagine! Coming all this way thinking you're going to meet your husband. . . "

"The way I see it, there's a thousand ships ready to go, and a lot of angry men ready to fight. If Agamemnon calls off the war, they might just turn against him. . ."

"The girl's arrived. She's very pretty."

"The mother's found out. She's raging around like a madwoman. . ."

"The daughter's weeping and begging her father. He must be a hard-hearted man."

"I've just heard ~ it's official. The sacrifice is tomorrow, on the shore. You'll have to be early if you want a good view. . ."

Iphigenia stood beside the makeshift altar, her face half-hidden behind her long, dark hair. She was no longer crying ~ she had used up all her tears pleading with her father. He had told her that, although it broke his heart, he had to obey Artemis. Iphigenia couldn't understand it. She'd always been so sure that her father loved her more than anything in the world. Surely he wouldn't do such a terrible thing?

Her mother, Clytemnestra, stood beside her, seething with rage. She would not look at her husband, but her eyes burned with hatred. One day, she vowed, she'd make him pay for putting his country before their child.

Agamemnon showed no emotion. But those who looked closely saw that as he picked up the knife, his hand was shaking.

With almost the whole Greek army watching from a respectful distance, he slowly approached his daughter.

"Silence!" called a herald.

The crowd hardly breathed. The only sound came from the waves lapping against the shore as Iphigenia closed her eyes and bent her head forward. Agamemnon raised the knife, while Clytemnestra, powerless to intervene, shook with grief and fury.

There was a moment of stillness. Agamemnon swallowed hard and tightened his grip on the handle. The blade glistened in the morning sun as it started to move. . .

Suddenly there was a huge flash of light. The knife clattered to the ground, and Agamemnon stepped back in fright. Iphigenia screamed, then vanished into thin air. And there, in front of the altar, instead of the girl, was a baby deer!

As the crowd gasped in amazement, Clytemnestra looked wildly around until her eye fell upon Calchas.

"What's happening?" she screamed. "Where's my daughter?"

Calchas sighed and slowly made his way to the altar. After inspecting the deer closely, he said, "I think it's all right, madam. Yes ~ everything seems to be all right."

"All right? What do you mean, all right? She's disappeared! How on earth can that be all right?" shouted Clytemnestra.

"She'll be safe now. No one will harm her. Artemis must have taken pity on her at the last minute and decided to make do with a deer instead. I've seen this happen before," nodded Calchas wisely.

"But where *is* she?" Clytemnestra hissed, infuriated at the old man's slowness.

"She's probably been taken to one of Artemis's temples, to be a priestess. That's what usually happens in cases like this."

"And when will I see her again?"

There was a pause.

"You probably won't, Madam. But you can be sure that she'll be well looked after."

Clytemnestra was speechless. First she'd had to face up to her daughter being sacrificed, then she'd seen her vanish before her very eyes, and now this irritating old man was saying she'd never see her again. It was all too much.

She silenced Calchas with a withering glance. She glared resentfully, her eyes blazing with anger and sorrow, at her husband. Then, taking a last, long look at the altar, Clytemnestra began to walk back to the tents.

When she was some distance away, Agamemnon turned to Calchas.

"So what do we do now?" he asked wearily. "I've lost my daughter and there's still no wind blowing."

"We sacrifice the deer instead," replied the old man. So they quickly performed the sacrifice to Artemis, following Calchas's instructions.

Agamemnon held his breath. At first, nothing happened. Then he became aware of a gentle breeze on his face.

"It's not strong enough," he said to Calchas. "I can hardly feel it."

"Be patient, sir," replied the soothsayer calmly, heaving the dead deer onto the fire. Agamemnon felt the breeze ruffle his hair. Then, very, very slowly, the smoke started billowing out across the sand, and the dry grass that grew behind the beach started to sway from side to side.

"At last!" whispered Agamemnon. "At last!" And, heaving a huge sigh of relief, he began to hurry back to the camp.

The wind grew stronger throughout the day, and, by the next morning, it was blowing hard. The goddess Artemis had kept to her promise. The conditions were perfect.

So, several years after the Trojan prince, Paris, had stolen away with Helen in the middle of the night, an army of one hundred thousand Greek men climbed on board ship, and sails were unfurled.

Not knowing what horrors or glories might await them there, uncertain whether they would ever win back the beautiful Helen, but full of excitement and ready for war, the soldiers gazed ahead at the horizon as a thousand Greek ships set sail for Troy.

CHAPTER THREE

THE ARGUMENT

Achilles stood in the doorway of his tent, gazing out at the world. The sun was high in the sky, and all around was the hustle and bustle of the Greek camp. Away to the east, across a wide grassy plain, stood the high walls and towers of the city of Troy itself.

Achilles sighed and cast his mind back. He remembered the long sea crossing from Greece; his first glimpse of this land, and the daunting sight of the fortified city. What excitement he'd felt, as they disembarked and unloaded the horses, weapons and supplies! How certain he'd been that they would fight their way into the city and capture it; how proudly he had led his soldiers into battle!

He turned and looked across the plain. Somewhere among those golden towers was Helen herself. Perhaps she was wandering through a sunlit room, or resting in a walled garden, away from the noise of the war. Achilles felt frustrated. Menelaus's beautiful wife ~ the cause of all this conflict ~ was so near, and yet so impossible to reach.

"We must find a way in," he muttered, as he stepped back into the tent. "We must."

"What's that?" asked his closest friend, Patroclus, who was mending his bow.

"I just can't believe we've been here all this time and still haven't found a way into Troy," said Achilles.

"No one could accuse us of not trying," said Patroclus.

"I know," sighed Achilles. Patroclus was right. Whenever the Trojan army marched out of the gates to defend their city, the Greeks were there on the plain, fighting as hard as they could.

"But they always seem to force us back," continued Patroclus. "I don't know how they do it ~ their army's half the size of ours. Still, if anyone can beat them, it's you."

Achilles smiled.

"You're by far our best soldier," said Patroclus. "Everyone says so."

For a moment, Achilles let his mind wander. The noise of battle filled his head: swords clashing against shields, arrows whistling through the air, voices shouting orders. His muscles grew tense. "If only I could find Paris on the battlefield," he thought. "I'd like to see how long that cowardly, wife-stealing little traitor would last against my sword."

For a moment, Achilles let his mind wander. . .

The noise of battle filled his head

Patroclus interrupted his daydream.

"Maybe," he suggested thoughtfully, "maybe we're doing something wrong. Maybe Agamemnon's not keeping the gods happy."

Suddenly a shout went up from outside.

"The gates are opening! The Trojans are coming out!"

"Good!" said Achilles. "Pass me my helmet. This time I'm really going to go for it!"

"Maybe tomorrow we'll be marching triumphantly through Troy!" grinned Patroclus, standing aside to let Achilles pass.

"Let's hope so," said Achilles, gritting his teeth as he stepped out into the sunlight.

Meanwhile, on the slopes of Mount Olympus, where the gods lived, Apollo, the god of the sun, was lazing under an olive tree strumming his lyre. Sparrows chirped in the branches, and a breeze rustled the leaves.

As his fingers brushed the strings of the instrument, Apollo hummed a tune.

"La la da daaaa. . . "

He paused for a minute. Something had distracted him. He listened hard, but heard nothing.

"La la da daaaaaa. . . "

He stopped again. This time, he was certain he'd heard something. Sure enough, after a few moments, the faint sound of a human voice came wafting through the air.

"Apollo!" it called. "Lord Apollo, can you hear me?"

Apollo groaned. It was Chryses, the priest at one of his temples.

"Oh, what does he want!" grumbled Apollo, placing his lyre carefully on the grass and struggling to his feet to hear properly.

"Apollo! It's Chryses. Are you there?"

"Yes, I'm here!" the god shouted back. "What's the matter?"

"It's my daughter," replied Chryses. "The Greek soldiers came rampaging through the country and raided the temple, and they've taken her away. They stole your statue and some treasure. . . and then. . . " his voice quivered, "they found Chryseis ~ my lovely daughter ~ crying behind the altar. I begged them to leave her, but they dragged her back to their camp."

Apollo frowned. "Have you tried speaking to someone in charge?" he asked.

"Yes," replied Chryses. "I gathered up all the treasures I had left, and went to see King Agamemnon. I pleaded with him to give back my daughter, and offered him a whole sackful of gifts. But. . . but. . . "

"But what?" asked Apollo gently.

Chryses sounded shaky. "He said the soldiers had given Chryseis to him," he said, "and he liked her so much, he wanted her as his special servant. He even said he was going to take her back to Greece with him!" Chryses' voice rose to a wail.

"Does Agamemnon realize who you are?" asked Apollo.

"Yes he does," replied Chryses. "I told him I was one of your priests and that you'd be angry if he didn't give my daughter back."

"I *am* angry," said Apollo. "Leave it with me. I'll deal with it ~ don't you worry."

Back at the Greek camp, Agamemnon was getting impatient. He'd called all the other leaders to his tent for an urgent meeting with Calchas the soothsayer. But Calchas, as usual, was late.

"Where is he?" he grumbled. "As if we all have time to sit around waiting for him!"

"He's an old man, sir," said Achilles. "I suppose he can't walk very fast."

Agamemnon snorted. "Well, I'm tired of waiting. We'll start without him. Ulysses, what's the latest news on this sickness?"

In the past few days, a deadly disease had spread through the camp. Ulysses had been trying to find out what was causing it.

"It's horrible," he shuddered. "I still don't know what it is, but I know I don't want to catch it. They all have the same symptoms ~ exhaustion, shaking limbs, staring eyes. Then they keel over and die. And the whole process happens within a day. I've never seen anything like it before."

Agamemnon frowned. His brother Menelaus looked worried. "I hope the gods are on our side, Agamemnon," he began. "You haven't done anything to upset them again, have you? I mean—"

"Calchas, there you are!" Agamemnon interrupted. "Here at last. Come on in."

Calchas hovered in the doorway, leaning on his stick and looking around nervously. Then, with everyone's eyes on him, he hobbled to the middle of the tent.

"Now," said Agamemnon briskly, "I'm sure you know about this strange sickness that's spreading around the camp. Well, I want to know why it's happening and how to put a stop to it."

Calchas tried to stay calm. He cleared his throat, but as he spoke he couldn't get rid of the tremor in his voice.

"It's Apollo, sir," he mumbled.

"What?" shouted the king. "I can't hear you. Speak up."

"I said, it's Apollo!" said Calchas, far too loudly.

"Apollo? What about Apollo?"

"He's angry with you," said Calchas.

"Oh," said Agamemnon, looking slightly embarrassed and avoiding his brother's eyes. "What have I done this time? Come on, come on, spit it out!"

"It's to do with your new servant girl, sir ~ Chryseis." Calchas paused and glanced warily at Agamemnon. The king said nothing, so the old man continued:

"Her father was very upset that you wouldn't give her back, so he told Apollo. Apollo was so angry, he sent a plague. That's why all the soldiers are dying."

"So what do I have to do to be forgiven?" Agamemnon asked huffily. "Another sacrifice, I suppose?"

"No," said Calchas. "He just wants you to give the girl back to her father."

At this, Agamemnon looked annoyed. "I don't think that'll be necessary," he said decisively. "A sacrifice would be much more suitable, I'm sure."

The truth was, Agamemnon wanted to keep Chryseis. She was an excellent servant, and she was also very beautiful. Agamemnon liked the idea that, as commander, he should have the best-looking servant girl of all.

There was a pause. Then Achilles spoke. "Sir," he said. "You have other servant girls. Is she really so special?"

"Are you arguing with me?" Agamemnon growled.

"No. . ." protested Achilles. "It's just that with so many men dying, it seems only right to give the girl back."

"Oh, it seems only right, does it?" said the king in icy tones. "Well, Achilles. I'll tell you what I'll do. I'll give the girl back ~ on one condition."

Achilles looked pleased ~ he hadn't thought Agamemnon would give in so easily.

"What's that?" he asked.

"That you give me your girl instead," Agamemnon replied.

"Look," Menelaus intervened, "let's not get into a fight. There's a lot at stake ~ we should concentrate on the war and getting Helen back."

"He's right," added Ulysses wisely. "We'll never win if we stand here bickering."

Agamemnon ignored them.

"I've seen that girl of yours around," he went on, still talking to Achilles.

"She's very pretty, isn't she? Not quite as pretty as Chryseis, of course, but she'll do. What's her name? Bristia? Brismene?"

"It's Briseis," said Achilles quietly.

"Ah, Briseis. Yes. Good. Well, that's all right then."

"Sir," said Achilles. "I can't agree to this."

"What do you mean, you can't agree!" exploded the king. "I don't care whether you agree or not. I'm in charge here. I make the decisions and I say the discussion is over."

He looked around the tent. "You can all go now."

Achilles went white. He took a breath as if to speak again, but the king spoke first.

"I said, you can GO!" he roared.

"Sir," Achilles said, shaking with rage. "If you do this, I will withdraw from the fighting and order my soldiers to follow me."

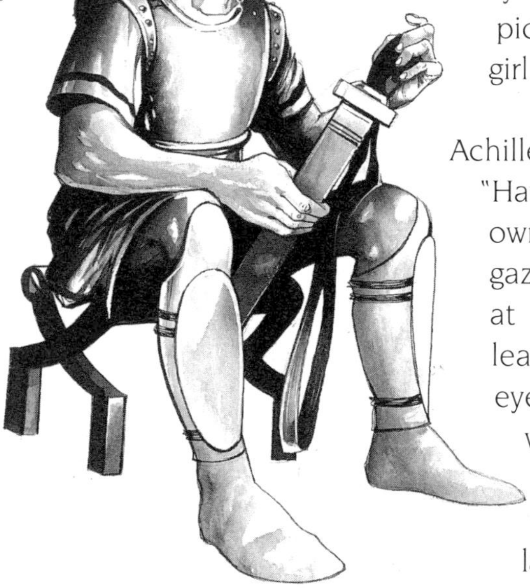

"Do what you like," Agamemnon retorted. "I'll send my heralds to pick up the girl."

"All right," Achilles fumed. "Have it your own way." He gazed around at the other leaders, his eyes flashing with anger. Then, with one last furious glance in Agamemnon's direction, he stood up and stormed out of the tent.

Achilles's mother, the goddess Thetis, was perched on a rock in the Aegean Sea, watching the dolphins. She loved the way they leaped out of the water, their bodies so graceful and streamlined. When they swam up and surrounded her rock, she reached out and patted the nearest one. As it swam off, Thetis decided she would turn herself into a dolphin.

She was just getting to her feet when she suddenly shivered.

Thetis knew what that strange feeling meant. Something was wrong with Achilles.

She could always tell when her son was in trouble, and now all her efforts to keep him away from the war had failed, it could be something serious.

Right away, Thetis turned herself into a seagull, and flew as fast as she could across the sea to the Trojan shore. She saw the Greek ships lined up on the beach below, and swooped down to the camp. Landing softly just outside Achilles's tent, she quickly changed back to her normal shape and stepped inside.

Achilles was sitting on the ground, staring sulkily at the floor. He looked up grumpily when he heard the tent flap rustle, and was startled to see his mother.

"Mother? What are you doing here?" he demanded.

Thetis bustled over and hugged him.

"Just looking after my little boy, that's all," she twittered. She was relieved to find he wasn't hurt. "What's wrong, my darling?"

"Nothing," mumbled Achilles.

"Now come on, dear," Thetis said. "I'm your mother! I know something's up."

"It's Agamemnon," shouted Achilles suddenly. "How dare he treat me like this? I'm his finest soldier ~ everyone says so ~ you'd think he'd respect me. Instead. . ."

Achilles was so cross, he almost burst into tears.

What?" asked Thetis. "What did he do to my poor boy?"

So Achilles told his mother all about the argument, and how the king's heralds had come to his tent and taken Briseis away.

"And I've refused to fight any more," he concluded. "I've withdrawn my soldiers and I hope the army's struggling without us. I never thought I'd say that ~ I did want us to capture Troy ~ but he's made me furious. . . treating me like a nobody, shouting at me as if I were a child ~ how dare he?"

"It's outrageous, that's what it is!" agreed Thetis. "That stupid commander just doesn't appreciate you, and I've a good mind to tell him so! In fact," she murmured, a sly smile spreading across her face, "I'd like to teach him a proper lesson."

"Mother. . ." said Achilles anxiously. "Don't do anything silly, will you?"

"Silly? Me?" said Thetis. "Of course not. I'll just pull a few strings, that's all! You leave it to me, dear." And she was gone.

It was early in the morning, and up on Mount Olympus, Zeus was trying to sit very still on his throne while Aphrodite combed the tangles out of his hair.

"Do stop fidgeting, Father!" she scolded.

"Well, it's taking so long," grumbled Zeus. "And it hurts!"

"If you'd let me comb it more often, it wouldn't get so tangled. I comb mine every day and see how smooth and silky it is?"

Aphrodite tossed her head so that her dark hair tumbled over her shoulders. Zeus smiled. He was just about to tell her how pretty she was when Hermes marched in.

"There's someone here to see you, Father," he announced loudly.

"Who is it?" asked Zeus. "Ah, Thetis! What a nice surprise. What can I do for you?"

Thetis kneeled at Zeus's feet.

"Oh Zeus, it's Achilles," she began. "He's been treated so badly by Agamemnon, and I was wondering if you might be able to help?" She squeezed his hand imploringly.

"That depends on what you want me to do," said Zeus, peering anxiously at the doorway. If Hera came in and saw Thetis holding his hand, there would be trouble.

"I want you to let the Trojans win the war," said Thetis. "To punish Agamemnon."

"Ah," said Zeus, scratching his beard. "I'm not sure Hera would be happy about that ~ you know she hates the Trojans after all that business with Paris and the apple."

"Well don't tell her then!" suggested Aphrodite, beaming at Thetis.

"Hmm. . . I don't know," said Zeus. "The Trojans did steal Helen."

"Please," begged Thetis, gazing up at him. "It breaks my heart to see my son so unhappy." And her eyes filled with tears.

"All right, all right," said Zeus kindly. "Leave it with me. Ah, that'll be Hera," he said, hearing familiar footsteps. He shook off Thetis's hand and jumped to his feet. "I think I'll go and meet her."

As he hurried out, Athene, the goddess of wisdom and war, entered the room. Her grey eyes stared suspiciously at Aphrodite and Thetis, who were smiling coyly.

"What's going on?" she demanded. "You're not interfering in the war, I hope?"

"Oh, it's not us," laughed Thetis. "It's not our fault if Zeus decides to help the Trojans along a little, is it, Aphrodite dear?"

"But the Greeks should win!" said Athene angrily. "You know they're the ones who've been wronged!"

"We don't know any such thing," said Aphrodite sweetly. And taking Thetis by the arm, she swept out of the room.

CHAPTER FOUR

THE DUEL

Deep inside the city of Troy, Helen was standing at her loom weaving a big, bright wall hanging. She'd been working on it ever since she'd arrived at King Priam's palace many years before.

At first, she'd been happy enough. Paris's family were kind to her, and she was so excited about being with him that she didn't really care where she was.

But as time had passed, she'd begun to feel a little homesick. Paris seemed to spend most of his days out with his friends, and Helen had to admit that he wasn't as wonderful as she'd first thought. Sometimes she even missed Menelaus, and she often felt guilty about leaving him.

Then the war had started. The dreadful, violent war. Hundreds of men had lost their lives, and all because of her. She'd begun to weave pictures into her work, showing scenes from the war ~ pictures of Greeks and Trojans fighting and killing each other. Somehow, it made her feel better.

As she bent down to select a new spool of thread from her basket, Andromache burst into the room. Her eyes were shining and she was clearly out of breath.

"I thought I'd find you here," she said, glancing scornfully at the wall hanging. "Can't you find something more useful to do?"

Andromache was married to Paris's brother, Hector. But unlike her husband, she wasn't very fond of Helen, and blamed her for all Troy's troubles. Seeing Andromache always made Helen feel guilty. She knew Hector spent a lot more time on the battlefield than Paris did.

"I have some news I think you should know about," continued Andromache. "The men have been complaining to Hector, saying they're tired of fighting and asking him to do something about it. He's so brave ~ do you know what he did? In the middle of a battle, he walked between the two armies, holding up his spear and shouting for silence. And they all went quiet and listened. Then he suggested to the Greek leaders that there should be a duel, and they've agreed to it!"

"A duel?" said Helen in surprise. "But who will he fight?"

"It won't be Hector fighting, you silly goose," said Andromache. "It'll be your darling Paris. And he'll be fighting Menelaus."

Helen felt a pang of guilt at the sound of her husband's name.

"But why?" she asked innocently, although of course, she knew. "Why are they fighting a duel?"

"Oh, why do you think?" snapped Andromache. "To try to end the war, of course. And guess what prize the lucky winner gets?"

"I. . . I don't know," stammered Helen.

"He gets you!" crowed Andromache. "You're the prize!"

Blushing, Helen pretended to rummage in her basket again. She wished Andromache would stop tormenting her. But to her despair, Andromache continued.

"Both sides have agreed to stop fighting so the duel can take place," she said. "It's so exciting, don't you think? This is the first truce since the war began ~ and the first chance for peace."

"But. . . does Paris want to fight a duel?" asked Helen.

"I don't think Hector gave him any choice!" laughed Andromache.

"When's it going to start?"

"Any minute now," said Andromache as she left the room. "Priam's gone up to one of the towers to watch."

Helen stood and hesitated for a moment. Then she picked up her cloak and hurried out of the palace.

When she came to the city wall, King Priam and some of the other old men were up on the tower, waiting for the duel to begin.

Helen rarely left the palace, and they were surprised to see her climbing the steps. As she approached, her hair shimmered in the sunlight.

"Well," one old man remarked, "she really is a beauty ~ no wonder they're all fighting over her."

"She's brought us nothing but trouble," his companion muttered.

Priam smiled. He knew that many of his people blamed Helen for all the misery the war had caused, but he was still fond of her.

"Helen, my dear," he called gently. "Have you heard? There's going to be a duel." He took her trembling arm as she approached.

"So it's true," she said, quietly. "I suppose it's a good thing if it helps to end the war, but. . . oh, sometimes I wish Paris and I had never met!"

Priam too had wished this many times, but he didn't want to say so. He just said, "Well, maybe this duel will settle things one way or another."

Helen looked the other way, hoping that Priam wouldn't see the tears in her eyes. How could she explain that, though she had run away from Menelaus, she hated the thought of Paris killing him? But neither did she have any wish to see Paris meet an early death on the plain below. She couldn't bear the thought of either of the two men dying for her sake.

As she gazed down at the troops, she realized with a shock

that she recognized some of the Greek soldiers. There was King Ulysses! Helen remembered him well ~ he'd been one of her admirers. And there was Agamemnon, her brother-in-law, the leader of the Greek army. Helen searched for Menelaus, but couldn't spot him.

Suddenly a loud cry went up from the old men nearby.

"They're ready! It's about to begin!"

Helen couldn't stand this any more. Leaving them jostling for the best position on the wall, she slipped away and hurried back to the palace.

Meanwhile, down on the plain, Menelaus was eager to start fighting. He paced to and fro impatiently while Hector and Ulysses measured out the ground. At last he had a chance to get his revenge on the man who had stolen his wife. Paris might be better-looking, but Menelaus was older, and a more experienced fighter. He'd survived similar duels in the past and knew what to expect: each man had just one chance with his spear. After that, it was down to a swordfight.

He glanced over to where his rival was waiting, surrounded by Trojan soldiers. As he watched, Paris took off his big bronze helmet, ran his fingers through his dark curls, then put the helmet on again.

Menelaus scowled in disgust and tightened his grip on his long, bronze-tipped spear. He could hardly wait.

"Everything is ready!" Agamemnon shouted. "We've drawn lots and Paris is to throw first."

Menelaus nodded. He took a deep breath and strode purposefully over to the position that had been marked for him. Paris took up his place opposite, and the rest of the soldiers stood some distance away, each army behind its own contestant.

Menelaus looked on calmly as Paris prepared himself. Even though the younger man was to throw first, he was feeling confident. He trusted in his mighty shield, and in Paris's lack of ability.

As he watched, the Trojan prince paced back a short way across the dusty ground, took a run-up, and hurled the weapon with all his might. It sailed through the sky, its long shadow shooting across the plain, and Menelaus eyed it carefully. When it began to drop, he stepped forward and positioned his shield with expert skill.

Yes! Perfect! Paris's spear clattered noisily against the shield and bounced off to one side. A triumphant shout went up from the Greek soldiers, and Menelaus felt his heart fill with a sense of pride, mixed with determination.

Meanwhile, Paris stood in the dust, staring dejectedly at his wasted effort.

Menelaus now raised his own weapon above his shoulder, and took a step back. Focusing hard on the distant figure cowering behind his shield, Menelaus summoned up every ounce of his strength and, with an almighty grunt of exertion, launched his spear into the blue air. It tore through the sky at terrifying speed, and the armies gasped as it plunged into Paris's shield.

The Trojan stumbled and fell, taking the full force of the blow. The crowd held its breath. Was he hurt? Menelaus waited.

Then, Paris slowly got up.

"Missed!" growled Menelaus angrily. As Paris tugged the spear out of his shield, everyone saw that his breastplate was torn on one side. He had escaped death by inches.

This only increased Menelaus's determination to finish his rival off once and for all. By rights, Paris should be dead already.

Menelaus wasted no time. "DIE!" he screamed, charging at his enemy with his sword drawn.

As he ran, he burned with deadly hatred for Paris. He thought of Helen in that traitor's arms. How he longed to get his revenge! The next few seconds were his chance. Nothing could stop him now.

Paris glanced quickly around the battlefield. For a moment he looked as if he was about to run. But when he caught sight of his comrades' expectant faces, he stood his ground and drew his sword.

His legs trembled, and he cringed defensively as the Greek fighter rushed at him. Empowered by fury, Menelaus had the strength of a lion. He raised his gleaming blade and brought it crashing down onto his enemy's helmet. Paris staggered back, dropped his sword and fell to his knees as Menelaus struck again.

"Aaargh!" moaned Paris in terror, covering his face with his hands.

Menelaus struck a third time, desperately trying to knock the helmet from Paris's head; but with the third blow, his silver blade splintered and shattered.

Menelaus stared in utter confusion at the useless sword hilt left in his hand.

"My lord Zeus. . ." he muttered desperately. "Zeus, please help me!"

Meanwhile, Paris was struggling to stand up. But before he succeeded, Menelaus dropped the broken hilt and grabbed at Paris's helmet. Clenching his fist around the Trojan's horsehair plume, he dragged Paris down again, and began to haul him along the ground, heading for the Greek side of the field.

"Viper! Wretch! Treacherous coward!" Menelaus panted, grabbing a breath with each awkward, heavy step. Paris struggled and choked as the helmet's strap dug deeper into his throat. He tried to scream for help, but he could hardly breathe. Menelaus tugged at him harder, deliberately throttling him. If he couldn't kill Paris any other way, Menelaus decided, this would have to do.

Paris writhed about and thrashed his arms wildly. He was vaguely aware of rows of faces staring at him as he began to lose consciousness. When Menelaus looked down and saw Paris's handsome face turning purple, and felt the Trojan's body relax, he knew his opponent would soon be dead.

Then, just when Paris was about to breathe his last, the helmet strap snapped. Menelaus lurched back as the helmet came away in his hands. He stared at it, amazed.

Paris cringed defensively as the Greek fighter rushed at him

The thick leather band was neatly severed.

Menelaus knew it was impossible that the strap had broken under Paris's weight; it was far too thick and strong. That Trojan must have a god on his side. He stared despairingly at the sky.

"Zeus," he whispered, "where are you? Athene, give me strength!"

At that moment, as Paris was staggering to his feet, Menelaus spotted a spear lying nearby. He darted over, picked it up, and whirled around to face his enemy.

Demoralized, weaponless and utterly exhausted, Paris stood alone in the middle of the battleground, staring groggily at Menelaus. He was at point-blank range. "Now then, Trojan prince," Menelaus murmured menacingly under his breath. "This time I've got you, you miserable traitor." And he hurled his spear, as fast as a lightening bolt, straight as an arrow and with deadly accuracy, straight at Paris's heart.

"Duck!" someone shouted.

But Paris was gone. And where he had been standing, there was nothing but a swirl of mist.

Hera and Athene were watching the action from the slopes of Mount Olympus. Athene was particularly enjoying herself ~ there was nothing she liked better than a good duel, and she knew Menelaus was going to win. She'd done enough to help him, after all ~ she'd guided his weapons, given him the idea of grabbing Paris's helmet, and helped him spot his spear again at the end. There was simply no competition. So when Paris disappeared, both goddesses were shocked.

"Hey, what's going on?" Athene complained, peering down at the scene. "Menelaus was meant to win!"

"Hmmm," said Hera, frowning. "I think I can guess what's happened. Follow me."

She led Athene up the mountainside until they reached the palace at the top. Hera strode through the halls and passages, searching for her husband. Athene hurried along behind her, the plume on her helmet bobbing as she went.

They found Zeus sipping a cup of nectar beside a shady pool in the courtyard. Aphrodite was sitting at his feet, carefully inspecting her reflection in the clear water.

Hera marched up to them."I thought I'd find you here," she said, eyeing Aphrodite suspiciously. Aphrodite just smiled.

"Hera, my dear," said Zeus guiltily. "And Athene. I haven't seen either of you all day. Wherever have you been?"

"Watching the duel," replied Hera, glaring at him.

"Ah yes, the duel," said Zeus, trying to avoid her eyes.

"And we want to know what's going on," continued Hera.

Zeus scratched his beard and stole a nervous look at Aphrodite.

"I saw that meddling fool Thetis leaving the palace the other day. You're plotting something with her, aren't you?" said Hera. "It's no good trying to hide it – I can always tell when you're up to your tricks."

Aphrodite giggled.

"Oh, I'm sure you're involved too," snapped Hera. "You'd do anything to help that pretty Trojan prince of yours."

Aphrodite shrugged.

"All I did was make a little mist," she said innocently. "There can't be any harm in that, can there?"

Hera and Athene exchanged disgusted glances, Athene's eyes flashing with fury.

"I knew it!" exploded Hera. "So where have you hidden him?"

"He's where he belongs ~ safe in the city with Helen," laughed Aphrodite, twirling her finger around in the sparkling water.

"Don't you realize what you've done?" fumed Athene, staring at her half-sister. "That would have been it ~ the whole war would have been over! The Greeks would have won! Now you've ruined everything!"

"I suppose you let her interfere?" Hera hissed at Zeus. "Well, it's clear whose side you're on. So what happens now?"

Zeus hesitated, racking his brains to try to think of a solution that would please everyone. He'd promised Thetis he would help the Trojans, but on the other hand he could hardly pretend that Paris had won the duel when he'd disappeared before the end.

He decided to try for a compromise.

"It seems to me," he began slowly, "that Menelaus has won the duel."

Athene smiled smugly.

"So my feeling is," Zeus went on, "that Helen should be returned to her husband and the Greeks should sail home. That way, the war will be over without Troy having to be destroyed."

"No!" shouted Aphrodite. "They can't give Helen back ~ she's Paris's wife now. They never will give her back, anyway!" she added childishly.

"Well then," argued Hera, "if the Trojans are going to be difficult, they deserve to be attacked."

"Hear, hear!" shouted Athene. "The Greeks will just have to destroy the city, won't they, if they can't get Helen any other way."

"Anyway," Aphrodite sulked, "Menelaus didn't win the duel, did he? Nobody won it."

"Exactly," said Hera, agreeing with Aphrodite for once. "Nobody won it. It was unfinished and there's no winner. The war must go on!"

Zeus sighed as he looked from one to the other.

"All right," he said at last. "I suppose the war will have to go on. Athene ~ can you make sure of that?"

"Of course, Father," replied the goddess of war, smiling triumphantly at Hera. "Just leave it to me."

Back on the plain, Menelaus was beside himself with rage.

"Coward!" he roared. "How typical of a Trojan to cheat his way out of things!"

"Calm down," Agamemnon said. "It's obvious that you've won the duel. As soon as I can find Hector, I'll speak to him about getting Helen back. Has anyone seen him?"

"I've sent Ajax to look for him," Ulysses reported.

"We'll wait forever if Ajax is looking ~ his brain's about the size of a berry," complained Menelaus. "If only Achilles were here. . . "

Agamemnon glared at him.

While the leaders were discussing the situation, the two armies were growing restless. The Greeks were shouting for Paris to be brought back to finish the duel. The Trojans were jeering, claiming Paris had won by outwitting Menelaus.

They were all so busy hurling insults that no one noticed Athene appearing quietly at the side of a Trojan soldier, whose name was Pandarus. She leaned forward, put her mouth very close to his ear and whispered something. Then she vanished.

All of a sudden, Pandarus stepped out from the crowd with his bow and arrow. He drew back the bowstring, took aim and fired a shot straight at Menelaus.

A roar went up from the crowd. Then Menelaus clutched his waist and fell to his knees. Gritting his teeth bravely, he grasped the arrow with both hands, and twisted it out with a groan of agony.

Agamemnon knelt down beside him.

"How deep is the wound?" he asked anxiously.

"Not too deep," gasped his brother, as blood trickled down his thigh. "I'll survive."

He winced in pain. "I'll need a doctor to stop the bleeding. . . but how could this happen?" he groaned in frustration. "We were so close. . ."

Ulysses immediately sent for a doctor, and Agamemnon got to his feet, seething with anger.

"I *thought* we agreed on a truce," he thundered. "Why should we have to keep to the cease-fire if the Trojans can't?"

"Maybe it was a mistake," said Ulysses reasonably. "Perhaps we shouldn't—"

"I don't care what it was," Agamemnon shouted. "It's clear that they can't be trusted. Give the order ~ tell the troops that from now on, the ceasefire is over. Let the fighting begin again!"

CHAPTER FIVE

HECTOR RUNS RIOT

As dawn rose, Agamemnon lay tossing and turning in his bed, unable to sleep. For the last few days, the Trojans had been fighting fiercely. With each battle they'd driven the Greeks back across the plain, away from the city and closer to the shore. Soon they'd be able to attack the camp and destroy the Greek ships.

The Trojan leader, Hector, was the main problem now. Since Paris had failed in his own attempt to win the war, his older brother had returned to the fray with more strength than ever. The man was so brave ~ he didn't seem to fear anything. And he was as tall and powerful as Achilles himself.

Agamemnon felt ashamed. If only he hadn't offended Achilles!

But it was too late now. He turned over again and sighed.

Hector leaned heavily against the gates of Troy, as the sun beat down remorselessly on his heavy breastplate and sweltering iron helmet.

His heart was pounding. Behind him he could hear men shouting and weapons clashing as the battle raged. He wiped away the beads of sweat that were trickling down the back of his neck. The fighting had started early that morning, and every muscle in his body was worn out and aching. He badly needed a rest.

He set off down the dusty streets inside the city, his sword swinging at his side. Children stopped their games and turned to stare.

"Look! It's Hector!" they whispered. And, they picked up their toy swords and pretended to fight, dreaming of the day when they would be able to carry a real weapon into battle.

When he reached the palace, Hector headed for his wife's chamber.

"Andromache?" he called.

Andromache appeared in the doorway, with their baby in her arms, looking relieved. "Hector!" she grinned. "I was just thinking about you."

Hector smiled and kissed her cheek. Then he bent down until his face was close to the child's. "And how's my little boy?" he murmured.

For a moment, the baby stared up in terror at the huge bronze helmet with its nodding horsehair plume. Then he buried his face in his mother's dress and started to scream.

"Come on, Astyanax," Hector cooed gently. "Come to Daddy." But the baby went on wailing.

"It's that ugly helmet!" declared Andromache. "Take it off, you'll scare him to death. And you've got blood all over you!"

"All right," said Hector, lifting the

helmet from his head and placing it carefully on the ground. He took the baby in his arms and cuddled him. "But I'll have to go back in a few minutes."

"Now don't go overdoing it, Hector," warned Andromache. "I know what you're like. This battle's been going on all day and you must be exhausted."

"But we're nearly there," Hector argued. "Just a couple more days and we can bring those Greeks to their knees. They haven't got Achilles, and if we really try—"

He broke off. Andromache was looking at him sulkily.

"You always put the war first!" she complained. "But what about us? Your wife and child?"

"Look, I have no choice," Hector pleaded. "They need me. It's not as if Paris is going to lead the troops, is it? I'm the only one who can do it. And we're so close to winning. When we've won, I'll spend more time with you ~ I promise."

"But must you go back immediately?" Andromache asked.

"You know I must," replied her husband. He passed the baby back to her. "And on my way I'm going to find that good-for-nothing brother of mine. We need everyone we can get ~ even Paris," he added, grimacing.

"I think he's with Helen," said Andromache. Hector laughed bitterly.

"Well, what a surprise!" he snarled. "Of course it's too much to expect him to leave his darling Helen!"

Then his tone changed. "Pray for us, Andromache," he said. "Pray to Zeus to let us win this war."

Andromache smiled up at him.

"I will," she said, standing on tiptoe to kiss him goodbye.

Hector sighed and picked up his helmet. He strode along the passage that led to Helen's chamber. From the doorway, he saw his brother sprawling lazily on a couch, cramming a handful of grapes into his mouth. The sticky juice dribbled down his chin and dripped onto the front of his tunic.

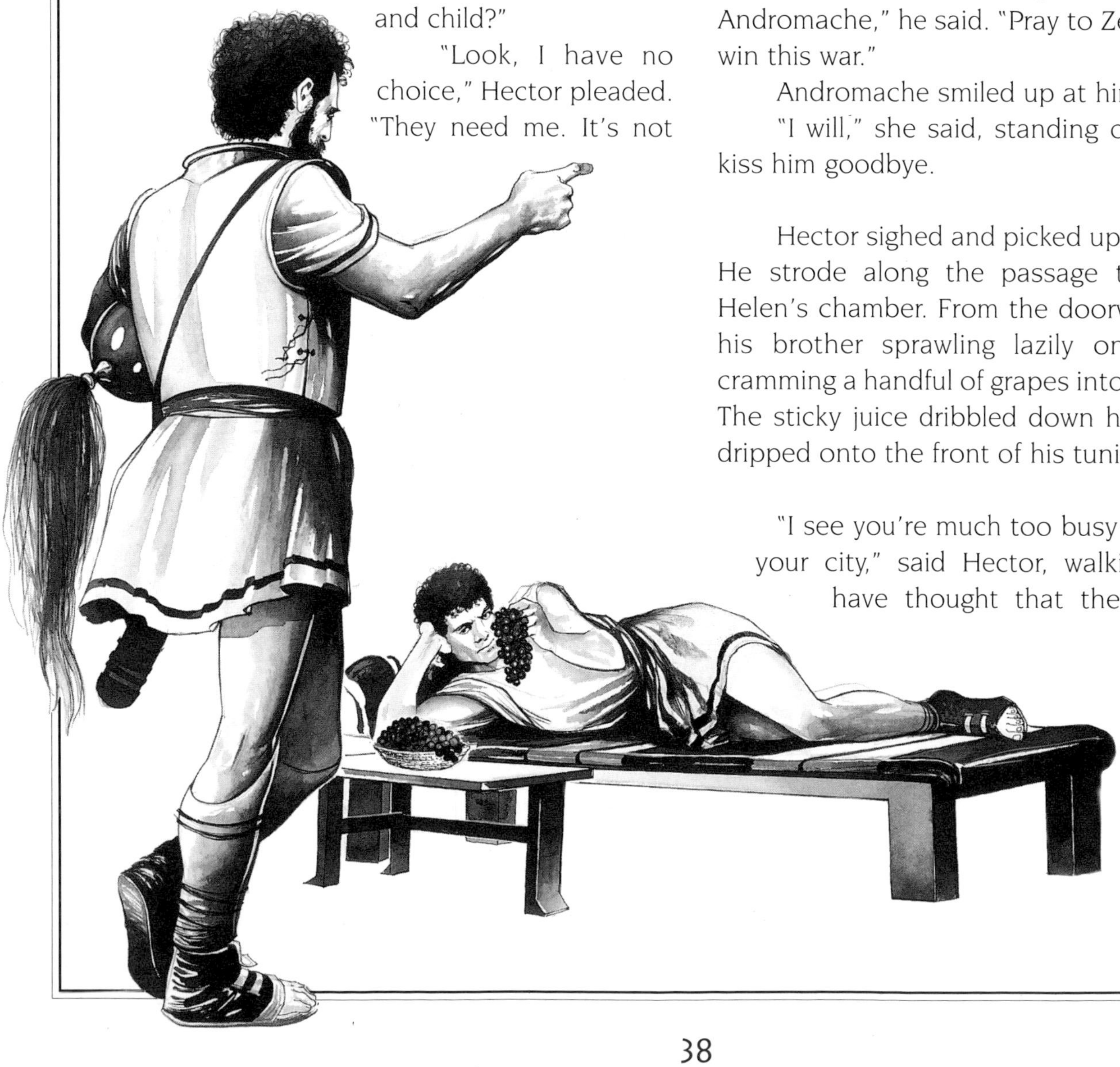

"I see you're much too busy to fight for your city," said Hector, walking in. "I'd have thought that the man who caused this war would be first on the battlefield."

Paris leaped to his feet, knocking the basket of grapes onto the floor.

"Hector!" he began. "I was just on my way." Hector snorted.

"How's the battle going?" asked Helen, who was sitting spinning wool.

"All right thanks," said Hector briskly. "But it would help if all our soldiers were fighting," he added, glaring at his brother.

Paris was fumbling with the fastenings on his breastplate.

"You go on ahead," he said. "I'll catch up with you."

"No," Hector insisted sternly. "You'll come with me. Now."

A few minutes later, Paris kissed Helen, slung his shield over his shoulder and grabbed his spear.

"I'm ready!" he announced.

"About time too," muttered Hector.

That night, Agamemnon still couldn't sleep. It had been another bad day, and many Greeks had lost their lives. He knew this couldn't go on ~ soon they'd have no choice but to give up ~ but what was the answer? They needed a plan, and fast.

He got up, slipped on his sandals and wrapped himself in a fur cloak. As he stepped out of the tent, he shivered in the chilly night air. The stars twinkled as Agamemnon paced nervously around the camp, racking his brains. In the distance, he could just make out the guards' fires burning along the tops of the walls of Troy.

Then, as he gazed out across the plain, an idea suddenly came to him. He stood there for a few more moments, then he smiled to himself, turned, and hurried back to his tent.

At first light, he called a meeting with the other leaders.

"I've had an idea," he said. The others looked at him expectantly.

"Well, we want to prevent the Trojans from reaching the ships," he began.

"Right," said Menelaus. "And?"

"And they're getting closer. So I propose we build a wall."

"A wall?" said Ulysses, frowning.

"Yes!" said Agamemnon excitedly. "A huge, strong wall between us and the Trojans, with battlements along the top, a ditch, gates, everything. Then they won't be able to get to the shore. If we start now, we could have it finished in a day or so!"

"Is this really going to work?" Ulysses said, tentatively. "I mean, wouldn't we be better coming up with a plan of attack?"

"Of course it's going to work!" said Agamemnon. "Look, Ulysses, I'll put you in charge. Then you can make sure it works."

It didn't take Ulysses long to produce a design for the wall. First they would dig a deep ditch. The soil from the ditch would be used to make a ridge, and the wall would be built on top of that.

"How will we get through it?" asked Nestor, examining Ulysses's drawing carefully.

"Well," said Ulysses, "There'll be gateways here, and here. And when we ride into battle, we'll go around the wall, at this end. We'll keep that area heavily guarded, of course. The other end will be blocked by the sea. And," he added, "we'll put pointed stakes in the ditch, sticking out of the ground. They should scare off those Trojans."

Ulysses also worked out a system of shifts, so that some soldiers could work on the wall while others were fighting.

The first group started work that morning. Half of them dug the ditch, while the other half piled up the soil to form the ridge. There was no shade on the plain, and it was hot, sweaty work.

By midday, the ditch and the ridge were both finished. The exhausted soldiers trudged off to join the fighting and a second group took over. Again, they split into two teams ~ one gathering all the stones they could find, the other building them into a wall. They fitted the stones together as closely as they could, then filled the gaps with soil.

Whenever he saw the men beginning to tire, Ulysses moved among them, offering words of encouragement and helping with various tasks. When the wall had reached its full height, the last group of soldiers took their turn. They built battlements along the top of the wall, and lashed pieces of wood together to make huge, heavy gates.

The sun was just starting to set as the Greeks began their final task. They sharpened hundreds of wooden stakes and planted them firmly in the floor of the ditch, with their pointed ends facing up.

In the evening, when the day's fighting was over and the wall was complete, Agamemnon went to inspect it.

"A fine wall," he said, sounding impressed and clapping Ulysses on the back. But deep down, he was less confident.

"I hope it works," he said anxiously under his breath. "It's got to work."

And with that, he headed for his tent, hoping for some sleep at last.

The following day, Hector was convinced the Greeks would give up. They were definitely fading fast ~ the day before, they'd had far fewer men than usual.

Brandishing his spear, he ordered his driver to take him wherever the battle was fiercest. One minute, he was attacking savagely from his chariot; the next, he fought on foot. And as the day wore on, the Trojans drove the Greeks farther and farther back. Soon, they would reach the ships.

Hector was on top of his chariot, about to urge his troops on with a rallying cry, when he saw something in the distance.

"What on earth is that?" he said.

It was a flag. A bold, bright battle flag, fluttering in the wind.

"What's it doing up there?" demanded Hector. The flag was far too high to be on top of a chariot. Then, as Hector peered through the forest of spears, horses and chariots ahead of him, he could make out the shape of the wall looming in the distance.

"Those shifty Greek cowards!" he cursed, staring at the broad, imposing structure. "Pathetic cheats! That does it!" he shouted. "If they think a pile of old stones is going to stop me, they're WRONG!" And he urged his soldiers onward, storming ahead into the thick of battle with more determination than ever.

Meanwhile, Agamemnon tried to rally his troops. He caught sight of Diomedes tearing past in his chariot, and yelled at him.

"Get to the front and keep attacking. Don't let them think we've given up. We must force them back!"

Raising his arm in acknowledgement, Diomedes disappeared into the fray. As Agamemnon turned to tell his driver which way to go, he found himself almost face to face with a young Trojan soldier. And before the Greek leader could raise his weapon, the boy lunged forward with his spear. For an instant, Agamemnon was aware of an excruciating pain shooting up his arm. Then he slipped into unconsciousness.

When he awoke, he was back at the camp. He couldn't remember what had happened. He tried to sit up, but the pain in his arm forced him back.

"Is anybody there?" he shouted.

The army doctor hurried into the tent, accompanied by Briseis ~ the servant girl Agamemnon had stolen from Achilles.

"Now, now, sir," said the doctor. "You mustn't get excited. You have a nasty wound on your arm and you've been asleep for several hours."

"Several hours!" exploded the king. "But what about the battle? What's going on? Are we winning?"

"Things aren't looking good, sir," replied the doctor, while Briseis tried to persuade Agamemnon to sip some water. "Menelaus and Nestor are still on the field ~ and Ajax too. But we've lost a lot of men, and many more are wounded."

Agamemnon sighed and pushed the cup away. "What about Ulysses?" he asked anxiously. "And Diomedes?"

"Both wounded, sir. They've had to withdraw. Ulysses has been stabbed in the ribs and Diomedes was shot in the foot ~ by one of Paris's arrows, I'm told."

Agamemnon covered his face with the sheet. He couldn't bear to hear any more.

The plain was a seething mass of horses, chariots and foot soldiers, and the noise was deafening. The air was so thick with the dust kicked up by the horses' thundering hoofs that the men could hardly breathe. Bodies littered the ground as Hector spurred on his men.

Ajax, the strongest Greek left on the field, fought valiantly, doing his best to keep the Trojans back. But one by one, the Greek soldiers fell and the Trojans inched forward, until the battle was raging right in front of the wall.

As they forced the last of the Greeks back behind the wall, Hector roared at his men to cross

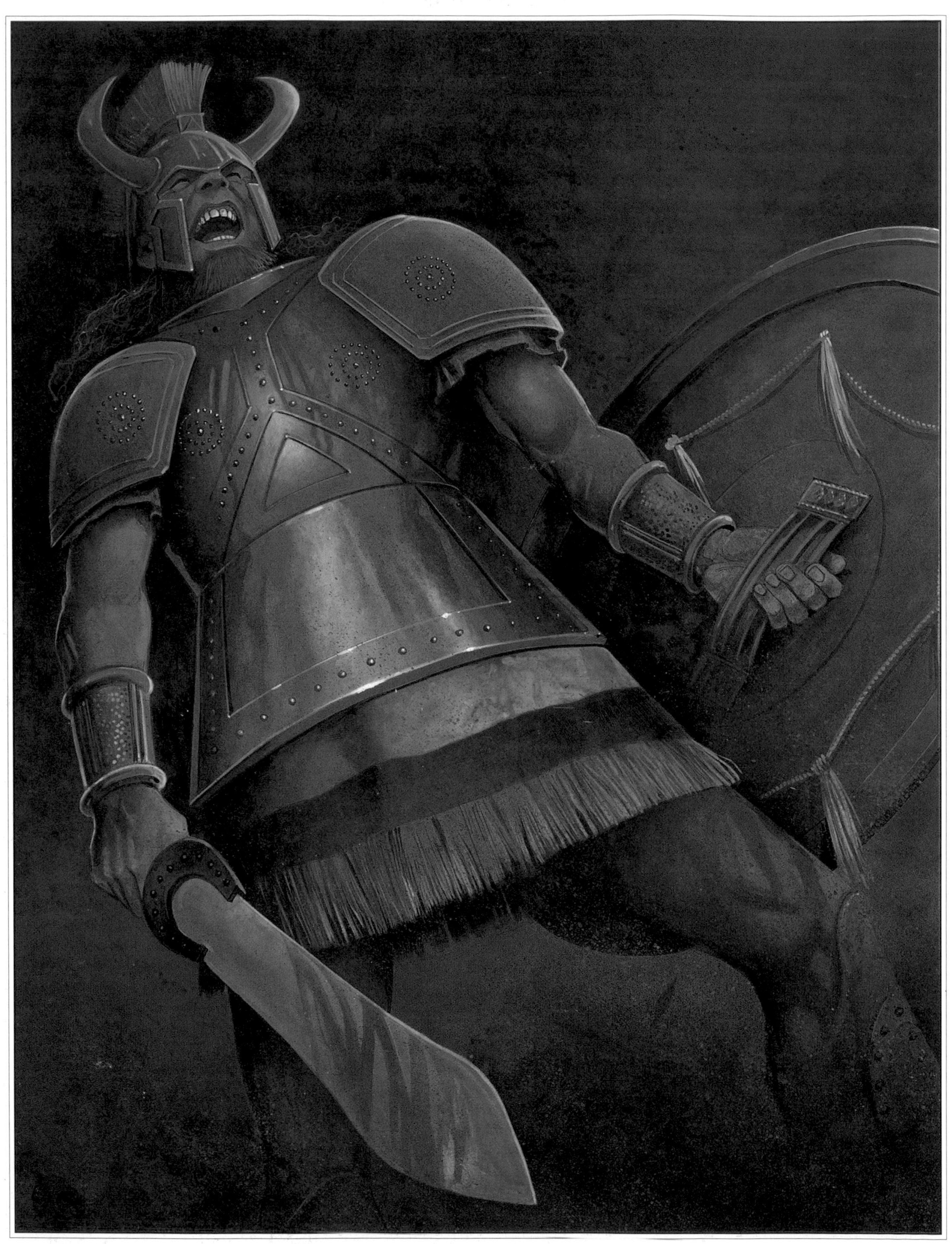

Ajax, the strongest Greek left on the field, fought valiantly

the ditch. It was too wide for the horses to jump, so the Trojans abandoned their chariots and leaped in on foot. They tried to avoid the sharp stakes, but many soldiers were impaled on the spikes and hung there in agony, bleeding to death. The rest scrambled out on the other side of the ditch and up the ridge, heading for the wall itself.

The Greeks climbed the battlements and began hurling stones and arrows onto the Trojan troops, who were attempting to dismantle the wall from below. Wrenching stones from it wherever they could, they tried to tear it down. But the wall stood firm.

"The gates!" screamed Hector, weaving through the stakes at the bottom of the ditch. "Attack the weakest point!"

The Trojan soldiers charged along the ridge, congregating at the central gate. Scores of them pounded on it with spears, swords, stones ~ even their bare hands.

As soon as Hector reached the gate, he snatched up a huge rock that was lying at his feet. Groaning, he lifted it above his head and, with an almighty yell, smashed it with full force against the gate. The wooden door splintered from top to bottom. Tearing away the pieces, Hector made an opening large enough to step through.

Seconds later, the Greeks were horrified to see Hector appearing on their side of the wall, his spear in his hand and his eyes flashing wildly.

"To the ships!" he roared. "Burn them!"

And as the Trojan army swarmed through the hole behind him, the Greeks started to retreat in terror.

Hera was sitting on her golden throne in Zeus's palace, fuming with rage. The Trojans were winning the war and it was all because that silly busybody Thetis had cajoled Zeus into helping her. And of course, he was too weak to say no.

Well, she'd show him!

She strode along to her chamber, locked the door and set to work. First, she had a long bath. She scrubbed her skin until it was spotlessly clean, and rubbed scented oil all over her body from head to toe. She rummaged through her wardrobe and pulled out her most beautiful dress ~ Athene had made it for her and had painstakingly embroidered it with hundreds of peacocks. When she'd fastened the dress with a golden brooch at her throat, she tied a shimmering sash around her waist. Finally, she combed out her long, dark hair and pinned it up on her head in a cascade of curls.

When she was ready, she put on her sandals and hurried to the kitchen. Pleased to find that there was

no one there, she quickly filled a basket with a loaf of freshly-baked barley bread, a lump of goat's cheese, some figs, a pot of honey and a large flask of wine. Then she slipped out of the palace.

She made her way down the mountainside until she reached a small cave. She listened for a moment, then bent down and stepped through the entrance.

"Sleep!" she called into the pitch darkness. "Are you there?"

There was a rustling, followed by a loud yawn. Then a drowsy voice said, "Who's there?"

"It's Queen Hera. Wake up."

Sleep sighed. Then Hera heard him get out of bed and stumble across the cave. A soft light appeared, and Sleep stood there in his nightgown, holding a lamp in one hand and rubbing his eyes with the other.

"What can I do for you, Madam?" he said, stifling another yawn.

Hera went up to him and whispered in his ear. He nodded sleepily and shuffled over to an old wooden chest at the back of the cave. After a lot of rummaging around, he pulled out a tiny silver bottle.

"Now, you won't use too much, will you?" he asked groggily, handing it to Hera.

"I'll use just as much as I need," she said brusquely, popping the bottle into her basket. "Thank you, Sleep. Goodbye!"

"Goodbye," mumbled Sleep, who was already halfway back to bed. As Hera stepped out into the sunlight, she heard the sound of heavy snoring.

A little way down the mountainside, Hera found Zeus sitting under an oak tree.

"Hera, my dear!" he exclaimed. "How very beautiful you're looking today."

"I thought we could take a walk through the forest," said Hera, flashing what she hoped was a charming smile.

"What a splendid idea," said Zeus, scrambling to his feet and brushing leaves from his tunic.

"I've brought some food," said Hera.

"Even better!" said Zeus. "Off we go!"

They walked hand in hand through the forest, talking, and laughing and stopping to look at unusual birds. Zeus couldn't help wondering why his wife was being so nice to him. Still, it made a pleasant change from her usual bad temper. And she looked and smelled divine.

After a while, they sat down in a sunny clearing carpeted with yellow crocuses. Hera spread the food out on a cloth, and Zeus ate as much as he could. He also drank a lot of wine, and soon felt very tired. Lying down on the soft grass, he fell fast asleep.

Hera waited a few minutes. Then she reached into the basket and found the silver bottle. She pulled out the stopper and sprinkled the contents onto Zeus's face. The sparkling droplets were as clear as raindrops. Zeus twitched his nose, but didn't wake. Hera packed the remains of the meal into the basket and crept away.

As soon as she arrived back at the palace, she went to find Athene.

"I need your help," she said. "I've put Zeus to sleep for a while, and I want you to help the Greek army," continued Hera. "Those Trojans are doing far too well."

Athene flew down to where the battle was still raging. The Greeks had almost given up hope. The goddess made herself invisible and flitted from one soldier to another, whispering secret words of encouragement in their ears.

With a sudden burst of energy, the Greek army started to fight back. Hector threw a spear at Ajax, which hit his shield and bounced away. Immediately, Ajax picked up a rock and hurled it straight at Hector's head. It hit him on the throat, and he toppled back. He staggered around in a daze for a few seconds, clutching his neck. Then he dropped to the dusty ground.

Shouting triumphantly, the Greeks surged forward, while the Trojans rushed to protect their leader. Fighting off the worst of the attack, they carried him to safety and lifted him into his chariot. The driver turned the horses and headed for the city.

Slowly, Zeus drifted back to full consciousness. For a moment, he wondered where he was. Then he remembered the walk and the picnic, and felt very suspicious. Hera was up to something.

Struggling to his feet, he rubbed his eyes and looked down on the battle. He was shocked at what he saw. The Greeks had forced the Trojans back through the wall and across the ditch. Athene was on the battlefield, helping the Greeks. And Hector, amazingly, was out of the action.

Guessing that he'd been tricked, Zeus stormed back to the palace in a furious temper. Hera was nowhere to be found.

"Hermes!" he bellowed.

Hermes appeared instantly.

"Yes, Father?" he said.

"Go to the battlefield and tell Athene to keep out of this war. And on your way, find Apollo and tell him to come and see me."

"Yes, Father," said Hermes. He scurried off, and a few minutes later, Apollo strolled in.

"Hermes said you wanted to see me, Father," he said.

"Yes," said Zeus. "I want you to go down to Troy, stop Hector's chariot and make sure he gets back to the battle."

A short while later, Hector was fully recovered and fiercer than ever. The Greeks were shocked to see him. And without Athene's help, they were in trouble again.

"This war's not over yet!" said Zeus, looking down at the Trojans advancing over the plain, across the ditch and back through the gate. Once more, the battle raged close to the shore. At last, Hector reached one of the ships. He tried to climb onto it, but Ajax was quicker and leaped up first. He desperately fought Hector off with his sword.

"Bring me fire!" shouted Hector to the men nearest him. "We'll burn the ships!"

Zeus sighed with satisfaction.

"What a good thing I woke up when I did," he said to himself. "Just wait till I find that wife of mine. . . "

CHAPTER SIX

BRAVE PATROCLUS

All was calm around Achilles's tent. When he had withdrawn from the war, he had moved his men along the coast, away from the main camp. Now the only sounds to break the peaceful silence were the waves lapping gently on the shore, horses gently chomping the clover, and soldiers chatting idly or training for battle with their spears and bows.

They had obeyed their leader's orders to leave the fighting, but the truth was that many of them felt frustrated and longed to return to the battle as soon as possible. There was a feeling of restlessness in the air.

Inside the tent, Achilles was sitting on a stool, strumming his lyre. Patroclus, his closest comrade, was cutting up a leg of lamb and threading the pieces onto spits. He was just about to put them over the fire when he heard voices outside.

"Achilles!" called a herald's voice. "Ulysses is here to see you."

Achilles leaped to his feet and strode over to the doorway. "Well, well," he exclaimed. "Visitors! Come on in." And in walked Ulysses with two heralds.

"Please, sit down," said Achilles. "Patroclus, cut some more meat and pour some wine for our guests. It's a long time since we've entertained anyone in this tent!"

"Achilles, I'll come straight to the point. I have a message for you," said Ulysses, wincing at the pain from his sore rib as he lowered himself onto a couch. "From Agamemnon."

Achilles smiled and said nothing.

"He wants you back."

Achilles remained silent.

"He's really desperate, Achilles. So desperate, he's even talking about giving up and sailing home. I don't know if you've heard ~ Hector's reached the ships. . . "

Achilles's smile faded.

". . . and he's setting fire to them. Ajax is trying to fight him off, but we're in terrible trouble. So many of us are wounded, and on top of that, the men are completely exhausted. You're our only hope."

There was a long pause. The meat spat and crackled on the fire.

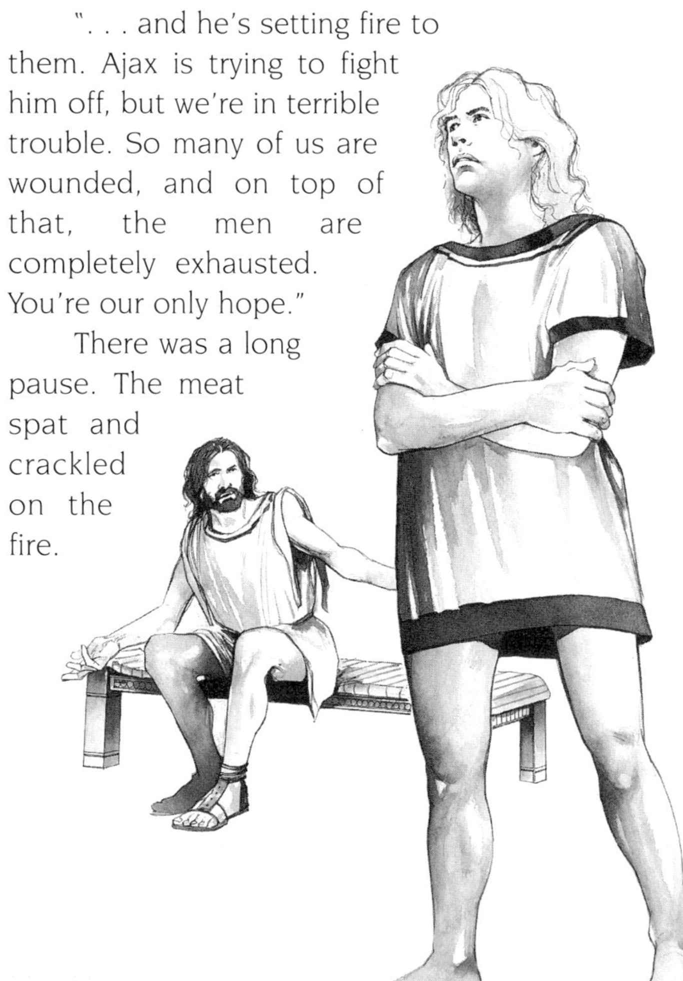

At last, Achilles spoke. "I gave everything to his precious war for years," he said angrily, "and what thanks did I get? He's treated me shamefully. I can't forgive him."

"He's willing to return the girl to you," said Ulysses.

"Now that he's desperate!" snorted Achilles.

"And anything else you want," Ulysses added hastily. "Gold, horses. . . please, Achilles. I'm begging you!"

Again, there was silence. Patroclus sprinkled salt onto the meat and heaped it onto the plates. A servant girl brought in baskets of freshly-baked bread.

Then Achilles said, "You can tell Agamemnon I'll return to the fighting. . . "

Ulysses held his breath and Patroclus glanced up.

". . . when Hector reaches my ships, and not before. Now, let's eat."

Some time later, when the meal was over and the guests had gone, Patroclus was left alone in the tent. As he cleared away the plates and leftover food, his eye fell upon a pile of shiny objects on the floor ~ Achilles's huge sword, his helmet and his shield. He stared at them for a while. And suddenly, an idea came into his mind.

The battle was still raging near the ships on the other side of the Greek camp. Ajax was worn out. His shoulder ached from the weight of his shield, his breath came in painful gasps, and sweat soaked his tunic. One moment he'd been standing on the beach brandishing his sword; the next he was rolling across the ground empty-handed ~ the sword had been knocked from his grasp by Hector's own weapon.

Waves of utter despair swept over Ajax. What hope was there of victory now? The Trojans were advancing in their hundreds, spurred on by the sight of the spreading flames. He, Menelaus and Nestor had done their utmost to keep the enemy away from the ships, but they'd failed. Ajax watched helplessly as Hector raised his clenched fist in an arrogant gesture of triumph against a fiery backdrop of burning masts and sails.

Suddenly, a distant movement caught his eye. He glanced over to the far end of the beach and could hardly believe what he saw. A splendid chariot, pulled by two golden horses, was thundering along the shore. Hundreds of soldiers charged behind it. As the chariot drew closer, Ajax shouted to Menelaus who was fighting nearby.

"Look! Over there!"

Menelaus turned to look, and his jaw fell open in amazement. There was no mistaking the two horses tossing their shimmering golden manes. Their names were Xanthus and Balius ~ and everyone knew who they belonged to.

"Achilles," breathed Menelaus.

One after another, the Greek soldiers spotted the approaching horde. Slowly their astonishment turned to relief, and then to joy. Achilles had come to save them!

The new arrivals galloped into the fray and joined in the fighting immediately, their shiny bronze breastplates conspicuous among the blood-spattered ones around them.

Meanwhile, Ajax was staring hard at their leader. Achilles must have lost weight during his time away from the action, Ajax decided. His usually tall, sturdy frame looked more slender, and his helmet seemed slightly loose. And there was something different about the way he was standing. . .

Then Ajax guessed the truth.

"It's not Achilles!" he muttered to himself. "It's Patroclus!"

By the time the other soldiers realized this, Patroclus and his men had reached the ships, and were attacking the maurauding Trojans. The latest recruits were bursting with energy, and their enthusiasm rubbed off on their weary comrades.

And Patroclus himself was like a man inspired. Waving Achilles's silver-hilted sword above his head, he swept through the ranks, shouting orders to the driver, Automedon. As the Trojans began to retreat, Patroclus thought of what Achilles had said after he'd given him permission to go.

"Just drive them away from the ships ~ don't try to take the city. You'll never do it."

"If only I could, though. . . " thought Patroclus to himself. "If only I could lead the army to victory and march through Troy in triumph. Achilles would be so proud of me ~ I know he would."

Hector was in trouble. At first, he'd tried to stand his ground, urging his men to do the same. But as he watched them being gradually swept back, defeat written all over their tired faces, he began to lose confidence. Though he kept battling away, the Greek spears and arrows seemed to be zipping through the air far more quickly than before. He found himself being beaten back until he was right under the Greek wall.

Leaning against the ridge for a moment, to catch his breath, he heard Paris's voice shouting at him.

"Hector! Look out!"

Hector spun around to see a Greek archer aiming an arrow at his head. Crouching, Hector scrambled up the ridge and through a gate, and just managed to throw himself behind the wall as the arrow whistled past him.

He stopped for a moment, gasping loudly. Then, glancing across to the other side of the ditch, he saw his chariot and horses still standing there. Suddenly, he wanted only to return to safety. He had been a match for every man on the field. But Achilles was in a different league.

It took some time to get across the ditch. Hector had to pick his way carefully around the sharp stakes that protruded from the ground, treading awkwardly on mangled bodies. At last, he climbed up the other side. Weapons rained down around him. Ducking behind his shield, he made a run for the chariot, leaped in and shouted at the driver.

"Head for the city!"

The driver hesitated, unable to believe that Hector was really deserting his men. Then he quickly grabbed the reins and urged on the horses.

At that moment, Patroclus reached the wall. Through the open gate, he glimpsed Hector's chariot hurtling into the distance. Snatching the reins from his driver, he guided the horses up the slope of the ridge and through the gateway. Then, to the amazement of the soldiers nearby, they soared over the ditch, pulling the chariot behind them, and landed safely on the other side ~ a distance no ordinary horses could ever have jumped. And they galloped off across the plain, in pursuit of Hector.

High up on Olympus, Zeus was keeping a sharp eye on the battle. When he saw Hector fleeing, he summoned Apollo, who made himself invisible, slipped into the chariot beside Hector and whispered in his ear.

As Hector neared the city walls, he began to have second thoughts about what he was doing. He imagined his father's shocked face when he admitted that he'd run away. He could almost hear the whispers that would spread through the city. . .

"Hector's a coward!"

"Calls himself a hero!"

"Not much of a leader!"

"Whoa!" Hector yelled, grabbing the reins from his driver, and bringing the horses to a stop. Then he turned the chariot, so that it once more faced the Greek army.

Patroclus was amazed to see the Trojan leader turn around again. Undeterred, he spurred on his team. When Hector's chariot was not far away, he pulled hard on the reins to slow the horses. Then, his heart pounding with fear and excitement, he jumped to the ground and hurled his spear at Hector with all his strength.

Patroclus's aim was good, and the weapon tore through the air straight at the Trojan chariot. Hector darted to one side to avoid it, but his driver was not so quick. The spear's bronze tip struck him in the neck with full force, knocking him out of the chariot and onto the dusty ground.

Hector realized immediately that the man was dead.

The first thing he felt was a jolt of fear. For a moment, he hesitated. Then Apollo

Gripped by panic, he turned and ran

whispered in his ear again, and he began to burn with the desire for revenge. Tossing the reins aside, he took his sword, sprang from the chariot and charged at Patroclus.

Patroclus bravely stood his ground, trying to control his nerves. The Trojan leader was a fearsome sight, with his helmet plumes trailing behind him and his huge shield glinting in the evening sun.

"Stay calm," Patroclus told himself desperately. Hector thundered nearer. As soon as he was within striking distance, Patroclus instinctively raised his sword. But before he could use it, Hector lifted his own weapon and, in one quick swipe, knocked Patroclus's helmet right off his head.

Horrified, Patroclus watched the helmet thud onto the sun-baked mud and roll under the horses' feet. He looked up again. Hector's piercing eyes gleamed menacingly through the eye-slits in his helmet as he moved closer. Patroclus could hear the rasping sound of his breathing.

He glanced from left to right, in the hope that help was nearby. He was alone. He tried to pull his shield closer, but his hands were slippery with sweat. The shield slid from his grip and fell to the ground.

With neither helmet nor shield, Patroclus knew he had no chance. Gripped by panic, he turned and ran.

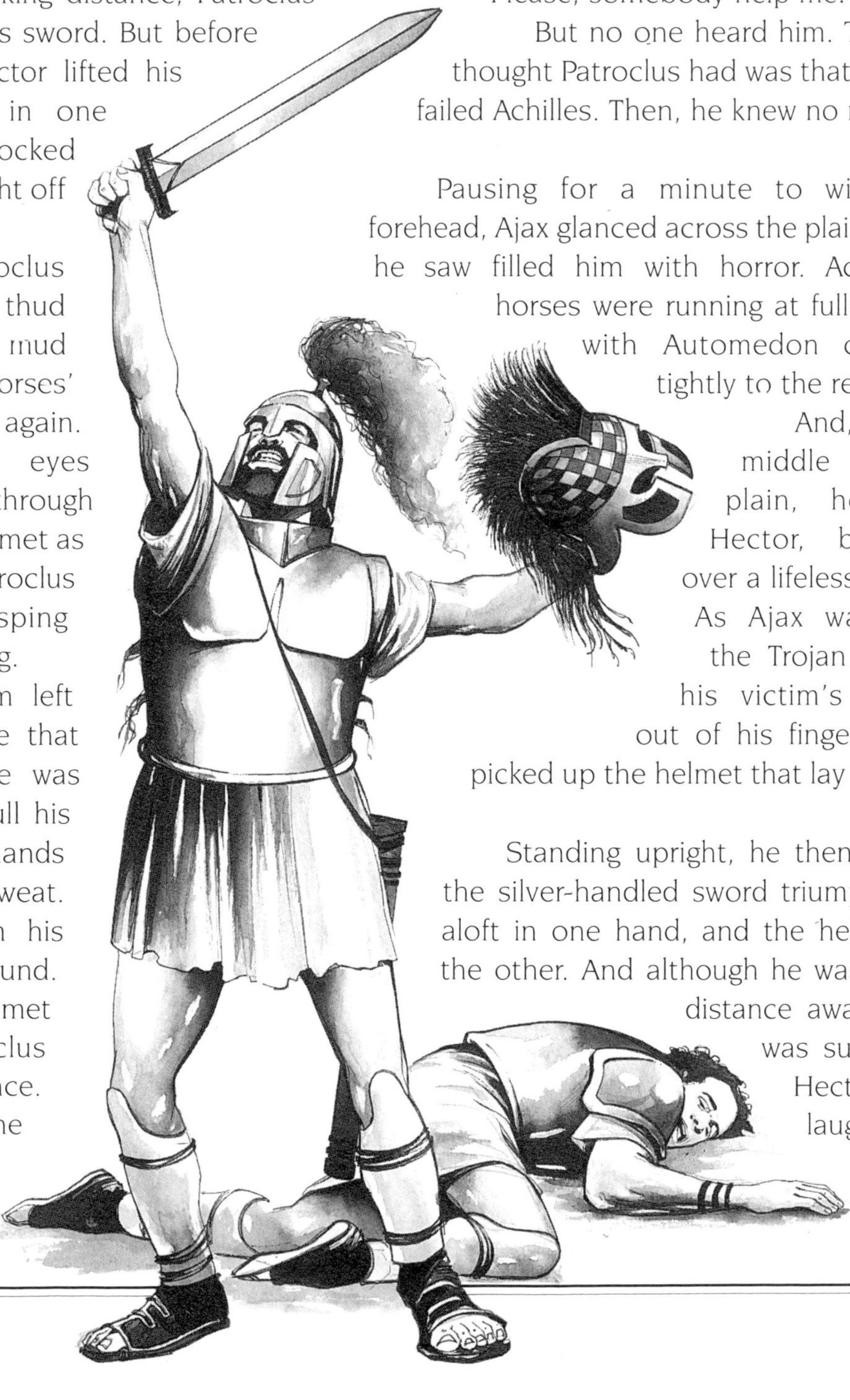

He hadn't taken more than a few steps when his arm was seized in a vice-like grip. Struggling frantically, he tried to wrench himself free. Then he felt a sharp stab of pain. Dizziness swept over him. He looked down and saw a glint of silver, laced with his own red blood. Then he slumped to the ground.

For a few seconds he lay there, concentrating on each breath. He tried to call out, but he had no voice left.

"Help me!" he croaked hoarsely. "Please, somebody help me!"

But no one heard him. The last thought Patroclus had was that he had failed Achilles. Then, he knew no more.

Pausing for a minute to wipe his forehead, Ajax glanced across the plain. What he saw filled him with horror. Achilles's horses were running at full speed, with Automedon clinging tightly to the reins.

And, in the middle of the plain, he saw Hector, bending over a lifeless figure. As Ajax watched, the Trojan forced his victim's sword out of his fingers, and picked up the helmet that lay nearby.

Standing upright, he then raised the silver-handled sword triumphantly aloft in one hand, and the helmet in the other. And although he was some distance away, Ajax was sure that Hector was laughing.

CHAPTER SEVEN

REVENGE!

Hephaestus, the blacksmith of the gods, was working at his forge on Mount Olympus. He was wearing nothing but a loincloth, and as he pumped his bellows to fan the flames, sweat trickled down his hairy chest. Just as he was about to start beating a small piece of silver into shape on his anvil, he heard a knock at the door.

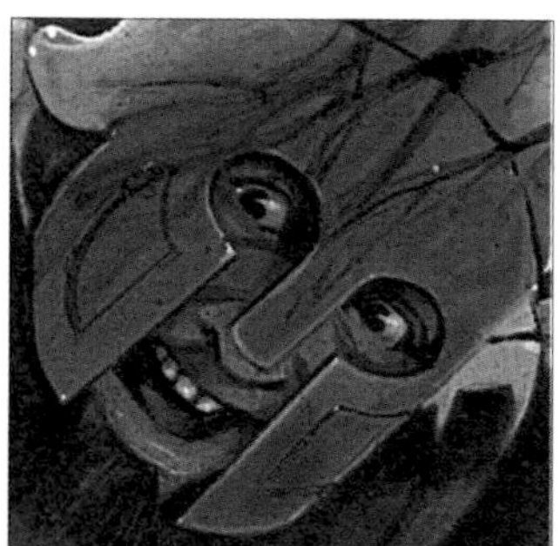

"Come in," he called.

The door swung open.

"Hello, Hephaestus," said Thetis. "Are you very busy?"

"I'm never too busy for you," smiled the smith, hobbling over to greet her. Many of the gods and goddesses teased Hephaestus because of his limp, but not Thetis. "Come and sit down."

He took her by the hand and led her over to a beautiful silver chair. Lowering himself onto a matching footstool, he picked up his tunic from where it lay crumpled on the floor and pulled it over his head.

"How can I help you?" he asked.

Thetis glanced at him, and he noticed that she had tear stains on her cheeks.

"It's Achilles," she began. "He's in a terrible state, Hephaestus. I've never seen him like this before."

"Whatever's happened?"

"Well," Thetis explained, "Patroclus persuaded Achilles to let him go into battle, and now he's dead ~ killed by Hector. Achilles is furious ~ furious with Hector, and furious with himself for letting Patroclus fight. Now he wants to rejoin the battle to take revenge. And I want to help him."

Hephaestus looked a little confused.

"Yes, yes, I know I wanted the Trojans to win," said Thetis uncomfortably, "but I ~ well, I've changed my mind. For Achilles's sake. The thing is," she went on, "he lent his helmet, sword and shield to Patroclus, and Hector's stolen them. So I was wondering. . . "

"If I'd make new ones for him?" smiled Hephaestus.

Thetis nodded.

"It would be a pleasure."

"I need them by dawn," said Thetis.

"Don't you worry," said the smith kindly, getting to his feet.

Hephaestus made his way back over to the furnace, pulling off his tunic as he went. He picked up his bellows and fanned the flames until they flared up fiercely. Then he threw pieces of shining metal onto the fire ~ first gold, then silver, then bronze. While he waited for them to soften, he rummaged in his toolbox for his best hammer and tongs.

Early the next morning, Agamemnon went to find Menelaus.

"You look exhausted!" said his brother, as

Agamemnon trudged into the tent

"I haven't been sleeping very well," Agamemnon grunted. "My arm's still in agony. And anyway, how can I sleep when we're on the verge of defeat? What are we going to do, Menelaus?"

Menelaus stared at the ground.

"If we have another day like yesterday, it will finish us," continued Agamemnon. "We need to come up with another plan."

"But the men are worn out," Menelaus said. "They can't keep Hector away from the ships forever. If only I'd won the duel," he went on frustratedly. "We'd be on our way home now, and I'd have Helen back. . . "

Agamemnon changed the subject. Is there any news about Patroclus?" he asked.

"Ajax managed to drag his body off the battlefield late last night," Menelaus sighed. "His breastplate was gone, and his helmet too. They took him to Achilles's tent, and they've been up all night mourning. Terrible business," he reflected.

"Well, I hope the great Achilles feels guilty today," snarled Agamemnon.

Then he noticed Menelaus's expression change. "What is it?" he said. "What's the matter?"

Menelaus had a clear view of the entrance. He was staring, transfixed, no longer seeming to hear a word his brother was saying.

Agamemnon turned around.

There, standing in the doorway was Achilles. On his head was a huge shining helmet, crowned by a rippling crest of horsehair. A mighty bronze sword, its silver hilt studded with gold, hung from his waist. And on his arm he carried an enormous shield, newly riveted and polished until it gleamed like a mirror. Gold, silver and bronze sparkled in the lamplight, casting swirling reflections onto the sides of the tent.

Achilles said nothing. But his eyes were glinting with determination.

In the end it was Menelaus who broke the silence. "Achilles!" he cried, striding over and clasping the warrior's free hand. "Welcome back!"

Agamemnon was more reserved. He stood up and eyed the armed man carefully.

"So," he said at last. "Now you're ready to fight, are you?"

"Yes, sir," said Achilles proudly. "I'm ready."

The battle now raged more fiercely than ever. The pattern of the day before began to repeat itself, as the Trojans forced the Greeks ever closer to the wall.

Hector himself was exhausted, but brimming

with confidence. He was wearing the helmet and breastplate that he had taken from Patroclus, and was determined that, today, he'd fight his way back to the ships and burn every single one. He spotted Paris and beckoned to him.

"I don't want you sneaking off back to the city today," he said sternly.

"Of course not," said Paris. Then he added, "We're doing well, aren't we?"

"We need to do better if we're going to burn the ships. I want every man to be— "

"What's that?" interrupted Paris.

"What?" said Hector irritably. Why would Paris never concentrate?

"Over there ~ near the wall," continued Paris. "It looks like. . . it is. . . it's Achilles's chariot again!"

"Well I wonder who's in it today," said Hector. They glanced at each other, then stared back across to where the golden horses were darting in and out of the battle.

"It can't be. . . " murmured Paris.

Hector screwed up his eyes trying to get a better view. There was the driver, Automedon ~ but who was standing behind him? Whoever it was, he was wearing a splendid helmet and holding the biggest shield Hector had ever seen.

"Surely it can't be. . . " He couldn't bring himself to say the name aloud. But the longer he watched, the more uneasy he felt.

The unknown soldier was tall, strong and broad-shouldered, with a commanding presence. He wielded his sword with great skill, leaning out of the moving chariot to strike at anyone within reach. Soldiers fell to the ground all around him, and Hector saw, to his horror, that the Trojan army was on the retreat, beaten back by the new arrival.

"It *is* him," muttered Hector. His earlier confidence began to drain away and he shot an anxious glance at Paris. "It's Achilles. . . "

"Hector, look!" shouted Paris suddenly. "Isn't that Polydorus?"

Polydorus was Priam's youngest son. Over the last few weeks, he'd been begging his parents to let him join the fighting. But Priam had insisted he wasn't yet old enough to get involved in the war.

Now it seemed that the boy had disobeyed his father. He shouldn't even have been outside the city, but his two brothers, watching in horror, saw him ride his horse right up to Achilles's chariot. Inexperienced as he was, Polydorus approached from the front, giving Achilles plenty of warning, and aimed his spear at his enemy's head. Achilles leaned expertly to one side, and the spear flew past.

Immediately, Achilles drew back his own spear to retaliate. Polydorus tried to turn his horse and ride away, but he was too slow. Achilles's spear shot through the air and tore into the middle of his back, knocking him sprawling from his horse.

Polydorus was dead.

Paris gasped and turned to his brother, but Hector had gone. He was already charging across the plain, heading for Achilles and vowing to seek revenge. When he was within striking distance, he hurled his spear with all the force he could muster, aiming for Achilles's back.

But the gods were still watching from Mount Olympus, and Athene quickly blew hard on the spear. It curved around in a wide arc until it was facing the other way. Then it landed gently on the ground.

At that moment, Achilles turned and saw Hector. The anger he already felt for the man

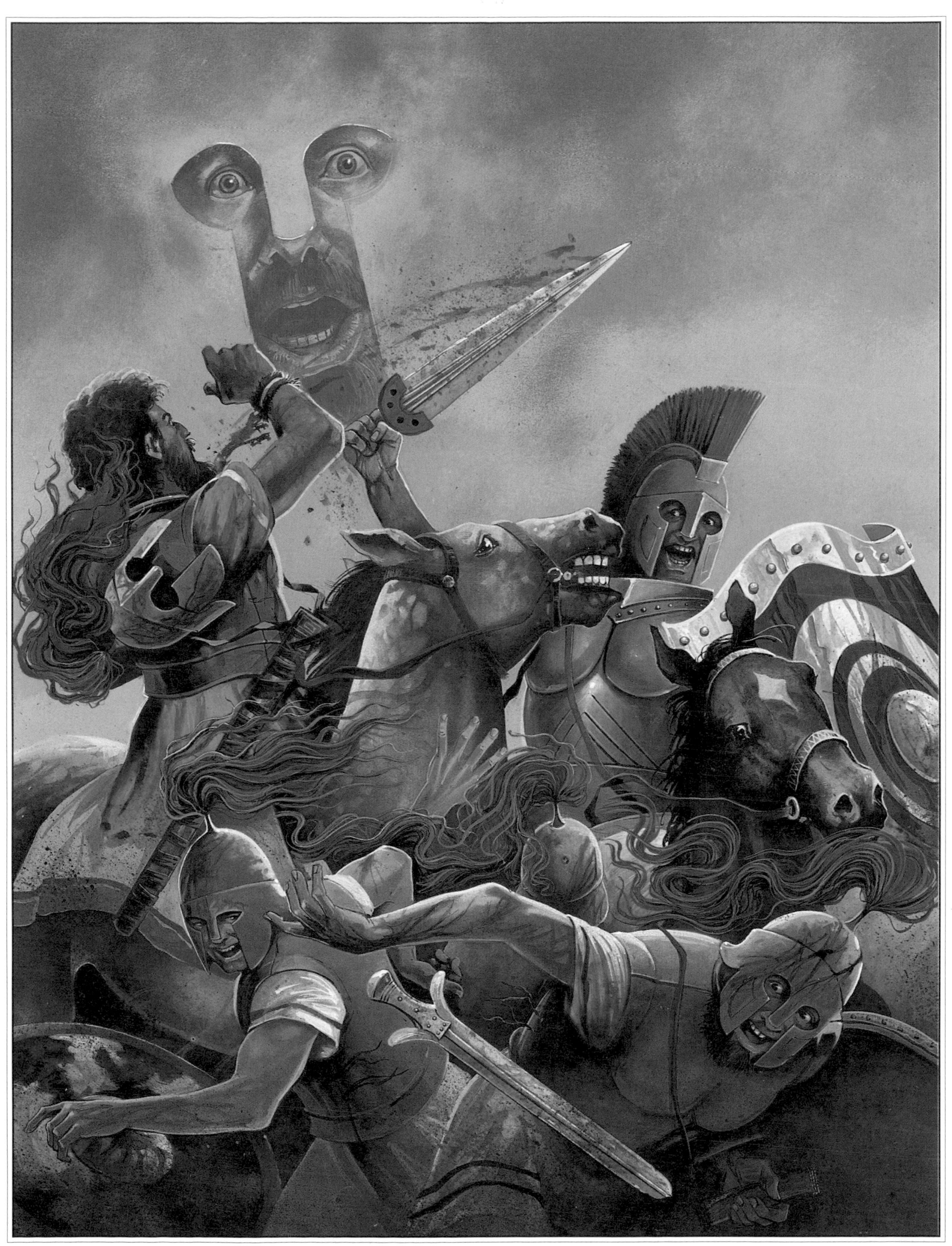

Hector saw, to his horror, that the Trojan army was on the retreat

who had killed his best friend turned to wild fury when he saw that the Trojan leader was wearing his helmet.

"Arrogant fool! How dare he!" he spat from between clenched teeth. Then he shouted, "Get me my spear!"

One of his comrades ran to the body of Polydorus, lying on the ground. He dragged the spear out, and delivered it to its owner.

"Charge!" yelled Achilles. And Xanthus and Balius, his magical golden horses, sprang into action. Raising his arm as the chariot hurtled forward, Achilles let out a terrifying roar. He was just about to throw his spear, when, all of a sudden, a heavy mist fell in front of him, shrouding Hector from view.

On Mount Olympus, Apollo smiled a satisfied smile.

Confused, Achilles lowered his arm and peered into the swirling whiteness. The Trojan leader had vanished from sight! Achilles was furious. He paused for a moment, then shouted into the void.

"I'll be back, Hector! You can hide yourself now, but I'll get you in the end!"

Then he wheeled his chariot around and headed back into the thick of the battle. Spurred on by rage, he fought like a madman all day. He killed dozens of soldiers, while his horses trampled over the bodies already scattered across the ground. And as more and more blood spattered the sides of his chariot, the Trojans began to flee back to the city.

Priam and Hecuba were watching from the city wall, but they couldn't see the other side of the battlefield. When they saw the Trojan army fleeing across the plain, Priam called out to a messenger.

"What's happening? Why are our men retreating?"

"It's Achilles!" panted the man. "He's back! He's slaughtering us, your majesty ~ the men can't stand up to him. And it looks as if he won't stop until he can find Hector."

Priam looked at his wife. Hecuba was wringing her hands and staring desperately out at the plain.

"Priam," she said, turning to him with tears in her eyes. "Please put a stop to this. Let the army back inside ~ just for a while. Just so they can recover their strength."

Priam squeezed her hands tightly. "If I do that, the Greeks will think we've surrendered," he said.

"But Hector's out there. And Paris. . ." The queen's tears welled up and she began to sob against his shoulder.

Priam knew she was right. With one last glance across the plain, the king made his way down the steps to the gateway. The guards leaped to their feet.

"Who's in charge here?" Priam demanded. A burly man stepped forward.

"I am, sir."

"Open the gates," Priam ordered.

There was silence. The guard stared at the king in disbelief.

"But, sir—" he protested.

"Do as I say," snapped Priam. "Now!" Then he climbed back up to the wall as the grating sound of the bars being pulled back echoed up the stone steps.

As soon as the gates were open, exhausted soldiers began to swarm into the city, thirsty and exhausted. Among the first to enter was Paris. When Hector had headed off to attack Achilles, Paris had stayed skulking as near to the gates as possible.

He joined his parents on the wall, but when he saw his mother rushing joyfully over to embrace him, he realized they knew nothing about what had happened to Polydorus. Trembling, he took a deep breath, preparing to break the grim news.

A while later, Hector rode close to the wall in his chariot.

"What's going on?" he yelled. " I can't fight a war with no soldiers! Close the gates!"

"No, Hector," Priam shouted back. "The men must come in for a rest. I can't let them all die."

"Hector!" wailed Hecuba with tears streaming down her face. "Come inside!"

"Achilles is coming!" shrieked Paris. "Get in, while you still can!"

"I'll go and ward him off!" Hector yelled up at them. And before his distraught mother could say anything, he had wheeled his horses around and set off across the plain.

The last of the Trojan soldiers surged through the gates, the Greeks hot on their heels. Priam scanned the plain desperately, but Hector was nowhere to be seen.

"We must close the gates to stop the Greeks from getting in," he said.

"No!" gasped Hecuba. "We can't leave our son outside to face Achilles alone."

"We can't risk Achilles getting into the city," said Priam, hurrying down the steps.

"Close the gates!" he called to the guards.

"No! " screamed Hecuba from above.

The guards hesitated.

"Close them!" ordered the king.

Slowly, the heavy wooden gates were heaved shut, and the bars drawn firmly across.

Achilles steadied himself as his chariot rumbled at breakneck speed closer and closer to the city. As he drew near to the gleaming walls of Troy, he saw that only Greek warriors were left outside. Those Trojan cowards had run for cover! Greek breastplates, swords and helmets adorned the soldiers who jostled around the enemy gates.

Achilles slowed his chariot.

Then he saw him. A tall, burly soldier, standing a little way along the walls, next to a battered chariot. No wonder he hadn't recognized this Trojan warrior at first sight. For he too was wearing a Greek helmet and a Greek breastplate ~ Achilles's own.

It was Hector.

"Murderer!" yelled Achilles, clutching his sword and springing down from the chariot. The Greek warriors made way for Achilles as he stormed relentlessly across the plain, his sword held out in front of him.

Hector stepped out from behind the chariot to face his opponent. Achilles, edging

closer, saw the Trojan grip his spear tightly. He saw Hector's big, powerful muscles and his determined stance.

But for a split second, through the slits in the stolen helmet, Achilles also glimpsed his enemy's eyes. And in them, the Greek saw something that gave him hope.

He saw fear.

"PREPARE TO DIE!" Achilles bellowed, rushing at Hector furiously.

The Trojan drew back his spear and tried to aim, but his courage deserted him. He dropped the spear clumsily, and, glancing helplessly from side to side, took the only course of action left open to him. He ran.

Up on the walls of Troy, Hecuba and Priam watched in horror, clutching each other's hands tightly.

"Don't look," whispered Priam, and his wife buried her face in his shoulder as he gathered her, sobbing, into his arms.

"Yes!" Achilles muttered under his breath, his determination fired up by the cowardice of the man who had killed his friend. "Now I'm going to get you once and for all!" Hector's stumbling, terrified figure was only paces away from him.

"REVENGE!" roared Achilles, as he closed in on his prey.

At that moment, the gods were engaged in a loud discussion about what exactly should be done.

"The Trojans have had their share of success," Hera pointed out. "It's time to let the Greeks win."

"I agree," said Athene.

"Well, if I'm not mistaken, you've already been helping your darling Achilles," said Apollo. "And don't pretend it was the wind that blew Hector's spear away."

"I'm not pretending," sniffed Athene. "And you're a fine one to talk! I think we all know where that strange mist came from, hiding your precious Hector just in time. And didn't he have a tiny little bit of help in killing poor Patroclus?"

Apollo scowled.

"All this bickering is getting us nowhere," sighed Zeus. "The point is, what are we going to do? Is Hector going to escape this time, or is Achilles going to kill him?"

At the thought of Hector being killed, Aphrodite burst into tears. Everyone else groaned. There was a stony silence. Then Zeus took a deep breath and spoke.

"I don't think we're going to come to an agreement on this. So there's only one thing to do. I'll have to get out my scales."

The others exchanged surprised glances. Zeus only ever used his scales as a last resort. Things must be serious.

Zeus got to his feet and rummaged on a shelf behind his throne.

"Aha!" he said at last, lifting down a pair of heavy golden weighing scales. After blowing the dust off them, he reached inside his robe and pulled out a small leather bag marked 'Death Powder'. Opening it carefully, he measured out two portions of the shiny black grains, one into each scale.

"The one on my left is Achilles's death portion," he explained. "And the one on my right is Hector's. Now then, let's see. . ."

Meanwhile, Andromache was in the palace, boiling a cauldron of hot water for Hector's evening bath. Humming softly as she plucked a clean linen towel from the chest, she wondered whether today had been as successful as Hector had hoped.

The baby gurgled in his high chair. "Hello little sparrow!" Andromache cooed. "Are you missing your father? I expect he'll be home soon – don't you fret."

Just then a servant girl appeared.

"Madam, there's a messenger here to see you," she said.

The messenger stepped into the room, cleared his throat and said loudly, "Madam, King Priam has sent me. You're to come to the city wall."

"Why, whatever's happened?" asked Andromache.

"I don't know, Madam. He just said you should come at once."

Something about his tone of voice scared Andromache. She seized her cloak, left her maidservant to look after the baby and hurried out of the palace.

At the wall, Priam ran to meet her. The minute she saw his face, she knew something was terribly wrong.

"What is it?" she cried, grabbing his outstretched hands. "Is it Hector? Is

he wounded? Tell me!"

Priam's face crumpled and he clung to her arm like a child.

Andromache shook him off and pushed her way through the crowd. Hecuba was crouching down, her back against the wall. Her face was covered by her hands.

Stepping past her, the fear rising in her throat, Andromache looked over the wall. For a moment, all she could see were hordes of Greeks. She scanned the battlefield.

Then she saw Hector. He was lying on the dusty ground.

Andromache's head started to spin. She clutched at the top of the wall to steady herself. "No!" she murmured, closing her eyes. "Please don't let it be true."

But when she looked again, he was still there. Andromache's legs gave way beneath her. Suddenly she remembered that she'd left the cauldron over the fire.

"The water will boil dry," she mumbled, then realized it didn't matter.

Hector wouldn't be coming home.

She felt Paris's hand on her shoulder.

"He was so brave," Paris lied, blocking out of his mind the image of his brother, running desperately from Achilles, hounded shamefully to death, like a fox or a rat.

"He fought back right up to the last minute," Paris went on. "You should be proud of him."

Andromache couldn't speak.

Priam stumbled up behind her and took her arm. Then the three of them, wife, brother and father-in-law, stood staring in silence at the body, while Hecuba sat on the ground next to them, weeping hopelessly.

As they watched, a Greek soldier walked up to the body and crouched on the ground next to it. Andromache had never seen him before, but she knew it must be Achilles.

When he stood up, they saw that he had tied long leather straps around Hector's ankles.

"What's he doing?" gasped Paris.

Achilles picked up the loose ends of the two straps and walked the short distance to his chariot.

He tied the straps to the back of it, climbed in and took hold of the reins.

"No!" groaned Priam, his voice choking with grief.

The horses jumped to a start. Andromache brought her hands up to her face, trembling with utter horror.

Then, at last, the hot, prickly tears began to squeeze from her eyes as she watched the Greek chariot charge at high speed across the Trojan plain, with the dead body of her beloved husband bumping along behind it in the dust.

CHAPTER EIGHT

BURYING THE DEAD

Achilles was miserable. Although he'd just killed Hector, he felt no sense of triumph. He felt depressed.

He'd just returned from his best friend's funeral. Patroclus had been given all the attention a hero deserved. The servants had made a huge pile of branches, and laid the body on top before setting light to the wood.

Achilles had stared numbly as the flames took hold. The fire burned all day, and the Greek soldiers came in groups to pay their respects. In the evening, all that was left of Patroclus's body was a heap of charred bones, which they had wrapped in soft material and placed in a golden urn.

Now, Achilles was left with a sad and empty feeling. He'd killed Hector, but where did that get him? He was one of the best fighters in the world, but he was powerless to bring back his dear friend and comrade. He was starting to wonder what the point of all this fighting was ~ so many meaningless deaths, and all for the sake of a woman. Would they ever win Helen back?

The urn containing Patroclus's bones now stood in a corner of Achilles's tent. As he stared at, it he heard someone behind him. Turning around, he saw his servant girl, Briseis. Agamemnon had returned her as soon as Achilles had rejoined the war.

Briseis came and put a sympathetic hand on his shoulder.

"I feel so guilty," confided Achilles. "Why did I let him go into battle? If only I'd refused, he'd still be here now, pouring the wine and . . . "

"He wanted to fight," Briseis reminded him. "It was his choice. At least they managed to retrieve his body. Think how much worse you'd feel if you hadn't even been able to give him a proper funeral."

Achilles just shrugged, so Briseis tried another approach. "Perhaps you should try to get some rest," she suggested. "Did you sleep at all last night?"

Achilles shook his head. He'd spent the night on the beach, watching the rhythmic movement of the dark waves on the shore.

After a long silence, he said, "I'm going to keep his bones."

"Aren't you going to bury them?" asked Briseis in surprise.

"When I die, I want my bones to be put in the same urn. Then we can be buried together."

For days, Achilles remained distraught. Every evening, when he returned from the battlefield and saw the urn in the corner, his feelings of anger and hopelessness welled up again. And he took out his frustration in a terrible way.

Hector's body still lay on the dirty ground behind the tent, the leather straps tied around his ankles.

Every night, as dusk fell, Achilles fastened the straps to the back of his chariot, and drove up and down the shore, dragging Hector's body behind him. When he was exhausted, he untied the straps and left the body sprawling face-down in the dirt.

From Zeus's palace, the gods were keeping an eye on Achilles, and becoming more and more concerned. Finally, Aphrodite could bear it no longer and called an urgent meeting.

"We must do something," she insisted. "We can't just stand by and watch him treat Hector's body so shamefully ~ it's not right."

"Hear, hear!" chimed in Apollo.

The king of the gods glanced at his wife."Hera?" he asked. "What do you think?"

Hera paused for a moment. Then she said, "I agree. I'm pleased that Achilles killed Hector," she continued, "and I still want the Greeks to win the war. . . but I agree that his treatment of Hector's body is wrong and should be stopped."

"Well!" exclaimed Apollo, raising his eyebrows. "I never thought I'd hear you sympathize with a Trojan!"

Hera scowled at him.

"Athene?" said Zeus, ignoring them.

"I agree with Hera," said Athene. "Hector's body should be returned to his parents to be buried. No one deserves to be treated like that ~ not even a Trojan."

"So we're all agreed," said Zeus, sounding relieved.

"The question is, what are we going to do about it?" asked Apollo.

"Couldn't we just steal the body and take it back to Troy?" suggested Athene.

"No," said Zeus firmly. "I want Achilles to give up the body of his own accord. Would somebody please summon Hermes?"

Meanwhile, in Troy, the whole city was in mourning. Priam and Hecuba were overcome by grief, and their daughter, Cassandra, did her best to comfort them. But Paris tried to avoid his parents. He couldn't help feeling that they blamed him for Hector's death ~ and probably for Polydorus's too.

Helen wandered the corridors, weeping for Hector, who'd always been kind to her. As for Andromache, she never left her chamber. She refused to see anyone except her servant girls and baby son.

One evening, Priam was sitting alone in the courtyard with his head in his hands. Suddenly Hermes appeared in front of him. Priam struggled to his feet. He recognized the messenger god immediately by the wings on his sandals.

"King Priam," Hermes announced. "Zeus has sent me. Load a wagon with treasure, find a driver and hitch up some mules. You must go to Achilles to ask for Hector's body."

"But he'll kill me!" he gasped.

"No he won't," replied Hermes. "I'll take care of you. Now do as I say."

And he disappeared.

So Priam ordered his men to get the wagon ready, and hurried to the storeroom with two servants. He found Hecuba there, sorting through a chest of Hector's things, her eyes red from crying. When he told her about Hermes, she burst into tears again.

"What?" she sobbed. "Go to Achilles's tent all by yourself? To the Greek camp? But they'll kill you! No, Priam! I've lost two sons ~ I can't bear to lose my husband too."

"It's an order from Zeus," said Priam gently, as he went over to a chest and lifted the lid. He picked out twelve fine fur cloaks, twelve soft wool blankets, and two silver goblets, and loaded the servants' arms with the gifts.

"You're not going, Priam," said Hecuba, her voice trembling. "You can't!"

"I have to go. It's our only chance to get Hector's body back. Do you want him to lie unburied in an enemy camp? Don't you think he deserves a proper funeral?"

A short while later, the treasure had been loaded onto the back of the wagon. Night had fallen and the courtyard was in darkness as Idaius, the driver, climbed onto the wagon seat. Hecuba watched in silence.

"Goodbye, Hecuba," said Priam, as he

Suddenly Hermes appeared in front of him

stepped into his chariot and picked up the reins. "Pray that I'll return safely."

And they drove out of the courtyard, along the city streets and through the gate onto the open plain.

Priam felt very nervous outside the city. He peered into the distance, scanning the field for enemies, but there was no one in sight. When they had been rolling across the plain for some time, the shadowy shape of the Greek wall loomed out of the darkness, eerily lit by the full moon.

Idaius stopped his horses.

"How will we get through?" he called quietly to Priam. "I'm sure there are sentries on guard ~ I can see their fires."

At once, as if in answer to his question, Hermes appeared.

"Follow me," he ordered. He led them close to the wall, then leaped into the air and soared up to the top. Balancing for a moment on the battlements, he quickly put all the sentries to sleep before flying down to open one of the gates.

"But the ditch—" whispered Idaius.

Almost as he spoke, a wooden bridge appeared, leading across the ditch to the open gate. Hermes beckoned silently and the two vehicles trundled safely through the gateway. Priam glanced back and saw the sentries fast asleep beside their fires, their heads lolling back, their mouths wide open.

With Hermes flying ahead, they made their way through the enemy camp. Priam felt sick. His palms were sweating so much, he could hardly hold the reins. He was terrified

that someone would hear them, but they drove unnoticed past rows of tents and ships, until at last they came to the far end.

"This is Achilles's tent," said Hermes, landing gracefully. "I'm going to leave you now, but I'll be back later."

Priam looked uncertain.

"What am I to do?" he asked.

"Go in and talk to him," replied Hermes. "Ask him for your son's body."

"But what if. . . ?" began Priam.

But Hermes had vanished.

Priam waited a while, then climbed shakily down from his chariot. "Wait for me here," he said to Idaius. He was quaking inside, but he took a deep breath and strode over to the tent.

Inside, Achilles and his companions had just finished eating. The table was strewn with the remains of their meal. Achilles himself was sitting on a chair with his back to the others, staring absent-mindedly into the distance, when, to his astonishment, an old man appeared in the doorway. Achilles leaped to his feet, and everyone else looked up.

Priam stood just inside the tent. He was too scared to say anything.

No one knew who he was, but they could tell by his appearance that he wasn't a Greek. Some of the men started to reach for their weapons, but Achilles motioned to them to keep still. After observing the stranger's face for several seconds, he sat down again.

"Well, old man," he said. "You gave us all a shock. We're not used to strangers arriving in the middle of the night without warning. Where have you come from?"

A note of gentleness in Achilles's voice gave Priam the courage to speak. Stepping forward and kneeling humbly at the young man's feet, he said simply, "Sir, my name is Priam, King of Troy." Amazed murmurs rippled around the tent.

"I've come here to beg you to give me back my son's body," continued Priam. "My wife was afraid, but I hoped you'd have pity. I couldn't live the rest of my life knowing Hector had not been buried. . . "

His voice began to quiver, and he glanced up, unsure whether to continue.

"There's a wagon full of gifts for you outside. . . " he added tentatively.

Achilles looked down at the old man's bloodshot eyes and wrinkled face. He was reminded of his own father, Peleus, far away in Greece. Achilles had gone to say goodbye to him before leaving for Troy, but that was years ago now. He realized with a shock that his father might not even be alive when the war ended.

"You're a brave man, Priam, to come here alone," he said at last. "Your son would be proud."

Priam just bowed his head.

"Please," said Achilles, "stay here

and rest for a while ~ you look exhausted. I'll have my men prepare some food for you."

"Sir," mumbled Priam. "You are very kind ~ but all I want is my son's body."

"You will have your son's body in due course, but there's something I must do first. Have some food while you're waiting."

"I couldn't eat anything, sir," replied the old man, "but I would be glad to rest ~ I have hardly slept since. . . "

Achilles nodded kindly. "I'll wake you as soon as we're ready."

Priam took some sips of water from a cup brought to him by Briseis. Then he slipped off his sandals, lay down and was asleep within minutes.

When the king awoke, it was dawn, and, for a moment, he wasn't sure where he was. Someone had spread a blanket over him while he slept. Pushing it aside, he got to his feet and stepped quietly outside.

His chariot stood where he had left it, the horses tethered to a post. Idaius was lying in the wagon seat, snoring loudly. And in the back of the wagon, in place of the gifts he had brought, Priam saw the body, carefully cleaned and wrapped in a beautiful cloak.

Hector's face was disfigured, but the old man recognized his son at once.

He reached out a hand and laid it gently on Hector's head. As he stood there, weeping silently, Hermes appeared once more.

"It's time to leave," he said.

Priam nodded and wiped away his tears. He shook Idaius awake and climbed into his chariot. Then they set off for home.

The battle was raging again near the city wall. With Hector dead and Achilles back in action, the Trojans were by far the weaker side. Paris had tried to take over from his brother, but he knew he could never command the same respect.

Since Hector's funeral, he'd been feeling guilty. He remembered his days as a shepherd and almost wished he'd never returned to Troy. He wished he could do something to make his parents as proud of him as they had been of Hector. The trouble was, he knew he wasn't brave enough.

Whenever the fighting grew fierce, Paris kept as close as possible to the city gate, so that he could escape if necessary. He was there now, lurking by the wall, his bow in his hand. Swords were clashing all around him, and dust was flying everywhere. Suddenly, he spotted Achilles nearby.

He lifted his bow. With trembling fingers, he positioned an arrow and drew back the string. But he couldn't bring himself to release it. Every time he was about to fire, his nerve failed. He couldn't help thinking of what Achilles might do to him if he survived. He'd kill him, just as mercilessly as he'd killed poor Hector. And Paris was terrified of dying.

Just as he was about to give up, he heard a strange voice whispering in his ear.

"Go on Paris! You can do it! Just take aim and fire. Think how proud your father will be. You'll be the avenger of your brother's death. The whole city will salute you as a hero. Go on! Fire!"

Paris was startled. He looked behind him but no one was there. Spurred on by the voice, he could feel his heart beating faster. Achilles was still within reach. Leaning back against the gatepost to steady himself, Paris raised his bow again, took aim ~ and fired.

The arrow sped away. Paris had aimed too low and, for a moment, it looked as if it would land harmlessly in the dust. But Apollo was watching. He took a deep breath and blew hard underneath the arrow, so that it skimmed along just above the ground.

Achilles was busy fighting with a Trojan soldier. He cursed as he felt a sudden thudding pain in his left heel. Someone's arrow must have lodged there. Now he'd have to go and have his foot bandaged, just as he was getting into his stride.

But when Achilles tried to reach for the arrow to pull it out, he stumbled and fell. Something was wrong. Why was the searing pain from his heel spreading through him, crippling his limbs and clutching at his heart?

"Help me!" he shouted, the blood draining from his face.

Ulysses was fighting nearby. He ran to Achilles's side and tried to pull the arrow out. Achilles screamed with pain and several Greek soldiers began to gather around.

"Get back to the battle!" ordered Ulysses. "I'll take care of him."

But the battle had come to a standstill. Both sides looked on in amazement. Someone had felled the mighty Achilles!

Paris could hardly believe his eyes. He saw Achilles lying curled up on the ground, the arrow still protruding from his foot at an awkward angle. For a while, Achilles's whole body seemed racked with tension. Then, at last, after a sudden jerking movement, he lay still.

Thetis was in her father's cave at the bottom of the sea. She was sitting on a giant shell, weaving garlands of seaweed and gossiping with her sisters. Suddenly, an icy chill ran through her body.

"What is it?" Nereus asked his

daughter, noticing she'd turned very pale.

"Achilles. . ." gasped Thetis urgently. "I ~ I think he's dead!"

The other sea nymphs stared at her.

"Dead!" Nereus exclaimed. "Surely not. How do you know?"

"I just know," sobbed Thetis. "But I don't understand. How can he be dead? I made him immortal! He's supposed to live forever. . . I must go to him immediately."

She glided up to the surface of the sea and burst out of the water, then flew as fast as she could until she came to Troy. Circling over a wide area, she desperately scanned the plain below for a glimpse of her beloved son.

Then she spotted a group of men carrying someone away from the fighting. Immediately she saw that it was Achilles.

She swooped closer until she could see his face ~ it was frighteningly white and lifeless, and she could no longer deny that he really was dead. Tears trickled down her cheeks, and she wiped them away as she quickly scanned his body for signs of injury. How could Achilles die?

But when she saw the wound in his foot where Paris's arrow had struck him, Thetis's thoughts went back to the day she'd dipped her baby son into the magical River Styx ~ holding him by his tiny heel.

"His heel!" she gasped, realizing with a shock what had happened. "His heel's still mortal ~ it never touched the water!"

And the prediction Chiron the centaur had made all those years ago began ringing in her ears. . . "The Greek army will never capture Troy unless Achilles fights with them, and Achilles will die fighting there."

That evening, Agamemnon sat in his tent, his head in his hands.

"Achilles," he groaned. "Our best fighter, and such a fine young man. Just when we were winning. . . Oh Menelaus, whatever next?" he sighed, staring wearily at his brother.

"It's as if we're cursed," said Menelaus grimly. He felt terrible. He still longed to get Helen back, but so many men were dying ~ so many great men, lost forever because of what he, Menelaus, wanted.

Just then, a herald appeared. "There's a servant girl to see you, sir," he announced.

Agamemnon looked up, surprised.

"All right," he sighed. "Show her in."

Briseis, Achilles's servant girl, slipped nervously into the tent. She had clearly been crying. Agamemnon looked at her kindly. "What can I do for you, Briseis?" he asked.

"I have to tell you something, sir," she said.

"Go on," said the king.

"It's something Achilles told me. He was keeping Patroclus's bones in a golden urn in his tent, and he said that when he died, he wanted his bones to be put into the same urn, so they could be buried together." She looked at Agamemnon. He nodded.

"Then that's what we'll do," he said. "After the funeral, we'll bury them together."

"Oh thank you, sir," said Briseis, running forward and kissing his hand. Then she turned and hurried out of the tent.

Ulysses, was sitting on the other side of the tent, watching the two brothers. He wished there was some way he could help them. Without Achilles, there was no way they could fight their way out of this.

He must be able to come up with a plan. If he really put his mind to it. . .

CHAPTER NINE

THE WOODEN HORSE

Early one morning, not long after Paris had killed Achilles, King Priam was wandering the streets of Troy.

Hecuba was still so upset about Hector, he could hardly bear to stay in the palace. And grief wasn't the only thing on Priam's mind ~ he was rapidly losing hope that the war would ever end. Since both sides had lost their best warriors, there was a lack of direction in the fighting.

After roaming around for some time, he found himself near the city wall. He climbed to the top and came upon a group of guards, deep in conversation. As soon as they saw him, they called him over.

"Your majesty, come and see!"

Priam joined them and looked over the wall. He could hardly believe his eyes.

Some distance from the city, in the middle of the plain, was a huge wooden horse.

"Whatever is it?" said Priam in bewilderment.

"Looks like a horse, sir," said a guard.

Priam glared at him.

"I can see that," he said impatiently. "But what on earth is it doing there?"

"No one knows, sir," replied the guard. "It was there at daybreak, so it must have arrived in the night. And that's not all, sir. The Greeks have gone. Vanished. Completely disappeared."

Priam stared at him in disbelief.

It's true, sir," said another guard. "A group of men have been to check. The camp's been dismantled and the ships that were left have gone. Looks like the Greeks have given up and sailed home."

Priam was stunned. But before he could even collect his thoughts, he heard voices at the gate below. A minute later, two guards appeared at the top of the steps, a young man between them. His clothes were filthy, and he looked terrified.

"We found him hiding near the shore, sir," said one of the guards. "He claims to be a deserter from the Greek army." As he spoke, he twisted the man's arm behind his back, causing him to cry out in pain.

"Let go of him," ordered Priam.

The guards reluctantly obeyed.

"Tell me who you are," Priam said.

"My name is Sinon, sir," replied the trembling prisoner.

"And you are with the Greek army?"

"Well, I was," replied the man, rubbing his sore arm. "But when I heard they were planning to sail back to Greece, I ran away and hid until they'd gone. I couldn't face the long journey back ~ there's nothing for me to go home for anyway. Besides, I'm sick of being ordered around. . . " He paused to draw breath and looked nervously up at Priam.

"Why have they gone?" asked Priam.

"King Agamemnon decided they were never going to break into the city, especially now that Achilles is dead. And Menelaus agreed that enough men had lost their lives and it was time to call a halt to the whole thing. So they packed up and left."

"And the horse?"

"It's a gift to Athene," said Sinon. "Calchas the soothsayer told Agamemnon it would ensure a safe journey. He also said. . . "

"Go on," said the king.

". . . that if the horse was brought inside the city gates, Athene would protect Troy and it would never be taken by enemies."

The guards exchanged suspicious glances, and Priam didn't know whether to believe the man or not. He decided to go home and think things over.

When Priam got back to the palace, Hecuba and Cassandra were waiting for him. News of the wooden horse and the Greeks' departure had already begun to spread, and when he told them what Sinon had said, Hecuba smiled for the first time in weeks.

"Maybe it's a sign that things are going to get better at last," she said. "What are you going to do?"

"Well, I don't see what harm it would do to bring the horse into the city," replied Priam. "And if the man's speaking the truth, it could do us a lot of good."

"*If* he's speaking the truth," interrupted Cassandra. "It's a trap, Father ~ I'm certain of it. Why should we believe what a Greek says?"

"He had an honest face," said Priam.

Cassandra groaned.

"Father, you're so trusting! Just because someone has 'an honest face', you're prepared to risk everything."

"But what's the risk?" asked her father.

"Oh never mind!" snapped Cassandra and she flounced out of the room.

Later that day, the gates were opened. Hordes of old people, servants, women and children swarmed out onto the plain. They'd been trapped in the city for so long, they hardly remembered what it was like to go outside. They crowded around the horse, jumping up to rap on its body, stroking its wooden legs and gasping at its incredible size. Mothers lifted up their children to see its long, tapering nose and pointed ears.

Long ropes were brought from the city and attached to the horse. Then fifty of the strongest men took hold of the ends and began to pull. Although the horse had been built on large wooden wheels, it was hard work moving it across the plain's rough surface. It seemed surprisingly heavy.

Puffing and panting, the men slowly dragged the horse closer and closer to the city, cheered on by hundreds of citizens. Through the gateway they guided the enormous object, being careful not to scrape its sides. They pulled it along the streets, all the way to the marketplace. And there it stood for the rest of the day ~ the most amazing sight anyone in Troy had ever seen.

That evening, the Trojans feasted until late into the night. For the first time in years, the city gates and walls could be left unguarded and everyone could enjoy themselves without fear of attack. The Greeks had gone. The war was over at last.

Finally, in the early hours of the morning, they sank into bed, exhausted but exhilarated, and slept soundly.

Inside the horse's hollow body, it was stiflingly hot. Menelaus wiped the sweat from his forehead and sighed loudly.

"Shhhh!" hissed Ulysses.

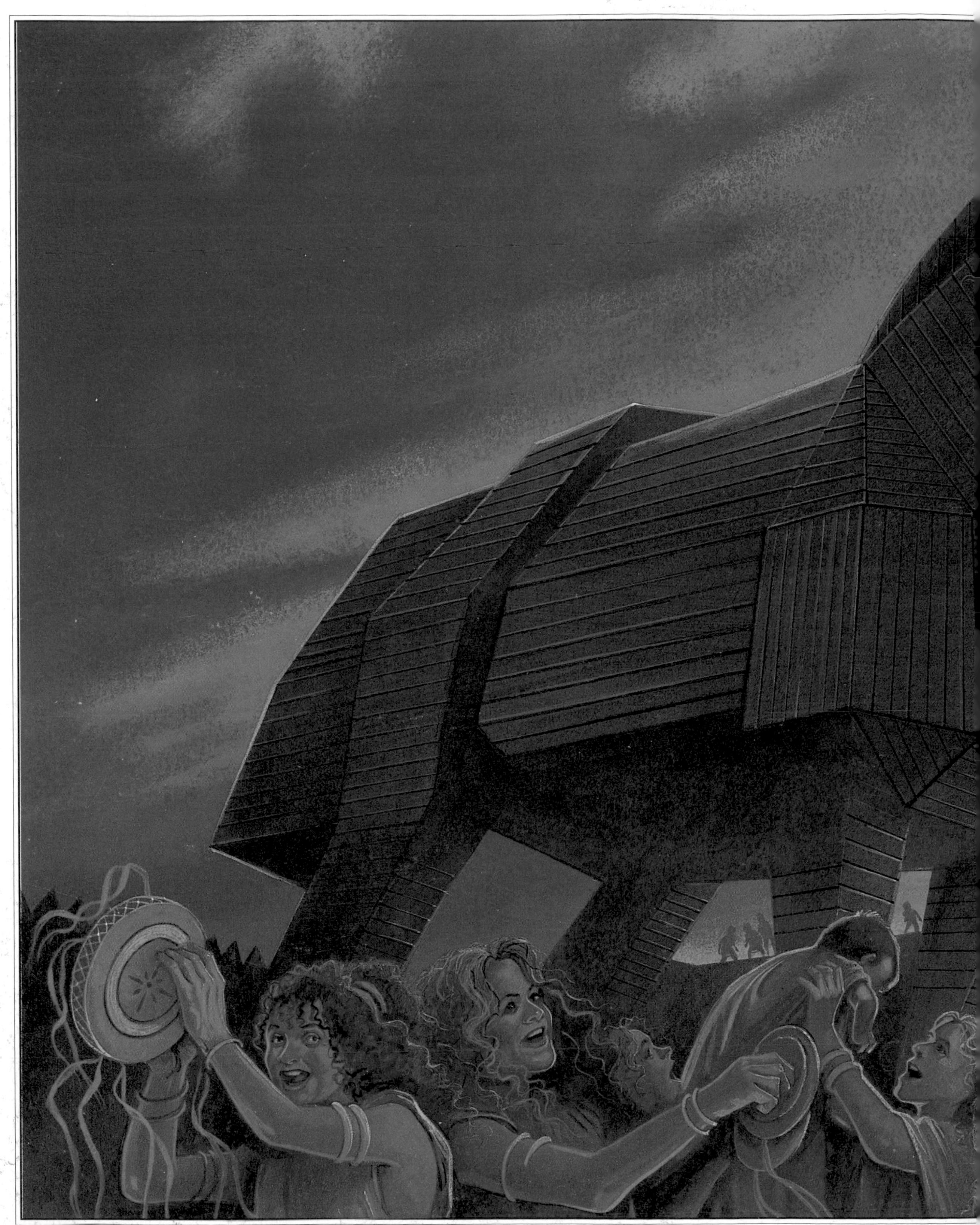

There it stood for the rest of the day...

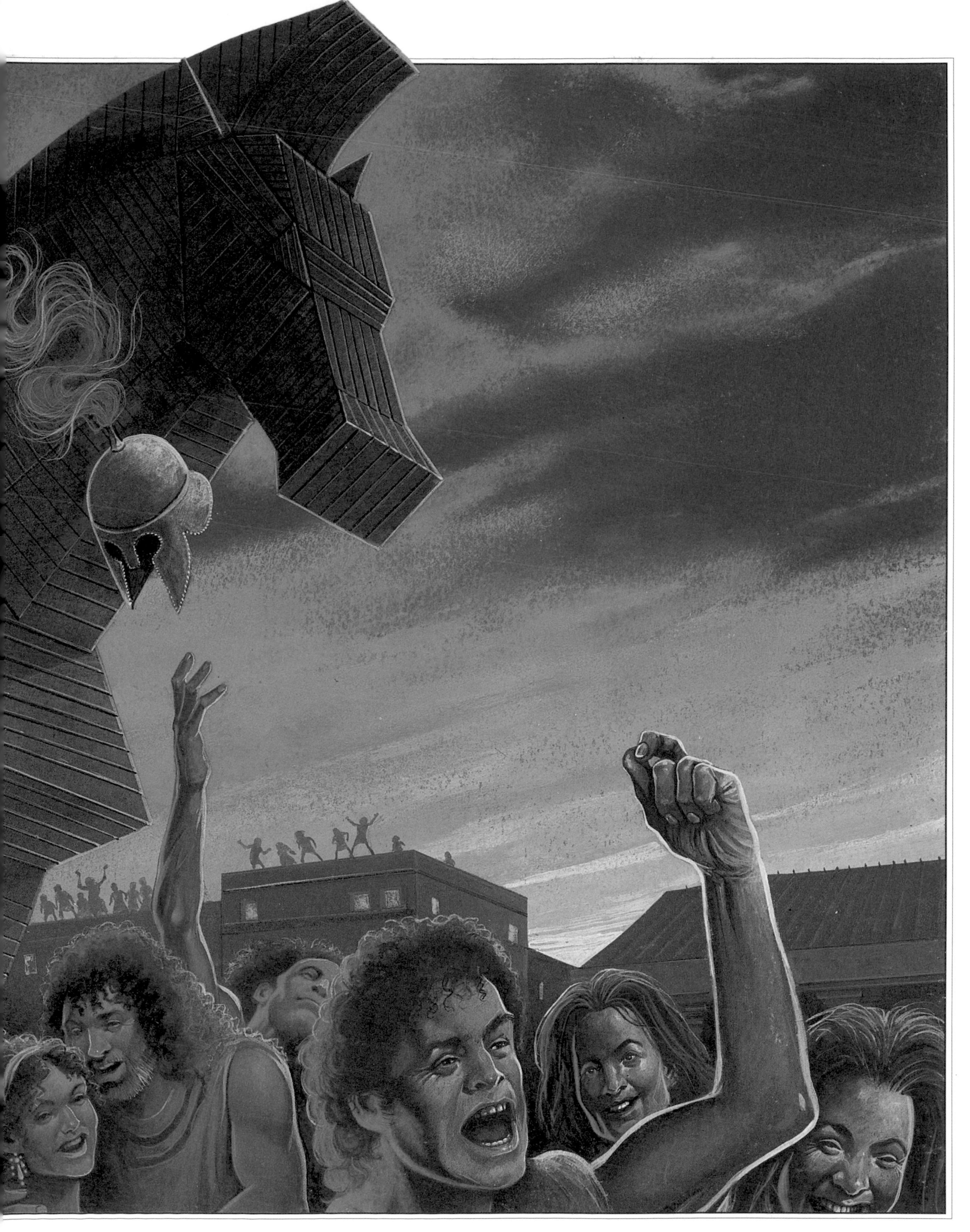

. . .the most amazing sight anyone in Troy had ever seen

"It's been quiet outside for ages now," whispered Menelaus. "Surely it's safe to take a look?"

The others murmured in agreement. There were twelve of them, and they'd been inside the horse since the previous night. The tension was awful. For hours now, they'd been sitting absolutely still, hardly daring to move, clutching their weapons to their bodies, for fear a slight rattle of metal against wood might give them away.

Nestor had his ear pressed against the side of the horse.

"There's no sign of life out there," he said. "They must have gone to bed by now."

Ulysses thought for a while. The horse had been his idea, so he felt responsible for the outcome. Things had gone smoothly so far, and he didn't want to waste all their hard work by being impatient at the last minute.

Still, it was very quiet outside. And they couldn't afford to wait too long. Once morning came, it would be too late. Ulysses decided it was time to act.

"All right," he said, quietly but firmly. "I'm going to run through the plan one more time. Is everyone listening?"

The others nodded.

"First," Ulysses whispered, "we climb out of the horse, get our bearings, then find the gates ~ all in total silence. When we find the

gates, we'll have to unlock them— "

"What if they're guarded?" interrupted Diomedes.

"We'll just have to hope they won't be," said Ulysses. "If Sinon was convincing enough, the Trojans should think we've gone for good. Then, hopefully, the rest of the army will have sailed back during the night and will be waiting outside the city."

"If Sinon managed to signal to them," said Nestor.

"How will we know if he did?" asked Diomedes.

"We won't!" snapped Menelaus.

"Be quiet!" hissed Ulysses. "Then, assuming the army is waiting outside the gates, we let them in ~ and destroy the city."

It sounded straightforward, but the men knew they were in a dangerous situation. They clenched their fists and breathed deeply to prepare themselves for the attack. It was their last chance.

"Diomedes," said Ulysses. "Open the trapdoor. And everyone else ~ keep still and don't make a sound."

Paris awoke suddenly. He lay still for a few minutes, wondering what had disturbed him. In the distance, he could hear shouting. At first, he thought it was just the celebrations still going on. But as the sounds grew louder, he wasn't so sure. Deciding to go and investigate, he slipped out of bed, dressed quickly and walked through the corridors.

As soon as he opened the palace gate, he realized that something was wrong. Over to his right, spirals of smoke were swirling up into the sky above the city. And the voices he'd heard before were coming closer all the time. They weren't the happy sounds of merrymakers wending their way home from a feast. They were the screams and shouts of terrified people.

"What's going on?" muttered Paris under his breath.

Then he spotted a group of bedraggled citizens tearing up the street. As they came closer, Paris stepped out into their path.

"What is it?" he shouted. "What's happening? Is your house on fire?"

The oldest member of the group slowed down enough to reply.

"More like the whole city, sir! The Greeks have come back ~ they're destroying everything and killing everyone. . . and they're heading this way!"

One of his companions tugged at his sleeve and they hurried away. Behind them came more people ~ small groups at first, then larger ones, until there was a constant stream of citizens fleeing past the palace. Old men stumbling along with sticks, families with screaming babies and toddlers, and younger, fitter people overtaking the slower ones, all of them frantic with fear.

As Paris watched, his mind raced. This could be his chance. If he acted now, he could save the city. He decided to go back to the palace for his weapons. Then he'd go and fight off those Greeks once and for all. He knew there wouldn't be many of them ~ probably just a small contingent that had returned to cause trouble.

Minutes later, Paris was back at the gate, fully armed. He strode through the city, heading in the opposite direction from everyone else. By now, the streets were so packed with people, he had to struggle to get through. As he approached the marketplace, the smell of burning wood filled the air. Blood-curdling screams rang out from the buildings as flames roared from windows and doorways.

In the panic, nobody recognized Paris. They jostled past him, desperate to get as far from the danger as possible.

"Don't go that way!" shouted a woman as she struggled by, a small child clinging to each arm. "The Greeks will kill you!"

Paris pushed on until, at last, he stepped into the marketplace. There stood the huge wooden horse, a trapdoor swinging open from its belly.

And instead of the small group of Greeks he had expected, he saw what looked like the whole army surging in his direction. In that enclosed and familiar space, the soldiers appeared much larger and far more formidable than they had out on the plain. Brandishing their mighty weapons and yelling war cries, they were killing everyone they could see, and destroying whatever stood in their path.

Paris immediately had second thoughts about being a hero. He turned to join the escaping hordes ~ just as an arrow came whistling through the air, heading straight for his back.

"Look out!" screamed an old woman.

But her warning came too late.

Before Paris knew what was going on, the arrow tore into his shoulder and pierced right through to his heart. He clutched at his chest, moaning with agony, as blood began to spurt from the wound.

Staggering forward a few steps, he grabbed hold of a marble pillar and leaned heavily against it. Slowly, his hands slipped down the pillar, smearing its smooth white surface with streaks of blood. Then he slumped onto the ground.

Priam was woken by a piercing scream. He climbed out of bed and stumbled to the door. Hecuba and Cassandra were in the corridor, weeping and shivering in their nightgowns, with a small group of servants.

"What is it?" asked Priam blearily. "Who screamed?"

One of the servants spoke up.

"The Greeks have come back, sir," he spluttered. "They're destroying the city. . . setting fire to everything, killing all the men, capturing the women and children—"

"They've killed Paris!" sobbed Hecuba. "He went out to try to fight them off and they've killed him!"

Priam stared at them, dazed with horror. His dear children, Polydorus, Hector, and now Paris too ~ all gone; sacrificed to this terrible, pointless war.

He recalled, so many years before, hearing the prediction that Paris, his baby son, would bring about the destruction of Troy. He thought, too late, of Cassandra's warnings. The king felt bewildered, trapped in a nightmare that never seemed to end. . . and he sank to his knees as the sound of clashing swords, heavy footsteps and shouts began to echo through the palace.

A maidservant came tearing along the corridor. "The soldiers are here!" she screamed. "They've broken through the palace gates ~ and they're coming this— "

But before she could finish, a group of Greek soldiers, led by Ulysses, burst through the door.

Priam stepped forward.

"I am King Priam," he said, his voice quivering, "and this is my home. I will hand over anything you ask for, but I beg you not to harm my family or my servants."

Ulysses stared at the old man for a few seconds, then looked away.

"Search the palace!" he ordered. "Kill the men and take the women as prisoners."

The soldiers split up into groups and set off in different directions. One of them grabbed Hecuba by the arm. She struggled, but he held her firmly and tied her hands together behind her back. Twisting around, she saw another soldier doing the same to Cassandra. He tied the rope tightly, and the girl cried out in pain.

"Loosen it!" commanded Ulysses immediately.

Two soldiers reappeared, bringing Helen and Andromache with them. Helen was weeping uncontrollably. As she passed Priam, she looked up at him and opened her mouth to speak. But she could say nothing.

All she knew was that she'd never meant it to end like this ~ so much destruction; so many horrific deaths. If only Paris could protect her. Or Menelaus. . .

The soldiers began to lead all the women away. Hecuba turned her head to look at Priam. His blank eyes stared confusedly. He glanced at her with faint recognition.

"Please don't hurt my husband!" she called over her shoulder. "He's an old man. . . "

But as she turned the corner, and Priam disappeared from view, she knew she would never see him again.

Feeling guilty and ashamed, Ulysses stared down at the ground. So this was how the war was to end. Women being dragged away from their homes, old men spending their last moments in terror, families being torn apart. . .

He remembered how excited he'd felt when they'd arrived at Troy and set up camp on the shore. How could he have imagined then that he'd still be here all these years later! He thought of his family in Ithaca ~ his wife Penelope, and Telemachus. He'd been away for so long, he wondered if he'd even recognize his son. Still, with any luck, he'd soon be home.

Shaking himself out of his reverie, he tightened his grip on his spear and marched off to search the palace.

The gods sat on the slopes of Mount Olympus, discussing the end of the war.

"I knew the Greeks would win in the end!" said Athene proudly.

"So did I," said Hera. Apollo snorted.

"I don't think it's anything to be proud of," said Zeus sternly. "War is such an unpleasant business. But those humans will keep killing each other," he sighed. "I'm just relieved it's all over. And," he added, turning to his wife, "I'm sorry. I ~ well, I haven't been myself recently." He didn't mention Thetis.

Hera said nothing. She just took his hand and smiled. Just then, Aphrodite wandered up, a scowl on her face. She'd been sulking ever since the war ended.

"Come on, my dear!" Zeus chided her gently. "Let's put this behind us, shall we?"

She looked up at him defiantly.

"It's all over now," Zeus said, "and thank goodness everything's back to normal. The Greeks have Helen back, and that's all there is to it!"

"Oh, look!" cried Aphrodite suddenly, her frown disappearing. "Look down there!"

They all got up and peered down at the Trojan shore, where the Greeks were packing up and preparing to leave.

"He's taking her back!" cried Aphrodite happily. "He still loves her! Oh, how sweet!"

Menelaus and Helen were standing together on the beach. As the first few Greek ships set off, their huge white sails billowing in the wind, Helen tossed her still beautiful curls and smiled up at her husband.

Menelaus, wiping away tears of joy from his face, bent down and kissed her tenderly. Then he took her gently by the arm, and, with one last glance over his shoulder at the Trojan plain, he led his wife up the gangplank and onto his ship.

CHAPTER TEN

THE SEARCH

Sitting in the sun outside Ulysses's palace at Ithaca, Telemachus sighed.

"If only. . ." he mumbled to himself. "If *only* he'd come back!"

Telemachus, the son Ulysses had left behind as a baby, was nearly twenty years old, and he had never known his father. He hadn't seen him since the day Ulysses had left to fight in the war at Troy, nineteen years ago, and he had been far too young to remember anything about it.

The war itself was over, of course ~ it had been won years ago. As news of the victory had arrived at Ithaca, everyone had waited eagerly for the return of their king, and grand preparations had been made to welcome him.

But Ulysses had never appeared.

No one seemed to know where he was. All the other Greek leaders were either dead, or safely home. But Ulysses and his men were still missing. Nevertheless, Telemachus and his mother, Queen Penelope could never quite give up hope that, one day, he might come home.

Telemachus sighed again, and turned to watch the party that seemed to be taking place on the lawn in front of the palace. A crowd of young men were drinking, eating, and generally enjoying themselves.

He watched Antinous and Eurymachus finishing a board game. Antinous, always a bad loser, tipped the board over and sent the pieces scattering into the grass.

Then he noticed Amphinomus directing some servants as they rolled a new barrel of wine out of the palace storeroom.

His father's wine.

Telemachus felt furious. Everything ~ the wine, the food, even the board game, belonged to Ulysses. But the young men of Ithaca hung around the palace, day after day, helping themselves. And there was absolutely nothing Telemachus could do to stop them.

He tried to imagine Ulysses marching into the palace grounds with a huge sword and chasing all the uninvited guests away. But it wasn't easy to imagine, as he wasn't even sure what his father looked like.

Just as he was wishing yet again that his father would come back, he saw a strange figure standing at the palace

gates. Telemachus got up at once to welcome him. Although he wasn't keen on the uninvited guests eating him out of house and home, he knew that a stranger should always be offered hospitality.

The visitor was tall and handsome, with unusual flashing grey eyes.

"Welcome to our house, sir!" said Telemachus, taking the man's long spear and beautiful shield. "Please come in and have something to eat."

He led the visitor into the hall and ordered a servant to prepare some food.

"So," began Telemachus, when his guest had sat down, "who are you, and what brings you to Ithaca?"

"My name is Mentes," began the stranger, "from Taphos. But never mind about that. Where's Ulysses? I was expecting to find him here."

Telemachus sat up, looking startled.

"Oh yes, I've heard he'll be home soon," said Mentes. "In fact, I assumed all those people out there had gathered to welcome him back."

"Just the opposite," said Telemachus wearily. "They all hope he's dead! They're my mother's suitors, you see ~ her admirers. They're trying to impress her, hoping she'll give up on ever seeing my father again, and choose one of them as a new husband. Well, I suppose she is a good catch ~ whoever marries her will be King of Ithaca, and get this palace and all my father's possessions."

Mentes opened his mouth to respond, but Telemachus couldn't be stopped.

"But they don't even behave like proper suitors," he moaned. "They just make a nuisance of themselves and have parties night and day at my father's expense. The stupid louts," he added angrily.

"So why doesn't your mother just choose one of them?" asked Mentes at last.

"She just can't seem to make up her mind," Telemachus frowned. "One minute, she says, 'I'm not getting married again! I'm sure Ulysses will be back soon.' The next minute, it's 'Oh, I'm sure Ulysses is never coming back! I promise, when I've finished this piece of weaving, I'll pick a new husband.'

"The trouble is," he went on, "she just can't give up hope that my father will come home. But she knows she'll have to do something soon. The suitors won't leave until she's made up her mind, and I can't get rid of them ~ there are just too many of them. And all the palace guards went off with my father to fight in the war. Anyway. . ." Telemachus moved closer to Mentes and lowered his voice. "I think my mother must secretly like having them around. If she didn't, she'd find a way to get them to leave."

"Well," said Mentes encouragingly, "you can be sure of one thing. The moment Ulysses gets back, he'll get rid of them!"

In one way, the stranger's words comforted Telemachus, but in another they made him feel even more downhearted. "But where *is* he?" he said. "If only he would come back. But he never does!"

"Listen, Telemachus," said Mentes, leaning forward conspiratorially, "I've got some advice for you. You're not a child any more, and it's time you did something. First, call a meeting and tell these people exactly what you think of them."

"I can't do that!" groaned Telemachus.

"Yes, you can, Telemachus! Take control! Show them who's in charge around here! And then," Mentes went on, "I think you should go on an expedition. Visit King Nestor in Pylos, and King Menelaus in Sparta. Ask them what's happened to your father. If you hear that he's dead, then come back and arrange a wedding for your mother. If not, you'd better get ready for a fight. Because when he does get home, you'll have to help him do something about this bunch of idiots!"

Telemachus was a little taken aback by this outburst. But he was even more surprised when Mentes, standing up and spreading his arms out like wings, shot up into the air and disappeared.

At that moment, Telemachus knew the stranger had not been Mentes of Taphos at all. The flashing grey eyes, the spear and the shield. . . Telemachus realized he had been visited by none other than Athene, the bold, beautiful goddess of wisdom and war.

He had better follow her advice.

"Gentlemen!" shouted Telemachus above the noise. His mother's admirers had all assembled at the meeting place, as he had requested. The old lords of Ithaca were there too. Many of them were the fathers of the suitors who were staying at the palace.

"Silence!" yelled Telemachus.

The crowd fell quiet, and the older men gazed at the prince in admiration. He had grown up to be almost as tall, strong and good-looking as his father.

Telemachus cleared his throat. "I've asked you here today," he said, in his most official-sounding voice, "to discuss a problem that's been bothering me recently."

He looked around him at the sneering faces of the suitors.

"Or, should I say, two problems," he continued. "First, as you know, my dear father Ulysses is still not home. Though I'm sure most of you can remember what a good, kind king he was."

A murmur of agreement passed among the older members of the audience.

"And secondly," said Telemachus, taking a deep breath, "you may have noticed that a mob of hangers-on has been pestering my mother, the queen. And I have to say that I think their conduct is disgraceful. They've invited themselves to stay at our palace, and are eating our food and drinking all our wine. It's high time they left me and my mother in peace. If they don't, it's not for me to say what terrible punishment the gods might inflict on them!"

With this Telemachus angrily threw his spear down on the ground.

At first, no one spoke. Then Antinous, who always acted like the leader of the suitors, stood up casually.

"Ooooh, Telemachus, you *are* in a bad mood!" he mocked. Several of the other suitors started sniggering. "So you think the way *we're* behaving is disgraceful, do you? What about your mother? She's the one who started all this. If she doesn't want to get married again, she should say so. But oh no, she leads us on, lets us think she's going to choose one of us any minute, and then keeps us waiting around for a decision! Who does she think she is ~ Helen of Troy?"

He put his hand on his hip, batted his eyelashes and imitated Penelope's voice.

" 'Oh, Antinous! ' " he cooed. " 'Oh, Amphinomus! Oh, you're all so gorgeous, I just don't know which one to choose!' "

The suitors roared with laughter.

"How dare you!" stormed Telemachus. "She's never said such a thing in her life! How dare you mock my mother! She's got a difficult decision to make!"

"And I'll tell you another thing," sneered Antinous, "she's a crafty one. Ages ago, she said to us, 'Oh, when I've just finished this piece of weaving, I'll choose a husband.' So we waited, and waited. And after a few years we thought it couldn't possibly be taking that long. Then, do you know what happened?"

Pretending not to know, the suitors jeered and shouted, "No, tell us what happened!"

Telemachus scowled and turned red. He'd heard this story many times before.

"One of her servants told us what she was up to," snorted Antinous, "and we caught her at it. Unpicking the weaving! Every night, she undid what she'd done during the day, so she'd never be finished!"

The suitors jeered louder than ever.

"Well, we've been keeping an eye on her since we found out about her little trick and we've made her finish it. So it's time she kept her promise. And, Telemachus, if Ulysses is gone, I suppose you must be the man of the house! So tell your mother to choose a husband, and make sure you throw a good wedding party. After that, we'll leave you alone! And not before!"

Antinous performed an elaborate bow and sat down with a smug look on his face.

"Right!" growled Telemachus furiously through gritted teeth, "I am going to Pylos and Sparta to look for my father. And when he comes back you'll be sorry. That's all I've got to say." He grabbed his spear from where it lay on the floor and stomped out.

"Huh!" said Leocritus, a young suitor, as the assembly gradually broke up. "Even if Ulysses did come back, there are loads of us, and only one of him. We'd kill him easily!"

"I don't think Telemachus will really go, anyway," put in Leodes. "He's too pathetic." Mumbling in agreement, the suitors all went back to the palace to start the day's drinking.

That night, while the suitors lay in a drunken stupor, a dark ship pulled quietly out of the bay. On its deck stood Telemachus, watching Ithaca disappear into the night. Next to him was the goddess Athene.

She had helped him prepare the ship, and found him a crew of thirty-six oarsmen. As soon as they had left the harbour, she called up a great wind from the north. And all night long, the ship cut its way smoothly and swiftly through the black waves.

The following morning, the ship sailed into the wide, welcoming bay at Pylos, and Telemachus and Athene made their way up the sandy beach. Athene was now disguised as Mentor, a nobleman from Ithaca.

Telemachus was nervous. "What will I say to him?" he panicked. "A wise old king like Nestor!" After his experience in Ithaca, he wasn't feeling very confident.

They could see the king in the middle of a large crowd outside the palace. Some kind of sacrifice was being made. Nestor, seeing them some way off, leaped up and began waving vigorously. Telemachus noticed that he was very old, with a jolly, round face, a tangled, grey beard and a small, golden crown. Now Nestor was urging the people around him to wave and beckon too.

"Visitors!" he cried as they approached. "Excellent! And very well-timed ~ we're just about to make a sacrifice to Poseidon! Got to keep the sea god happy, you know! Come and join the feast, the pair of you! Who are you, and where are you from?" He grasped Telemachus's hand and shook it warmly. "I must say, your face rings a bell! And you, sir!" He now shook Athene's hand so hard that her shield slipped from her shoulder.

She smiled. "Your majesty, my name is Mentor," she began. "But this friend of mine is a much more important guest." She prodded Telemachus.

Er . . royal sir," stumbled Telemachus. "Your Majesty. We are from Ithaca, and I am Telemachus. I'm searching for news of my father. I think you fought with him at Troy."

"Ulysses!" cried Nestor delightedly. "Of course! I knew you reminded me of someone! Oh, my dear boy, you're very welcome! I remember it as if it were yesterday, fighting alongside your father on the fields of Troy. What a great man he was!"

"Was?" said Telemachus, hesitantly. "Please, your majesty ~ don't spare my feelings. Tell me ~ is my father dead?"

"Dead? Ulysses? Oh, no, no, no, I shouldn't think so," said Nestor. "A great fighter like him? The most cunning, brilliant strategist in the world?" Nestor sat down so heavily that his old jowls wobbled.

"Well, actually, to tell you the truth, I don't really know," he said, rather more seriously. "The thing is, when we left Troy, we all got separated, you know. I eventually got home safely, and so did most of the others. Poor old Agamemnon, of course. . ."

Telemachus nodded sadly. Like everyone else, he'd heard the terrible story of what had

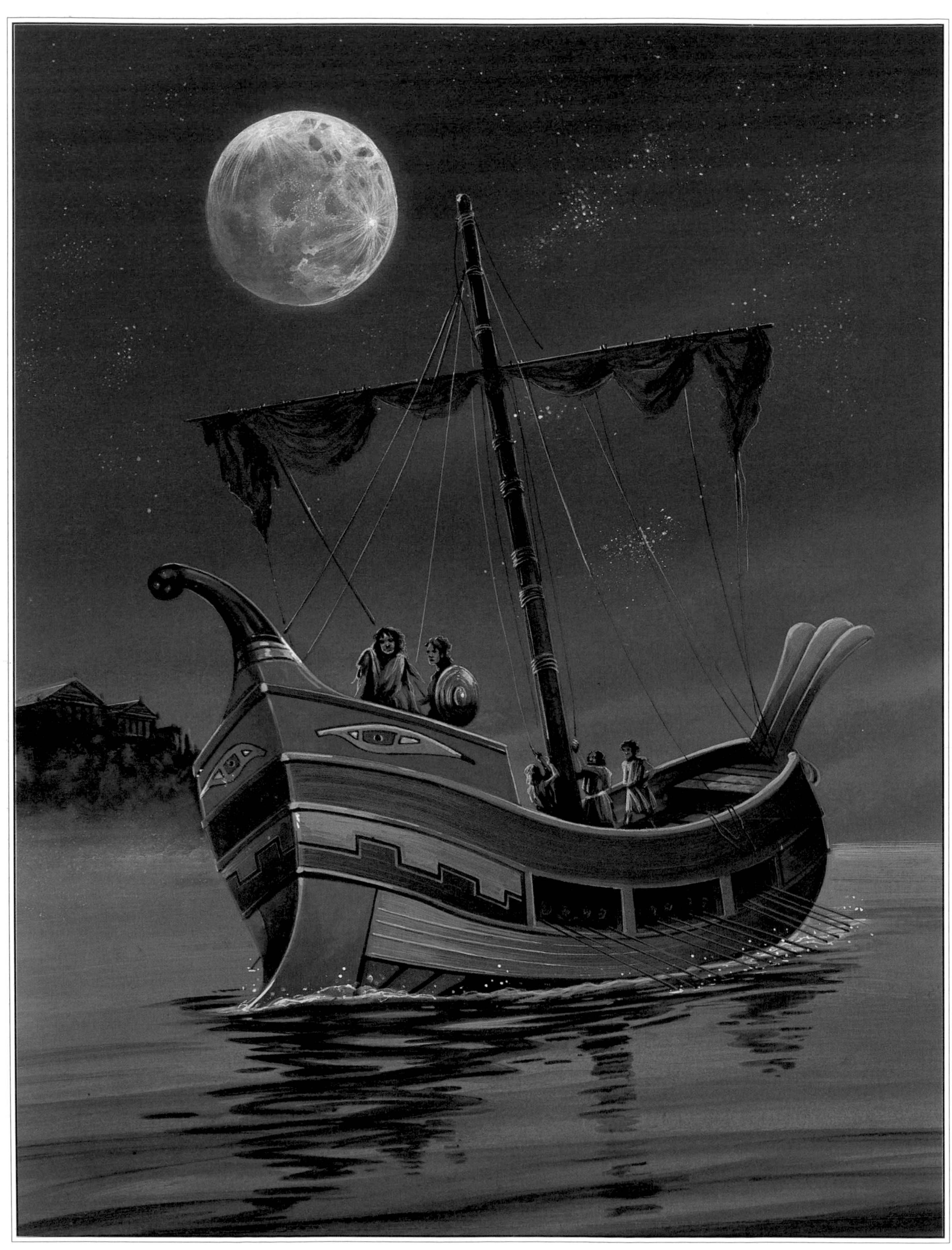

. . . a dark ship pulled quietly out of the bay

happened to Agamemnon, the leader of the Greek forces at Troy. He had returned triumphantly to his kingdom at Mycenae, only to discover that his wife Clytemnestra had taken up with another man, Aegisthus. And before he could do anything, Clytemnestra and Aegisthus murdered him.

"Tragic business," Nestor went on, shaking his head. "And Menelaus wasn't there to protect his brother, as he'd been blown off course and ended up in Egypt! So as you can see, we were all over the place. I think Ulysses was blown off to the south somewhere, but that's the last I heard of him.

"But don't you worry, my boy. I'm sure Ulysses can get himself out of any scrape!"

"We're desperate for him to come home," said Telemachus solemnly. "If only I were as clever as him, I might be able to get rid of the crowd of suitors that are plaguing us."

"Ah yes, I've heard about that!" Nestor nodded. "You could do with a bit of help from Athene ~ I must say she hasn't been much use lately!" He roared with laughter, while Athene spluttered into her wine.

"Listen, my boy," Nestor continued, kindly, "I truly believe that Ulysses is still alive. Here's what to do. Visit Menelaus. Oh, poor old Menelaus isn't much of a laugh these days, but he's been abroad more recently than I have. He might know something about Ulysses and where he is!"

The following evening, Telemachus found himself in Sparta, in the grand hall of King Menelaus. Next to him sat Peisistratus, Nestor's son. Nestor had sent them there in a chariot. The two young men had received a solemn welcome into the echoing palace, where they were now being given supper. The king had not yet asked them who they were.

"Peisistratus," whispered Telemachus to his companion, "isn't this palace incredible? It's so huge and full of treasures! This must be what Zeus's palace looks like!"

Menelaus heard him. He raised a sad, old eyebrow. His long hair, streaked with grey, hung down the sides of his old, weary face.

"I don't think so," he said, coldly. "I can hardly compare myself with Zeus."

"Sorry," mumbled Telemachus.

"After all the hardships I've suffered. Fighting a ten-year war to get my wife back from Troy. Being stuck abroad for eight years. Then coming home to find my brother dead. And losing my dear friend Ulysses."

"Ulysses?" said Telemachus, urgently. "That's what I—"

"Ulysses!" a woman's voice cried out behind them. "It can't be!" Menelaus's wife Helen had appeared in the doorway.

Telemachus couldn't help staring. She was much older than when she had run away to Troy, but Helen still glowed with beauty. No wonder Menelaus had wanted her back ~ badly enough to start the war against Troy, which had taken Ulysses away for so long.

"What are you talking about, woman?" grumbled Menelaus.

"You look just like him!" said Helen. "For a moment I thought. . . But you must be his son, Telemachus! You look just like him!"

"Your Majesty," broke in Telemachus, "I am Ulysses's son, and I must find out about my father. Please, sir, tell me all you know. Do you know where he is? Is he alive?"

"It happened in Egypt," began Menelaus.

Trembling, Telemachus put down his fork. He was sure he was about to hear some gruesome story about his father's death.

Menelaus told them that after the war, he had been stuck on an island called Pharos, waiting for a good wind. There he had met the god Proteus, the Old Man of the Sea, who promised he would help Menelaus get home and answer any questions he had.

"So I asked how I could get home," said Menelaus, "and do you know what he said the problem was? We hadn't been making enough sacrifices!" said Menelaus indignantly. "All we had to do was sacrifice to the gods, and we were off! It was that simple," he added huffily.

"But. . . what about Ulysses?" asked Telemachus nervously.

"Ah yes. I was coming to that. Well, of course, I asked Proteus if he had any news, and he told me where Ulysses was."

"Yes. . ?" said Telemachus.

"It's just a question of whether he can get back," mused Menelaus.

"So. . . where is he?" Telemachus asked, trying to hide his desperation.

"On an island," announced Menelaus. "Miles from anywhere. A nymph called Calypso is keeping him prisoner. According to Proteus, he sits on the beach, weeping for home, but Calypso won't let him go."

"He's alive!" cried Telemachus. "He's alive!" he shouted, hugging Peisistratus and laughing out loud. "Thank you, Menelaus! Come on, Peisistratus! I've got to go home!"

In the palace in Ithaca, a young merchant named Noemon stood before Antinous and the other suitors.

"I. . . I just came to find out if you knew where Telemachus was," he spluttered. "It's just that he's borrowed my ship to go to Pylos, and, well, I'll need it back soon."

"You lent Telemachus a ship?" shouted Antinous threateningly.

"Well. . . of course. He is the prince of Ithaca. Er, why?" asked Noemon weakly.

"That sneaky, impudent little rat!" fumed Antinous. "That stuck-up little TOAD! He's gone without telling us! Crept off in the night like a common thief! I'll show him. I'll teach him. I'll—"

"He did tell us, actually," put in Amphinomus. "At the assembly."

"Shut up," Antinous said coldly. "I'm going to put a stop to that little idiot's plans once and for all. He's not going to get away with this. Get me a ship! He'll come back past Asteris; everybody does. That's where we'll catch him." Antinous's fist closed around the handle of his sword.

"And kill him," he snarled.

CHAPTER ELEVEN

ESCAPE FROM CALYPSO

Dawn rose over Mount Olympus, bathing Zeus's palace in pink light. The gods were sitting in a circle in the palace courtyard, where they always assembled to discuss human problems.

The gods fell respectfully silent as Zeus walked in, his long, white cloak brushing the ground. But Athene was so eager to start that Zeus had hardly sat down on his throne before she began.

"What's the point of being a brave fighter and an excellent leader," she shouted, making some of the gods jump, "if you end up miserable and lonely, stuck on an island miles from anywhere?" Everyone looked blank. They had no idea what she was talking about.

"Look at poor Ulysses," Athene went on. "He's been a wonderful king, ruled the people of Ithaca as kindly as if they were his own children, and practically won the Trojan war single-handed," ~ here Zeus raised his eyebrows just a fraction ~ "and instead of being allowed to go home, he's left to languish on the island of Ogygia. He's been there for seven whole years! That nymph Calypso has him in her clutches, and there's no way he can escape without our help."

Zeus gave his daughter a weary smile. "Well," he sighed, sadly. "If people will mess with a Cyclops and upset my brother, what can they expect?"

Athene had to admit it was was true. Ulysses had blinded the Cyclops, Polyphemus ~ who just happened to be the son of Zeus's brother, the bad-tempered sea god Poseidon. From that day to this, Poseidon had done his utmost to stop Ulysses from getting home.

But Athene hated her uncle Poseidon far more than she blamed Ulysses. "Ulysses had to do what he did to escape," she said indignantly. "And Poseidon's nothing but a big old bully." Some of the gods looked around nervously. Then they remembered that Poseidon was away in Africa, where another huge sacrifice was being made for him.

"You're the leader of the gods!" Athene reminded her father. "You've got to do something while he's gone!"

"She's right," put in Hera. But Zeus had already made up his mind.

"Hermes," he said loudly, turning to his son. "The gods have decided that Ulysses has suffered enough. You are to go to Calypso and tell her she must let him leave her island at once. He will have to make his own boat, and after nineteen days at sea he will reach the land of the Phaeacians. They will help him return to Ithaca."

Zeus had spoken, and Hermes knew that Zeus must be obeyed. It was a long journey to Ogygia, Calypso's island, and he really didn't feel like going, but he tried to look enthusiastic as he put on some winged sandals. Then,

Then, casting an irritated glance at his half-sister Athene, Hermes leaped into the air and flew up, up into the misty early morning sky, and headed for Ogygia.

As the sun began to sink in the west, Hermes touched down at last on the sandy beach, and walked wearily along the shore in the direction of the cavern where Calypso lived. A copse of fragrant cypress trees grew around it, and in their branches sat horned owls and flocks of black choughs, who filled the air with their chattering and chirruping.

A vine, laden with bunches of ripe purple grapes, twisted and tangled around the cavern's entrance, and four tiny, crystal-clear streams trickled across the sand past Hermes's feet. When he stepped closer, he could smell the heady scent of cedar and juniper logs burning inside the cave, and hear the nymph singing softly to herself.

Even Hermes, who lived in the gorgeous palace of Zeus, had to admit that Calypso's home was beautiful. He stood and gazed, enjoying the relaxing sounds and scents and the warm sun on his back. Finally, he stepped into the shady cavern.

"Calypso?" he ventured.

"Hermes, my *dear*!" Calypso cried, leaping up from her weaving. She ran across the floor, grabbed Hermes by the shoulders and kissed him firmly on both cheeks. He blushed.

"And what brings you here?" she went on. "I haven't seen you in ages! You *have* turned out well! The gods must have been thinking of me, to send me such a handsome visitor! So, what can I do for you? But wait, don't answer yet. We must get some food inside you!"

"Oh," said Hermes. "Erm, I mean, thanks." He hadn't expected to stay for dinner, but now he realized he was feeling rather hungry after his long journey. Calypso was already putting a dish of ambrosia and a drink of sweet nectar in front of him.

As his eyes got used to the gloom, he looked around at Calypso's beautiful woven wall hangings and precious ornaments. But Ulysses was nowhere to be seen.

When he had eaten, Hermes knew it was time to deliver his message. He also knew it wasn't going to be easy.

"Calypso," he began. "The reason I'm here is. . . well. . . Zeus sent me. I wouldn't have come otherwise." Calypso looked hurt.

"I mean," Hermes said quickly, "it was an awful journey ~ really boring! There were no islands to rest on, and no one to offer me any sacrifices, and—" Calypso was staring at him. He'd better just say it. He took a deep breath. "I have a message for you," he said. "From Zeus. It's about Ulysses."

Calypso's face fell.

"Well, he has been here for seven years. And he really does want to get home to his wife. Zeus says you have to let him go."

Calypso was looking so heartbroken that Hermes didn't know what to do next. He knew she would have to obey Zeus. Everyone had to. So perhaps, Hermes thought, it would be better if he just left. "Calypso," he said. "I'm sorry—"

"This is absolutely typical of Zeus!" said Calypso suddenly. Her miserable expression had changed into one of fury. "Those gods just can't let anyone have any fun. I rescued Ulysses from the sea! I saved him, when they would have let him die! And now they won't let me keep him! It's outrageous!" She was standing up now, thumping on the table so that the plates rattled. Hermes could see she was close to tears.

"Well," he said nervously. "I'd better be going."

Calypso sat down heavily and covered her face with her hands.

"Thanks for dinner," Hermes mumbled. Then he backed out of the cavern, took off from the beach, and headed for home.

Calypso walked along the shore. She knew she had to obey Zeus, however unhappy it made her. She approached the rock where, every day, her captive sat gazing out to sea and weeping for his homeland.

As she got nearer, she could make out his shape. His head hung forward. His feet dangled in the water. His shoulders shook with wave after wave of deep, heavy sobs.

She knew he wanted to go home. But she couldn't help wishing he would rather stay. True, she had forced him to live with her like a husband for the past seven years.

Every night, he came home to her cavern, and was as polite as he could be. But, deep down, Calypso knew that however nice she was to him, whatever delicious food she cooked, and however many hot, scented baths she prepared for him, she could never win his heart or make him happy. Every day, he sat on his rock, sobbing wretchedly. All he wanted was to leave.

. . . thumping on the table so that the plates rattled

"Ulysses," she said softly, touching his shoulder. He looked up. His handsome face was wet with tears, his eyes were puffy, and his hair was bedraggled.

"Ulysses," the nymph said again. "I've had a message from Zeus. There's no need for you to stay here any longer. You're free to go."

Ulysses had been so miserable for so long that at first he didn't believe her. He was convinced this must be part of a plot to keep him on the island forever.

He pushed his hair out of his eyes, wiped away his tears, and stood up.

"Calypso," he began. "How can I escape, even if I am free to go? I have no boat or crew, and everyone knows that the seas around Ogygia are deadly. I'll just find myself washed up on your shores again. How do I know this isn't a trick?"

"Oh, Ulysses!" Calypso teased. "That just shows the crafty way your mind works, you wicked man! I promise you, Zeus has ordered me to let you go. I'll even help you build a ship. I swear I'll never try to harm you. How could I? It's not me that has been hard-hearted and unloving all these years! Not like some people!"

And yet, back at the cavern, Calypso couldn't resist trying one last time to persuade Ulysses to stay.

"So," she said, "I bet you're overjoyed to be going back to that wife of yours."

"Calypso," began Ulysses. "I don't mean to be rude. I just. . . "

"But Ulysses. . . " She leaned nearer to him. "She can't really be better-looking than me, can she? I mean! A mortal woman, more attractive than a nymph?"

Ulysses had to think quickly. "My lady," he said politely. "Of course, my wife's appearance could never compete with yours. She is a mere mortal, whereas you have perfect, unfading beauty. You are the most beautiful thing I have ever seen. Why, on that day, seven years ago, when you pulled me from the sea, I thought I was dreaming."

Calypso looked quite pleased.

"However," he added, "it is my home that I yearn for ~ to be among my own people, to feel the soil of Ithaca beneath my feet, and to see my son, Telemachus. He was only a baby when I left for Troy to fight in the war. He'll be a young man now."

Four days later, Ulysses's new ship bobbed proudly at its mooring, and Ulysses, wearing a set of new clothes that Calypso had given him, was itching to get going.

"So," he said, as brightly as possible, to Calypso. "This is it, then!"

Calypso didn't speak. She watched as he waded out to his boat, climbed on board and untied the mooring rope.

"Goodbye," he shouted, as a fresh wind, which Calypso had summoned up, nudged the boat away from the beach where she stood. "Goodbye, Calypso!"

Calypso watched until the ship was a small speck in the vast, shining ocean, and Ulysses was too tiny to see.

Ulysses couldn't remember when he had ever felt happier. The wind filled the sails, the sun was shining, and he was getting farther away from Ogygia by the minute. He was so excited, he couldn't even sleep. At night, he watched the stars and thought of Ithaca. And his boat sailed on safely for seventeen days, carried by the fair wind Calypso had summoned up for him.

On the morning of the eighteenth day, the sun rose on a beautiful sight. In front of him, rising up from the misty surface of the sea, was the mountainous land of the Phaeacians. Ulysses knew that these sea-loving people, who were close relations of the gods, would welcome him and help him on his way. As he sailed nearer to the land, Ulysses relaxed. He would soon be home.

"*Curse* him! Curse Ulysses! What on earth does that brother of mine think he's doing? I only have to go away for a few days and he goes and changes his mind without consulting me. Me, Poseidon, the mighty ruler of the waves! He'll regret this! Or at least," said Poseidon, remembering that Zeus, and not he, was ruler of the gods, "that puny little idiot Ulysses will regret it. He'll be sorry. There's no way he's getting back to Ithaca without a fight!"

Poseidon was on his way home from Africa. He had been taking a rest at the top of the Solymi mountains when he noticed the little ship. The last he'd heard, Ulysses was stuck on Ogygia, and that had suited the sea god very well. It served Ulysses right for injuring Poseidon's son, Polyphemus. But now, he seemed to have escaped.

However, Poseidon still had the upper hand. Ulysses was on the ocean, and that was where the mighty sea god could do his worst.

Poseidon grabbed his trident. "All right, Ulysses," he growled. "Now we'll see who's boss!"

Ulysses felt a cold wind on the back of his neck that made him shiver. He heard a very faint, low rumbling sound in the distance. He turned around.

Behind him, the sky was black. Thunder clouds were gathering on the horizon, and the wind whipped the waves up into frothy peaks.

And far away, below the darkest part of the sky, he could see a huge wave, the size of a cliff, rolling steadily closer. The wind began to toss and buffet the ship so that Ulysses could hardly stand upright. He clung to the helm, wrestling with the current and keeping a fearful eye on the menacing wall of water roaring in his direction.

He began to wonder if these were the last few moments of his life. "I should never have expected to make it home safely," he moaned, "with my record of bad luck! My friends who died at Troy were the lucky ones ~ buried and celebrated as great heroes. I wish I'd died there too, instead of suffering a lonely death here, in this cruel ocean!"

Ulysses was so wrapped up in this self-indulgent train of thought that he didn't realize the wave was almost on top of him. Suddenly it surged down with a thundering roar, crashing all over the deck, whirling the boat around and snapping the mast in two, like a matchstick. Ulysses's hands were torn from the helm and he was flung into the sea.

He found himself deep underwater, dragged down by the weight of his sodden clothes. The more he kicked and struggled, the heavier he seemed to become. His lungs were screaming for air, and when he opened his eyes, all he could see was a mass of swirling bubbles, filling his field of vision.

Finally, after fighting his way up until he thought his lungs would explode, he burst out on the surface of the sea, gasping desperately for air and coughing out salt water. He was exhausted, but he thrashed through the waves to catch up with the boat, which was drifting, battered and broken, without its mast or sail. Hauling himself aboard, he collapsed onto the deck.

He found himself deep underwater

And there he lay, almost comatose, clinging to a broken plank, while the winds threw the boat from side to side, and bolts of lightning plunged into the sea around him.

"Ha!" barked Poseidon. "That'll teach you. Not so smug now, eh, Ulysses?"

He packed up his trident and went on his way, satisfied with a job well done.

But someone else had been observing Poseidon's bullying. The goddess Ino, who was once human, but who now lived under the sea, was not so heartless.

"That poor Ulysses!" she said to herself. It almost made her cry to see how proudly and hopefully he had set out, and how near he had come to safety, only to have his boat smashed to pieces and his plans ruined. She decided to help him.

Ulysses groaned. He thought he must be hallucinating. Through the driving rain, he thought he saw a huge seagull perched on the ship's prow. He dragged himself closer. No, it was a woman ~ in a long, pale blue dress. The rain and wind didn't seem to affect her. She wasn't even wet. Instead, a gentle glow surrounded her.

At last, he recognized her.

"Ino. . ?" he whispered.

"Ulysses," Ino answered. Her voice was as soft as the lapping of tiny waves on the shore. "I will help you ~ but you must follow my instructions.

"Your ship is bound for the deep," she went on, "and you will not reach land under sail. Swim, Ulysses. It's your only hope." She unwound a shimmering veil from her shoulders and held it out to him. "Tie this around your waist, and you will swim ashore safely. The veil will protect you ~ as long as you are wearing it you cannot drown or be killed. But the moment you reach the shore, you must cast it back into the sea, and immediately turn your eyes away."

She was gone. Ulysses was left half-sitting, half-lying on the deck, clutching the veil. It felt as soft as a seagull's feather.

He looked around. Maybe the storm was beginning to die down, but the land looked too far away to swim to. Perhaps, if the weather was improving, he could make it in his damaged ship, after all. He had not really listened to the goddess.

Yes, the storm was definitely subsiding. He hauled himself upright. A beam of sunlight peeked through the clouds.

"So," said Ulysses out loud, "even when the sea god does his worst, he can't hurt me. Can you, Poseidon?" he shouted rudely. "Eh? Ruler of the waves? I'm going to get home safe and sound, whatever the sea throws at me. Just you watch!"

Poseidon stopped dead in his tracks. Was it Ulysses he could hear mocking him?

He turned around slowly.

"Ulysses!" he roared. "Ulysses, you, smug, arrogant, insignificant little FOOL!"

But all Ulysses heard was a sudden roar of wind, a huge thunderclap, and the terrible sound of another giant wave, even bigger than the first, which smashed down all over his crippled boat. This time the ship splintered into a thousand pieces, and Ulysses was plunged even deeper into the swirling sea. Kicking his way up to the surface, he fumbled with the silky veil and managed to tie it around his waist. When he finally emerged spluttering from the waves, there was nothing left of the ship at all.

For over a day, Ulysses was lost in the sea, sometimes drifting nearer to the land, sometimes being dragged away from it. Then, at last, the weather cleared, and he could swim closer to the Phaeacian coast.

At first, he couldn't find a safe place to come ashore. The waves crashed onto the sharp rocks with such force that Ulysses was sure he'd be battered to death.

"My whole journey has been for nothing," he groaned. "I'll break every bone in my body on those rocks. Or I'll get carried back out to sea, where I'll be drowned. Or eaten by a sea monster!" He had forgotten that the magic veil would protect him.

Then a large wave threw him straight at one of the sharpest rocks of all. He managed to grab the pointed tip of the rock with both hands, but the backwash dragged him off again, leaving pieces of skin clinging to the jagged stone.

Ulysses felt like giving up. He was sure he would never get home. He could relax, sink down into the dark depths, open his lungs to the salty water, and let the current take him. . .

Through half-closed eyes, he saw a gap between the rocks. He swam nearer, using the last few ounces of strength left in his body.

It was the mouth of a stream, surrounded by grassy banks. He could feel the cool current on his aching legs, where the stream flowed fast and fresh into the sea. For the first time since leaving Ogygia, Ulysses remembered to pray for help.

"River god," he groaned faintly to the stream. "Please, please help me. Take pity on a poor sailor, and bring me ashore."

The current slowed and stopped, and the sea became calm in front of Ulysses. He paddled up into the shallow, sandy mouth of the little river. There he fell on his knees, clumsily untied Ino's veil, and let it float back into the ocean, turning his face away. The flesh on his arms and legs was all swollen. His cut hands throbbed, and salt water streamed from his nostrils and mouth.

He had to sleep. He stumbled onto the bank and crawled over to a little grove of olive bushes near the rocks. Beneath their tightly-packed branches, where the thick foliage let in no light and fallen leaves covered the ground like a carpet, Ulysses lay down. His eyelids drooped drowsily and his heavy limbs sank into the leaf-litter. Finally, the goddess Athene sent Ulysses a deep, magical sleep, to renew and refresh him for all the troubles she knew lay ahead.

CHAPTER TWELVE

A ROYAL WELCOME

"Nausicaa!" hissed a voice in the princess's ear. "You haven't been there for ages! You'd better go at once!"

Nausicaa was having a very odd dream. In it her best friend, Eugenie, was talking to her. Nausicaa rolled over sleepily under the gold-stitched eiderdown that covered her bed.

"Haven't been where?" she murmured in her sleep.

"To the river to do your washing, of course!" Eugenie said. "Just in case!" She giggled.

"In case what?" Nausicaa didn't understand. She was a princess. She didn't have to do any washing.

"In case you get married," laughed Eugenie. This dream certainly was a little strange.

"It's important for a girl to do a lot of washing," Eugenie went on. "It's good for your reputation. All the most handsome men on the island have their eye on you, Nausicaa! I mean, you are the Princess of Phaeacia! They'll all be asking for your hand in marriage soon. And you'll need lots of clean clothes. I'm telling you, you'd better go to the river tomorrow."

What Nausicaa didn't realize was that Athene had entered her dream, disguised as Eugenie, and whispered to her as she slept. Athene wanted Nausicaa to go to the river so that she would find Ulysses.

And when Nausicaa woke up, she somehow did want to go to the river. It was true, she hadn't been there for ages. She could go with her maids and have a day out.

"Father," began Nausicaa carefully. She couldn't say she wanted to go to the river to prepare for getting married ~ that would be far too embarrassing.

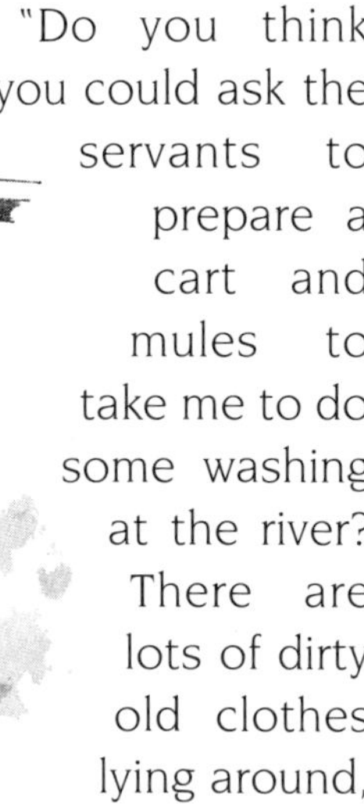

"Do you think you could ask the servants to prepare a cart and mules to take me to do some washing at the river? There are lots of dirty old clothes lying around, and you need clean things to wear for meetings, and my brothers need them for going to parties."

"Absolutely," said King Alcinous, asking no questions. He knew as well as Nausicaa did that the servants could do the washing. But he liked to indulge his only daughter. He let her do whatever she liked.

Soon, a wooden cart containing Nausicaa and her maids trundled to a halt next to the river, where a series of crystal-clear pools led down to the sea.

It didn't take the girls long to wash the small bundle of clothes which Nausicaa had managed to find. They rinsed them quickly, swishing them around in the water, and laid them out along the banks to dry in the hot sun. Then it was time to have some fun.

They bathed in the sparkling river, laughing and screaming as they splashed each other with droplets of water.

Ulysses, still in a deep sleep under the olive bush nearby, began to stir.

After their swim, Nausicaa and her maids sat on the bank in a group and rubbed each other with perfumed oil to keep their skin soft. Giggling, they combed their hair and tried on each other's clothes.

Ulysses thought he was having a dream about twittering sparrows.

When the sun was high overhead, Nausicaa's maids went to the cart to fetch the food. They feasted on the fresh fruit and cheese that the kitchen servants had packed for them, and made a small driftwood fire and toasted pieces of bread on sticks.

Ulysses started to dream of hot roast dinners. He turned over in his sleep.

Finally, the girls took a ball from the cart and began throwing it around. Their laughter grew louder as they ran to and fro.

Athene was watching. She made the ball veer off to one side after a particularly forceful throw. It ended up in the river, and started bobbing steadily down to the sea.

The girls shrieked.

Ulysses woke up with a start. He sat up, brushing off dry leaves, and remembered where he was. But what was going on? Who was making such a racket?

He got up, crawled out of the bush, and stumbled over to the river.

He saw a crowd of girls leaning over a deep pool with a stick, reaching for a ball. Nearby were the leftovers of a picnic.

Ulysses remembered that he hadn't eaten for days.

He was about to call to them when he realized that he had lost most of his clothes in the sea. But he had to ask for help. He quickly broke a branch from the bush and held it in front of him.

"Er. . . hello!" he called.

This time the girls screamed louder than ever. Half-naked, encrusted in sea salt, covered in dirty dead leaves, and with matted hair, Ulysses looked more like a wild animal than a man. Only Nausicaa stayed where she was, while her maids ran away over the grass and sand down to the sea.

Ulysses stared at the girl in front of him. She was incredibly beautiful.

"Lady, I beg your assistance," he began, politely. "If you are a lady, and not a goddess. For I have never seen a human as beautiful as

Ulysses looked more like a wild animal than a man

you. Your parents must be proud ~ and as for your husband, well, he'll be a lucky man.

"But I'm not so lucky. I've been at sea for nineteen days, and away from home for nineteen years, and now I find myself in yet another foreign land. Please would you be so kind as to direct me to the nearest town, and to give me a rag or blanket to wear?"

Nausicaa stared back at him. Then she remembered that, as princess of the country, she ought to welcome him.

"Sir," she said, "your politeness shows that you are wise and well-bred. I'm afraid your bad luck is the work of the gods, but while you're here in Phaeacia, we'll do what we can to help." She stepped closer to him. "I am Nausicaa, the daughter of Alcinous, King of the Phaeacians," she added.

When Ulysses had eaten the remains of the picnic, and bathed in the river, Nausicaa brought him a clean, dry tunic to wear. She was amazed at how different he looked. In the precious clothes, he suddenly seemed very handsome, with thick black hair and strong, muscular arms and legs.

"Sir," said Nausicaa, "we must go back to the city. I'd like to welcome you to my father's palace, but people would gossip if they saw me riding into town with a strange man. So when we reach the city walls, please wait in the forest until our cart has gone in. Then follow us, and come to the palace.

"Walk through the great hall until you find Arete, my mother. She will be sitting by the hearth, weaving a beautiful tapestry with purple thread. Ask her to help you. If you can win her sympathy, I'm sure you'll be able to get home to your own land."

After waiting, as Nausicaa had instructed, Ulysses stepped through the gates of the Phaeacian city. It was a beautiful place. Hundreds of white houses with blue-tiled roofs clustered around the port, where several tall ships were moored. In the distance, the jade sea shone in the sunlight.

There was no mistaking Alcinous's palace. It towered above all the houses, and was surrounded by a gleaming wall of bronze. Its garden overflowed with ripe pears and figs. Even though Ulysses was a king himself, he felt a little nervous about going in.

The goddess Athene shrouded him in a fine mist, so that no one could see him as he strode through the great hall. At the far end, flanked by guards and noblemen, he saw Arete, weaving her tapestry, just as Nausicaa had described. Nearby sat her husband, Alcinous, a king renowned for his kindness and generosity. Ulysses prayed that they would help him.

When Ulysses reached the royal couple, Athene made the mist disappear. Ulysses fell to his knees in front of the astounded queen, and began his speech.

"Queen Arete," he said. "May the gods grant you joy. I beg you to help me return home, for I have endured many hardships since I last saw my friends and family."

There was a shocked silence. Everyone stared at the stranger who had suddenly appeared among them. Then Echeneus, an old lord, said, "Alcinous, it seems you have a guest. Surely we should welcome him?"

The king nodded, stood up, smiled warmly at Ulysses, and led him to a seat.

"My lords," King Alcinous announced to the assembled noblemen, "it is time for you to make your way to your own homes. Tomorrow, we shall hold a general meeting, and arrange for our noble guest to be transported safely to his home."

Ulysses relaxed. Relief flooded through him. Perhaps, at last, his journey would soon be over.

Everyone was filled with excitement and curiosity about the new stranger in town.

This was partly because Athene had disguised herself as a messenger, and had spread the news that an amazing foreigner, who looked more like a god than a man, would be at the meeting place that morning. Soon the marketplace was filled with an eager, gossiping crowd of people, all trying to get a good look at the newcomer.

"People of Phaeacia!" shouted King Alcinous above the din.

"This noble stranger has asked us to help him on his way. As it is the Phaeacian custom to help all seafaring visitors, let us prepare a ship, and pick fifty-two of our best young oarsmen to row him to his destination. Although," he added, looking at Ulysses, "He's so handsome that, if he were willing, I wouldn't mind having him as a son-in-law."

The crowd laughed and cheered, and young men began pushing forward excitedly to offer themselves as oarsmen.

"When the ship is ready," Alcinous added, "the crew and all my noblemen will be invited to a feast at my palace, to entertain our visitor before he leaves."

A few hours later, the palace's great hall echoed to the sound of laughter and conversation. Empty bowls littered the tables. Servants walked from place to place, refilling the silver wine cups.

"So," said Alcinous, banging the table, "if everyone has feasted enough, I think it's time for a song! Call for Demodocus!"

Demodocus, King Alcinous's bard, was led in by a servant. For although he had the loveliest singing voice in Phaeacia, the bard was blind. Some said the gods had taken his sight away in exchange for his amazing talent.

He raised his little silver harp and plucked a single note. An expectant hush fell over the hall, and then the bard began to sing softly:

"My royal king, my fair and lovely queen," Demodocus began.

"I'll tell a famous story from the war,
When Ulysses devised a cunning ploy:
He told the Greeks to build a wooden horse,
And hiding in it, they invaded Troy."

Ulysses's stomach lurched when he heard what the song was going to be about. The Phaeacians obviously had no idea who he was, but the story of the Trojan War had obviously spread far and wide while he'd been away.

As the bard continued, Ulysses remembered his adventures at Troy, and the huge wooden horse he'd designed which had finally helped the Greeks to win the war. How he missed his old comrades ~ loyal Agamemnon, and brave Achilles. Both of them were dead now. And who knew what had happened to the others ~ his dear friends Menelaus, Nestor and Diomedes? He hadn't seen them for so long. Soon, the beautiful sound of the music began to make Ulysses weep for the friends he had lost.

Fortunately, he was wearing a heavy purple cloak, given to him by Alcinous. He used it to cover his face and hide his tears. He tried desperately to stop sobbing, reminding himself how bravely he had fought at Troy, but that only made it worse.

The longer Demodocus's song went on, the more Ulysses wept, until at last his shoulders shook with sobs. King Alcinous couldn't help noticing. He motioned to his servants to stop the bard.

"I'm afraid our entertainment isn't to everybody's liking," he said kindly. "My friend, what is upsetting you? You've been weeping bitterly ever since the bard started to sing, even though this entertainment was meant to please you."

Everyone stared as Ulysses lowered his cloak, revealing his tearstained face.

"My friend," King Alcinous went on, "I beg you, please tell us your name, and why you weep to hear a song about heroes, when you should rejoice. Where did you come from, and what have you seen on your travels? You know, talking about your troubles can help to soothe them. Come, sir. Tell us your story."

He reached out and placed a hand warmly on Ulysses's shoulder. Ulysses wiped his eyes and took a deep breath.

"You are very kind, your majesty," he began, "and honestly, your bard is the best I've ever heard. There's nothing at all wrong with his performance. It's my memories that are upsetting me. And since you ask, I will tell you who I am."

Only the clatter of a cup being put down broke the heavy silence. Everyone was agog with anticipation.

"I am. . . " Ulysses faltered. "I am the famous Ulysses, of whom your bard sings. The whole world speaks of my skill and bravery, yet only the gods know where I have been, and how I have failed so miserably to get home. This is my story. . ."

CHAPTER THIRTEEN

THE CYCLOPS

"It's a sad tale," Ulysses began. "I set off from Troy in triumph, with twelve ships full of treasures, and a fine crew of men. Yet when I crawled onto your shores two days ago, I was destitute and alone. When you hear of the terrible monsters we met, you'll be amazed anyone escaped alive. But I have to admit," Ulysses added, "it was partly my own pride that caused our problems. If only I hadn't taunted the Cyclops. . ."

"You've had dealings with a Cyclops?" gasped the king. An excited murmur spread among the guests.

"Sorry," said Alcinous. "Do carry on."

"When the Greeks left Troy, our fleet split up. Agamemnon and Menelaus went off with their ships, and I thought we'd have no problem at all getting home to Ithaca. But my convoy of ships ended up being blown right off course in a huge storm. We stayed awake for two days, trying to control the ships as they were battered and driven sideways by the gale. But we couldn't fight the wind. It blew us south, away from Ithaca and past the island of Cythera, into the open sea.

"Then we sailed for nine whole days with no sight of land, and we needed fresh water," said Ulysses, "so we pulled up at the first place we came to. It was the land of the Lotus-eaters. You'd think we'd have been happy to meet such friendly people. But their friendship was dangerous.

"As soon as we'd found some water and had some dinner, a few men went to find out who lived there. As it turned out, the natives had no desire to attack us. Oh no, they were only too willing to share everything they had.

"The next thing I knew, my men came stumbling out of the woods with huge grins on their faces, and sticky juice running down their chins.

" 'We want to stay here forever,' they cried, like innocent children at a party.

"They had been given the fruit of the Lotus plant. Like a drug, it made them forget that they had jobs to do, or even homes to go to. All they wanted was to spend their entire lives lazing around, eating Lotus fruit and forgetting all their troubles.

"Well, I wasn't falling for it. I personally dragged them back on board and chained them up in the galley. Then the rest of the crew rowed us away from that place forever.

"After that, as you can imagine, we were wary about landing anywhere else, but we still needed a rest. And the next place we came to was the home of the Cyclopes.

"Of course, I'd heard all the stories ~ that the Cyclopes were a savage people: uncivilized, stupid and dangerous. But I thought it couldn't be any worse than the land of the Lotus-eaters. I was wrong.

"We landed on a little offshore island. From there we looked across to the mainland, where we could see wisps of smoke rising through the trees. And we could hear these strange, booming voices. I was curious. I wanted to meet these people and find out just what they were like.

"So the next morning, I told the rest of the men to wait while I took my own ship and crew over to the mainland. And there, by the shore, was a cave. I decided this was the place to land, and I picked twelve men to go ashore with me. I also took along a goatskin of strong wine. I planned to have it handy to give as a gift, in case we needed to get on the right side of anyone.

"The owner wasn't at home, so we tiptoed into the cave to explore. Inside, it was absolutely enormous. There were pens filled with bleating lambs along one side, and all the Cyclops's possessions were lying around ~ tools, baskets, huge pails of milk, and some *massive* blocks of cheese.

"By the size of those pieces of cheese, we could tell this Cyclops was a particularly large giant. My men didn't want to hang around. They were all for trying to roll one of the pieces of cheese down to the boat and getting out of there. And that would have been by far the best thing to do," said Ulysses miserably. "But no, of course, I insisted on waiting until our friend the Cyclops came home.

"We were still debating what to do when we heard footsteps outside. To be honest, they were more like thunderbolts. The next thing we knew, a huge pile of firewood ~ whole trees and branches ~ crashed onto the floor inside the doorway, and we had to run for our lives. We scuttled to the back of the cave and hid there.

"Then, at last, we saw him towering in the cave entrance. He was vast. He looked more like a mountain than a person. And there, right in the middle of his forehead, staring wildly from side to side, was the gigantic,

single staring eye that all Cyclopes have."

All the guests in the hall drew in their breath in horror. Alcinous looked pale.

"Of course, I'd heard that the Cyclopes were ugly, one-eyed monsters," said Ulysses, "but until you see that single eye," ~ he looked around the hall, from one wide-eyed guest to another ~ "until you actually *see* it, you don't realize just how horrible it is.

"Anyway," Ulysses went on, "by then, it was too late to escape. The next thing the Cyclops did was to lift up a huge stone slab and use it to block the cave entrance. It was much too big for us to lift. You couldn't even move it if you had twenty horses to help you pull! That's how big it was. All we could do was sit there and hope he was in a good mood. That's when he spotted us.

"'Strangers!' he roared, in a voice so deep and booming we could feel the vibrations through the floor. 'Strangers! In my cave!?'

"We all huddled back against the wall, trembling. 'And who might you be, strangers?' he roared.

"I was terrified, but I put on my pleasantest, most charming voice. 'Greetings to you, sir!' I said. 'We are Greeks, on our way back from the battle of Troy, to our home in Ithaca. Of course,' I continued, trying to sound light-hearted, 'we didn't mean to come here, but we got a little, er, lost. And if you would be so kind, sir, in the name of almighty Zeus, could we beg you to help us on our way? Or might you entertain us in your beautiful home? Please?'

"He looked slightly puzzled for a moment. Then a frown passed over his big, stupid face.

" 'Hah!' he boomed. 'Zeus! In the name of Zeus! We Cyclopes don't give a fig for the name of Zeus! You must be an idiot if you think I'd help you for fear of him! But tell me,' he said, suddenly sounding more friendly, 'where's your ship, then? Eh? Is it along the coast? I'd quite like to see it.'

"I didn't trust him. I had to think fast.

" 'Er. . . our ship,' I said, 'yes, it's, well, shipwrecked. But we escaped. That's why we need your help. If you wouldn't mind.'

"In reply, the monstrous creature stretched out his huge, hairy hand and grabbed two of my men by the legs. Then he lifted them up and smashed their heads against the stony floor, killing them instantly. Their skulls split open and their brains spilled out onto the ground.

"We could only watch in horror, totally paralyzed with fear and disgust, as he proceeded to tear them up, limb by limb, and eat every scrap of them ~ skin and bones, even their clothes. Some of my men wept as the Cyclops crunched on their comrades' bodies, and licked his bloodstained lips."

King Alcinous's hand was over his mouth. He didn't look well.

"Then," Ulysses continued, "he washed it all down with an enormous slurp of milk, and lay down to sleep.

"My mind was racing, as you can imagine. I felt distraught, as I had lost two of my friends, and I was full of fury and hate for the Cyclops. And I felt bad for having insisted that we stayed in the cave, when we could have escaped so easily before he arrived.

"I desperately wanted to protect the remaining men. I took out my dagger, planning to stab the Cyclops and kill him.

"But I stopped myself just in time. If he was dead, we'd never escape. The huge stone slab over the cave door would trap us in there forever. I needed a better plan.

"The next morning, exactly the same thing happened. The Cyclops got up, milked his ewes, and then grabbed two more of my men for breakfast. We couldn't bear to look. We turned away in agony as we heard their heads being cracked open and their bodies being crunched up. Then the Cyclops opened up the doorway, drove his animals out, and replaced the stone slab.

"All morning, I racked my brains. I had to think of something. I, Ulysses, whose strategies had helped to win the Trojan War!

"It was a pole lying on the floor that finally gave me inspiration. It was probably just a walking stick, but to us it seemed

as big as a ship's mast. We couldn't possibly lift all of it. So we hacked away at it with our daggers and cut off a stake about the height of a man. I sharpened the end into a point, and hardened it in the fire. Then we hid our new weapon under piles of smelly sheep's dung.

"The Cyclops only had one eye. And I only had one job in mind for that stake."

"In came the Cyclops that evening, being careful to replace the slab behind him, and went through his ritual. He milked his ewes. He grabbed two of my terrified men, and killed them mercilessly. Then he gobbled them up in front of us.

"This was my chance. I took my goatskin of strong, rich wine and poured some into a bowl. I tapped him on the foot.

" 'Here, Cyclops,' I said, in a sweet, coaxing voice. 'Please try this fine wine, which I've brought especially for you. It will wash down that meal of tasty human flesh, which I can see you've enjoyed.'

" 'Shut up, stranger', thundered the Cyclops, grabbing the bowl from me. He tipped his head back and drained it.

" 'MMMmmm!' he said. 'Delicious. Well, stranger, perhaps I've changed my mind about you. Be good enough to pour me some more wine, and tell me your name, so that I can give you a special present.'

"I poured him three more bowls of wine, and though it wasn't much for someone his size, it was so strong that it soon had an effect. He grew clumsy, his speech became slurred, and he was more stupid than ever.

" 'So, sshtranger,' he drawled, 'what'sh your name, then. Uh?'

"I could hardly keep myself from grinning at my clever plan.

" 'Nobody', I told him. 'It's Nobody.'

" 'Well, Nobody,' slurred the Cyclops, with a stupid smirk. 'I'll tell you what your preshent will be.' Then he laughed a horrible, gurgling laugh, and said: 'I'll eat you lasht. Out of all your friends, I'll save you,' he guffawed, 'and eat you at the end. For dessert.'

"And then," Ulysses told all the spellbound guests in the hall, "he fell over with a crash, and lay unconscious on the floor. He was flat on his back, snoring, with his head twisted over to one side. Perfect.

"We put the point of the wooden stake in the fire again to heat it up. Then Eurylochus and three of my other men lifted it up and carried it over to the sleeping giant.

"While I leaned on the end of the pole, my friends twisted it, and together we drove it right into the middle of his big, round eyeball. Blood boiled and sizzled around the burning hot wood. Stinking smoke filled the air, and the heat singed his big, bushy eyebrow. We kept gouging and twisting until we had dug out the very roots of his horrible eye.

"Of course, he woke up and started struggling and thrashing about. He let out a huge, blood-curdling scream that echoed around the walls of the cave, and sat up, shaking us off him like breadcrumbs. He put his hands up to his face, grabbed the stake and yanked it out of his eye, which just made the blood flow even more quickly. It poured down his face and neck as he clutched in agony at the ragged, smoking eye-socket."

"My goodness," said King Alcinous, weakly. He had turned a delicate shade of green. Everyone else leaned closer, wide-eyed.

"What happened then?" asked Demodocus, the blind bard.

"Then," said Ulysses, "the second part of my cunning plan came into operation. The monster got up and started stumbling around

. . . and carried it over to the sleeping giant

the cave, tripping over milk pails and banging into the walls, yelling 'Help! Oh! Help me!' All the other giants ran from their homes, and shouted from outside: 'What, Polyphemus? What's the problem? Who hurt you?'

" 'Nobody!' bellowed the monstrous Cyclops. 'Nobody hurt me!'

" 'Well then,' shouted the others, sounding irritated, 'what did you wake us up for?' And off they went, while I laughed to myself about how well my plan was working.

"But we still had to get out of the cave. In the morning, after groaning loudly all night, the Cyclops felt for the stone slab, and managed to heave it out of the way. Then he slumped down in the cave entrance, and felt each sheep as it passed by, so we couldn't sneak out. But I had another idea.

"In the flock, there were lots of big rams. I tied them together in threes, using the Cyclops's yarn, and tied a man under each group. When the rams wandered out through the entrance, we would go too. Because, you see, the Cyclops only thought to feel the back of each sheep, not the underside.

"For myself, I picked the biggest ram of all. I clung onto his shaggy belly, and hung there upside-down as we waited for the animals to leave the cave.

"My ram, laden down with my weight, was the last to go. And as the giant stroked him, with me clinging on underneath for dear life, I realized that even the Cyclops had a kind word for someone ~ his sheep.

" 'Dear, sweet ram,' he burbled, 'you're usually the first to trot outside. Why are you so slow today? I expect it's because you're sorry for me! You're sad, aren't you, because your dear master has been blinded by that evil Nobody. Oh, if only you could speak, and tell me where he's hiding! I'd bash his brains out!'

"When I heard that, I clung on tighter than ever.

"Outside, I let go of the ram and untied my friends, and we ran down to our ship and rowed for the island. But as soon as we were clear of the shore, I couldn't resist shouting: 'So, Cyclops, you've got your just deserts, now, haven't you? Zeus has punished you for being so rude as to eat your own guests!'

"This infuriated him so much that he grabbed a huge boulder and hurled it at us. It sent up a huge wave that almost washed the boat back to the Cyclopes' shore.

" 'Ulysses,' groaned Eurylochus, 'please don't make him any angrier! Let's just get out of here as fast as possible!'

"But I just couldn't stop myself. 'Cyclops!' I boasted loudly, 'if anyone wants to know who blinded you, tell them it was Ulysses, King of Ithaca, son of Laertes!' "

" 'Ulysses!' growled the monster furiously. 'I'll make you pay for this!'

"Then he drew himself up to an enormous height, so that his shadow fell right across our ship, and reached up to the sky.

" 'Beloved father Poseidon,' he roared. 'Make sure Ulysses never gets home! Or if he does, let him arrive late, after years of misery, on an unknown ship, with all his comrades dead, and trouble brewing in his royal house!'

"And that," Ulysses concluded, "is why Poseidon has cursed me, and sends storms wherever I go. If only I had held my tongue," he said sadly, "I might be home already. In fact, we soon came so close to Ithaca that we could see the people waving on the shore, and I was sure I was about to see my family and friends once again. And yet it was not to be.

"But that," said Ulysses, reaching for his wine, "is another story.

CHAPTER FOURTEEN

CIRCE'S ISLAND

King Alcinous patted Ulysses on the back. "Well done!" he said, "an excellent story, and very well told. But tell us what happened next, and how you almost got back to Ithaca."

"Yes, tell us some more!" shouted a voice from the back of the hall.

"But your majesty, isn't it getting rather late?" protested Ulysses, smiling. In fact, he loved talking about his adventures, but it wouldn't be polite to carry on all night.

"Nonsense! The night is young!" cried Alcinous, who had now recovered completely from his queasiness. "Go on, sir, do!"

"Well," said Ulysses, "if you want. . ."

There was a ripple of enthusiastic agreement, and Ulysses began.

"After our encounter with the Cyclops," he said, "we sailed on sadly, grieving for our lost friends. But the next place we came to gave us a proper welcome.

"It was the home of Aeolus, who is, I must admit, rather strange. There he lives, in the lap of luxury, on the floating island of Aeolia. He and his wife have six daughters and six sons, and they're all married to each other! I told my men not to remark on it, of course. People say Aeolus is a friend of the gods.

"Well, Aeolus entertained us splendidly with wonderful food and wine, in exchange for news about what had happened at Troy. And when it was time for us to leave, he said he had a gift for me. 'Just a little something, to help you on your way,' he said. And do you know what it was?"

The guests all leaned closer.

"A bag of winds," said Ulysses proudly. "The best present any seafarer could have. He brought me this huge sack, which was bouncing and buffeting around as if it were full of fighting puppies. Inside, he had trapped the power of all the four winds for us to use on our journey, and tied the bag with a silver string.

"I really couldn't thank him enough!" said Ulysses. "But now that we had the winds, my men were eager to get back. So off we went. We had no problem sailing straight for Ithaca, and within a few days there we were, within sight of the shore. . ."

Ulysses's voice trailed off. He looked heartbroken. "It was so beautiful," he said, quietly. "We could see the people on the rocky beaches, tending their fires and waving to us. Behind them, the dark peak of Mount Neriton rose into the sky. It had been nearly eleven years since I'd seen it.

"I was so happy, and so relieved, that I felt I could relax at last. I lay down to rest on the deck while my men rowed us to land. And there I fell asleep. A fatal mistake.

"Eurylochus told me afterwards that while I was snoozing on the deck, some of the men started wondering what other presents

from Aeolus might be in the bag. 'I bet he's given him a pile of gold and silver, and he doesn't want to share it with us!' one of them said, and eventually they all agreed to have a look. What a disaster! As soon as they opened the bag, all four winds got out, and immediately produced a storm which blew us right back the way we'd come.

"I was woken by my men calling out in anguish as they saw their beloved homeland vanishing into the distance. But there was nothing I could do. The storm took hold, and I've never seen one like it in my life. It sank eleven of the twelve ships in my fleet. My own crew spent hours dragging shipwrecked men from the other boats out of the water. But I'm afraid many of them drowned.

"So, with a crowded ship, and most of the men so exhausted and depressed they were just about useless, we limped back to Aeolus's island.

"I felt pretty stupid, I can tell you. I thought he might help us out, but he was furious. 'You timewasters!' he snorted. 'I gave you every chance. If you can't manage to get home with a bag of winds, you must be cursed by the gods, and I don't want you hanging around! Be off with you!' And that was that.

"We were back to square one, traipsing from one place to another, and wondering how we'd ever get home again. And you can imagine that by now, my men were begging me not to explore any more. It seemed that everywhere we went we found trouble in one form or another. So when we stopped on a little forested island, I knew the wisest thing would be to stay on the shore, rest for a while, and then get going again.

"But I just couldn't resist it. I left them all asleep on the beach and climbed a nearby hill. And what did I see? A wisp of smoke, rising from a mountainside right in the middle of the island. I had to investigate.

"I went back and woke them up. They protested, but I was their leader, and complaining didn't do them any good. To make it fair, I split us into two groups ~ I was in charge of one, and I put Eurylochus in charge of the other. Then we drew straws, and Eurylochus's group got the job of finding out where that wisp of smoke was coming from.

"Eurylochus told me later about what had happened when they'd arrived. On the hillside, next to a sparkling mountain stream, his men had found a charming little stone cottage. Prowling around it were wolves and lions, drugged to make them tame. Instead of biting the men, they jumped up and licked their faces, like big friendly dogs.

"Through the doorway of the house, they saw a beautiful woman with green eyes. They immediately recognized her as Circe, the sorceress. There she was, weaving a magical cloth, and singing gently to herself.

"Well, as soon as she noticed them, she invited them inside, and they were so impressed by her beauty, and her soft, purring voice, that in they all trooped. Only Eurylochus, who suspected a trap, stayed behind. He waited in the garden, keeping a watchful eye on those slavering beasts.

"Inside, Circe offered the men some food: a mixture of cheese, honey and barley soaked in wine. But there was something else in it too ~ something more sinister. As soon as they'd eaten it, up got Circe and used her wand to poke and drive them out of the door. They'd all been turned into pigs!

"They had human feelings, but they looked and sounded like pigs. They even smelled like them, Eurylochus said.

"The next thing he knew, Circe was shooing the pigs into the yard.

She penned them all up in a pigsty, and Eurylochus came running back through the forest in desperation to find me.

"He wasn't too pleased about it, either. 'Ulysses!' he shouted, as he ran panting onto the beach, 'Now you've done it! Everywhere we go, your curiosity just gets more of our men killed. Or turned into pigs!' he added, 'because that's what happened! This is Circe's island! You've led us right into a witch's den!'

"I had to try to help my men," said Ulysses, "even though the others pleaded with me to set sail and abandon them. Off I went, tearing through the undergrowth, determined to get our men back, when I ran head on into Hermes.

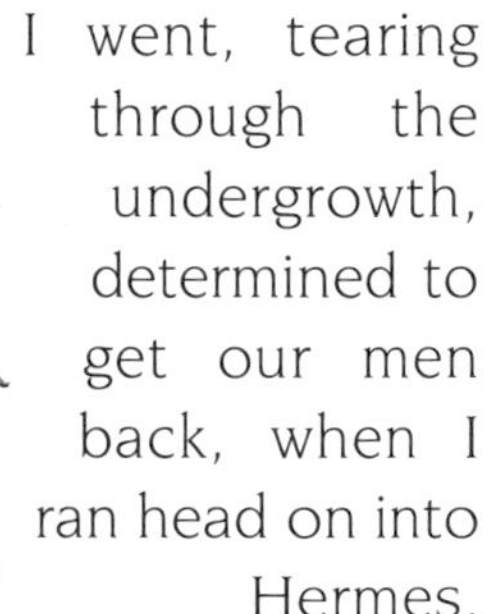

"'Hermes!' I panted 'What on earth are you doing here?'

" 'At your service,' the handsome young god grinned.

"I stopped and caught my breath, while Hermes coolly sat down on a log and put his feet up on a rock.

" 'I'm here to help you deal with Circe. I'm assuming you don't want to be turned into a pig too,' he said casually.

" I hadn't thought of that.

" 'Well, no,' I admitted.

" 'All right then,' he said, and he pulled a great big bush out of the ground and broke a piece off. It wasn't really necessary to uproot it, but the gods are so strong, they can do anything.

" 'Here's what you must do,' said Hermes. 'Eat this herb, which is called Moly. When you meet Circe, she'll give you drugged food, but the Moly will protect you. After you've eaten, draw your sword and threaten to kill her. She'll beg for mercy. Make her promise not to harm you, and she'll be in your power.'

"Well, it sounded easy enough," said Ulysses, "so I thanked Hermes, and set off for Circe's cottage

"Circe was waiting for me as I walked into the clearing and stepped past the drugged animals. She really was amazingly beautiful ~ tall, with long, dark hair, and large, clear green eyes, like a snake's. She was looking me slowly up and down with that bewitching stare.

" 'Come in, come in, my darling,' she said, in a soft, low, purring voice. But I didn't find it very romantic. I was too scared."

"She invited me to sit on a decorated silver chair while she prepared some dinner. I could see her mixing things into it, but I didn't say anything. I ate it all.

"Then she stood up and prodded me with her wand.

"I waited, fearful that at any second I would turn into a pig.

"But nothing happened. I wasn't a pig. The Moly had worked! I was quite surprised myself, actually. Then I remembered the next part of the plan, and drew my sword. 'Circe!' I shouted, rushing at her, 'Give me back my crewmen, or I'll cut your throat!'

"She crumpled onto the floor and flung her arms around my legs in terror. 'Who are you?' she cried. 'No one has ever resisted my magic before!'

"But then a change came over her. Her snake eyes narrowed, and she started to look very cunning. 'I know who you must be,' she said slinkily, starting to rub my leg. 'Only the famous Ulysses ~ the cleverest, boldest and most *handsome* of warriors,' she smiled, 'could possibly survive the drug that turns men into pigs. Oh Ulysses, *is* it you?' she wheedled. 'Please, stay with me for a while, and we can live together, like husband and wife.'

"It was embarrassing," said Ulysses, "but also flattering. And she was very good-looking. I was just about to accept, when I remembered my men, shut in the pigsty.

" 'Circe,' I said, forcefully, 'how do you expect me to trust you when you have turned my men into pigs? Turn them back immediately, and promise me you won't harm any of us. Then maybe I'll think about it.'

" 'Oh, Ulysses, you're *so* manly,' she purred, getting up. Then she leaned over and stroked my face softly, looking deep into my eyes. I tried to look away.

" 'It's a deal,' she said at last. 'I'll set the men free and promise not to hurt anyone, as long as you, my *gorgeous* warrior, promise to stay with me. For a year.'

"I had no choice. I had to agree ~ I didn't want to. But she led me out to the pig pen, and using her magic wand, prodded and poked the pigs. Their bristles fell off, their snouts shrank and, they were transformed into men again. They wept with joy to see each other. I knew I'd done the right thing.

"And so I fetched the others from the beach, and we all had to stay with Circe for a year. After her promise, she no longer had any power to trick us. And I must say, we had quite a pleasant time," Ulysses blushed. "Certainly, if I hadn't met Circe, I wouldn't have found out how to get home. Or rather," he added, "how to get this far. For I still haven't set foot on Ithaca since I left for Troy, nineteen years ago."

"That day shall soon come," said King Alcinous. "We can only show our gratitude to such a master storyteller by taking you safely home tomorrow. But tonight," he announced, "we shall hear some more of your tale."

"Yes, Ulysses," said Queen Arete, "what exactly did Circe teach you? How did you find out how to get back? Where did you go next?"

"Of all the places I've been to," said Ulysses, "the next one was the most frightening. I've met a lot of people. But there was one race I never thought I'd meet. Not until I'd fallen in battle, drowned at sea, or grown old and died by my own hearth, did I ever think I would talk to the dead.

"Here I am before you ~ living, breathing and healthy, thanks to your excellent dinner! But I, Ulysses," the warrior whispered, his hushed voice echoing gently through the hall, "I have been down to Hades, where the dead lie moaning for evermore. And I've survived to tell the tale."

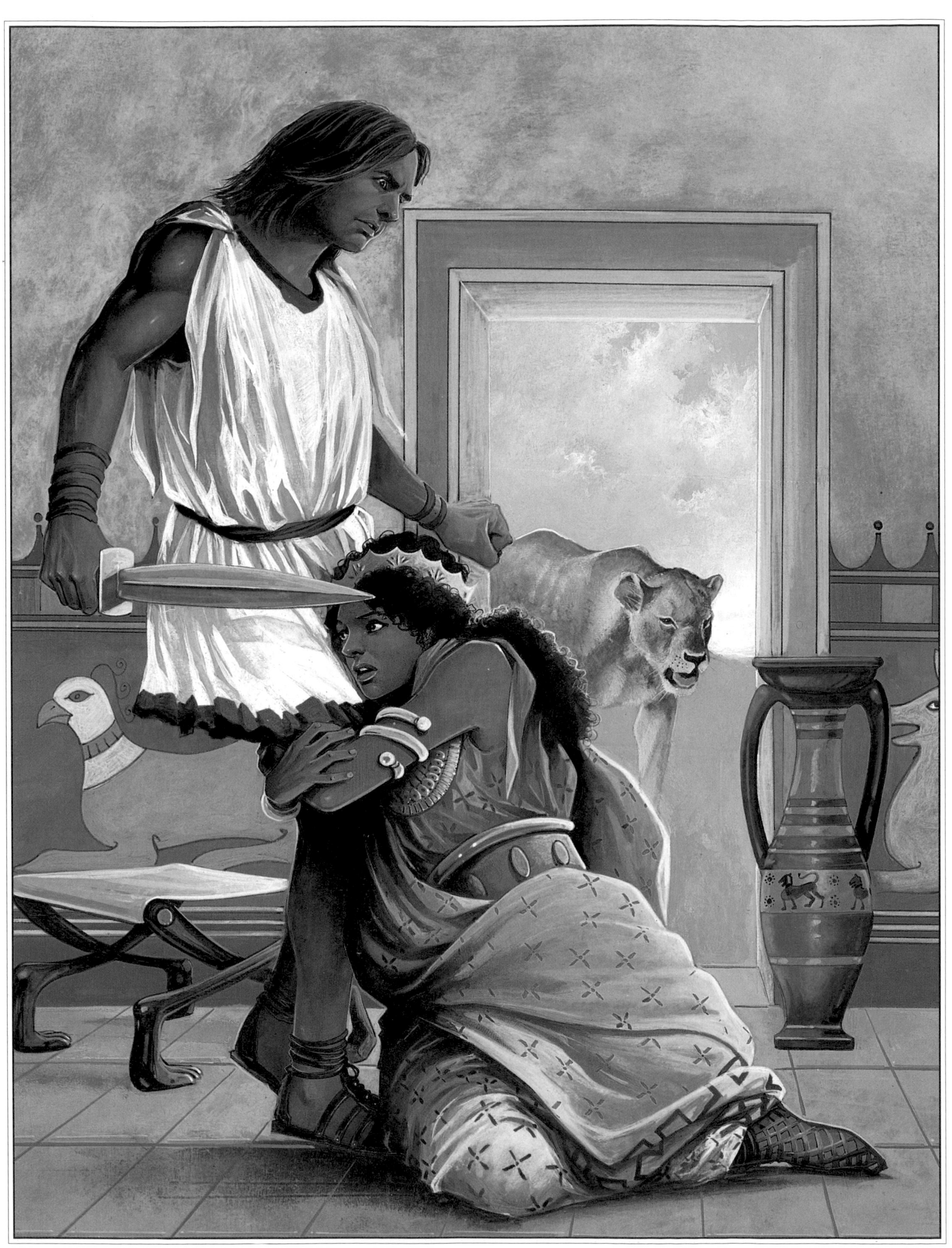

She crumpled onto the floor and flung her arms around my legs

CHAPTER FIFTEEN

THE LAND OF THE DEAD

"A year went by," began Ulysses, "and I knew I'd have to say something to Circe. I found her weaving as usual, but the expression on her face showed she knew what was coming. When I told her we had to leave, she looked very annoyed.

" 'How do you think you're going to make it home, then?' she asked, resentfully. I hadn't even thought about it. All I could say was, 'Well. . . we'll just set off, and hope for better luck.'

" 'There's only one way to be sure of a safe return,' said Circe, looking at me as if I was an idiot. 'You must visit Teiresias, the soothsayer.'

" 'But Teiresias is dead!' I protested. 'No one gets the benefit of his wisdom any more, Circe, not since he drank from the poisonous Well of Tilphosa.'

" 'Even the dead have a home,' she answered, and I realized what she was saying. If I was going to get Teiresias's advice, I would have to go to Hades itself.

"The Land of the Dead," Ulysses whispered, eerily. The hall had grown dark, and the servants were lighting lamps. The guests' wide-eyed faces glowed in the orange light.

"Circe told me how to get there. She said we would have to follow the current to the south, then go up the River of Ocean. Where two streams met, I was to dig a small trench and sacrifice a black ewe and a white ram, so that their blood filled the trench.

"Then, she said, the shadowy ghosts of the dead would rise out of the ground. 'But keep them away with your sword!' she warned. 'Don't let them drink the blood until Teiresias has had his turn!'

"I went to tell the men to get ready. And even then, we couldn't leave without a tragedy. Some of the crew were taking a nap in the sun on Circe's roof. When I called to them, one, Elpenor, forgot where he was, stumbled and fell off, breaking his neck.

"Elpenor always was a little clumsy. But I couldn't help wondering if that heartless Poseidon didn't have something to do with our endless string of catastrophes."

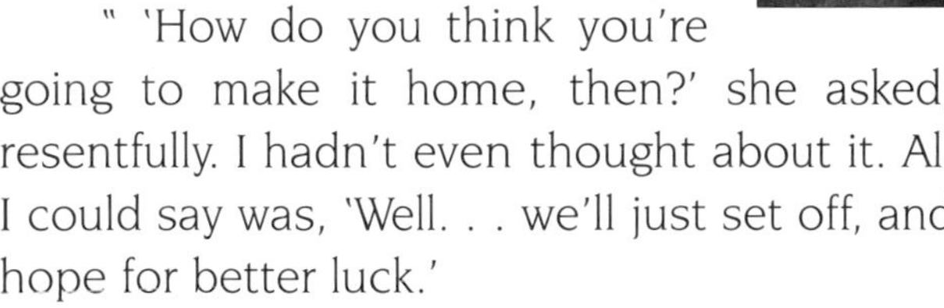

"Anyway, it wasn't long before we found ourselves sailing into the swirling mouth of the River of Ocean, away from the open sea. Circe had summoned up a wind to take us there.

"As we progressed inland, everything became strangely quiet. The wind dropped, and the water was flat calm. All around, the land was low and dark, covered with a creeping, greenish mist. Our ship pushed its way onward, slowly, magically, through the unearthly silence, into the Land of the Dead.

"We moored where Circe had told us to, and started walking across the swampy ground, dragging with us the ram and ewe for the sacrifice. Their bleats were the only sounds. The mist swirled around our legs as we came to the place where two streams joined, and there, I knelt down and used my dagger to dig a trench in the marshy soil.

"We were trembling by the time we came to sacrifice the sheep. Eurylochus and Polites held them still, while I slit their throats, turning to face the River of Ocean, as Circe had instructed. The animals fell, and their blood overflowed the little trench I had dug.

"We waited, staring hard into the mist. There was a low, murmuring sound, which grew into a quiet whimpering and moaning. Suddenly, I thought I could make out a face forming in the green shadows. But it wasn't Teiresias.

"It was my mother, Anticleia.

"I had no idea that she had died while I'd been gone.

" 'Mother!' I cried out to her, but suddenly her face became one of hundreds of moving, shifting, fluttering figures, filling the air around us. They were rising out of the ground faster and faster, armies of young soldiers with gaping spear wounds, brides struck down on their wedding day, children who had fallen sick, and old, withered men and women, with life's suffering behind them.

"Their horrible moaning and green, decaying faces made me panic. I felt the blood drain away from my face, and I thought I was about to faint, when I remembered that I must stop the dead from reaching the blood. Some of them were already creeping and swirling over to it.

"I grabbed my sword and held it shakily in front of the trench. 'Teiresias?' I called out. My voice sounded like a whimpering kitten. 'Teiresias, where are you?' I called again, feeling the panic rising in my throat.

"An old, bent figure could be seen feeling its way forward.

" 'Royal son of Laertes,' Teiresias croaked. His blind eyes roamed blankly. 'Allow me to drink, so that I may foresee your future.' Then he knelt, and I shrank back, terrified of being touched by his misty form. As he drank the warm blood, he began to look more solid, and his voice became more human.

" 'Oh, Teiresias,' I began, nervously. In one way, I didn't want to know my future. No man wants to know the date of his own death. But I had to know if we would get home, and how.

" 'Please tell me what. . . what will become of me,' I begged him.

"I felt like a coward. Me, Ulysses, reduced

to a quivering wreck in front of a blind old man, terrified of my own death. For death, after all, comes to everyone, and a warrior should not be afraid," Ulysses reminded his audience in the hall.

"Anyway, Teiresias gave me as full an answer as anyone could wish for. This is what he told me.

" 'My noble lord Ulysses, you are hoping for an easy way home. But Poseidon will fill your days with danger. He has not forgotten that you blinded his son, the Cyclops. But you and your crew may return home safely, if you follow my advice.

" 'You will come to the Island of the Sun, where the proud Sun god Apollo keeps his sturdy cattle. Whatever you do,' ~ and here Teiresias waved his bony finger at me ~ 'whatever you do, you must not kill the sheep and oxen of the Sun. Leave them untouched, and you will go home. But if a single one of the Sun's sacred animals is killed, you may never return. Or if you do, you will arrive late, after years of misery, on an unknown ship, with all your comrades dead, and trouble brewing in your royal house!'

"I shivered, realizing that these were the exact words the Cyclops had used when he called on Poseidon to curse me. But Teiresias was about to speak again.

" 'For when you do get home,' he went on, 'you'll find the place full of scoundrels harassing your wife and threatening your son. You'll have to fight them, Ulysses. And even when you've dealt with them, you'll have more journeys to make.

" 'But for you, I predict a happy ending. After a peaceful old age, death will come to you out of the sea, in a gentle disguise. This is the truth that I have told you. . .'

"Teiresias was starting to fade away. He grew misty at the edges.

" 'Teiresias!' I called. 'There's one more thing! I saw my mother here, among the dead. How can I speak to her?'

"Teiresias had almost turned back into a swirl of mist, but I heard him call faintly: 'The blood, Ulysses. You may speak to the dead, but they must drink the blood. . .' "

"I looked down at the murky pool of sheep's blood in the trench. How could I ask my mother to drink that?

" 'Mother?' I ventured. 'Mother!'

"She came up to me, out of the crowds of the dead. Her fluttering, shadowy form knelt and drank at the trench, and she stood up looking more solid and strong than when I had last seen her alive. 'Mother!' I cried, flinging my arms around her.

"My arms closed on nothing.

. . . hundreds of moving, shifting, fluttering figures,

filling the air around us . . .

" 'Oh, Ulysses, my darling son!' she cried, 'I am not made of flesh, and you cannot touch me. When we come here, our bodies decay. This is only my spirit that stands here before you. My darling, where have you been? Why didn't you come home? And if you're still alive, what are you doing here in Hades?'

" 'I have still not been home,' I replied. 'It seems as if I'm destined to wander all over the world. I came here to ask Teiresias about my future. But Mother, what happened in Ithaca? How did you die?'

" 'I died of grief for my lost son,' she wept. I could see tears welling up in her eyes, but still I couldn't touch and comfort her.

" 'I'm alive and safe, Mother,' I reassured her. I didn't tell her what Teiresias had said

about the difficult challenges ahead of me. 'Tell me. . . how is Penelope? And my father? And Telemachus,' I pleaded. 'Tell me how he has grown up.'

" 'Penelope's a good girl ~ I'm sure she'll wait for you,' she said absent-mindedly. 'Your father spends his time on the farm, away from the palace. It takes his mind off his troubles,' she added. 'But as for Telemachus ~ Ulysses, you would be so proud. He looks just like you, and I know he's going to grow up just as strong and brave as you are. But it's been hard for him, without a father. You must go back, Ulysses. Hurry back to the land of daylight, before it's too late!'

"My mother faded away, and I was left staring into the clouds of green mist. I was about to tell my companions to head back, when I noticed another green, shadowy form at my feet, bending down to drink the blood. I could see from his broad shoulders that this time it was a man, cut down by some disease or disaster in the prime of life.

"As he drained the trench to the bottom, the ghost took on a solid shape, and stood up before me. I was flabbergasted.

"I recognized those smiling eyes, the broad chest and imperious face of the man who'd been my beloved leader at Troy. I desperately wanted to throw my arms around him, to slap him on the back and shake him by the hand. But I couldn't.

" 'Agamemnon!' I gasped. 'What are you. . ? I thought you were alive! What happened?'

"The light in his eyes dimmed a little as Agamemnon looked down, almost with shame.

" 'I was killed,' he admitted. 'Well. . . murdered.'

" 'But. . . not at Troy!' I protested. 'You left with me. . . I saw your ships sailing off for home. Surely you made it?'

" 'Yes. . .' Agamemnon looked pained. 'My wife, Clytemnestra. And her. . . her lover, Aegisthus. They were waiting for me.'

" 'Oh, Agamemnon, that's terrible!' I cried, awkwardly. I didn't know what to say. My dear friend, one of the greatest warriors in the world, murdered by his own wife and her lover!

" 'After surviving Troy!' I went on. 'To get home, and. . . and have that happen.'

" 'I know,' agreed Agamemnon, grimacing apologetically. He looked up at me. 'She never forgave me, you know. Ever since that business with Iphigenia ~ the sacrifice, before we left for Troy. . .'

" 'But Iphegenia wasn't hurt ~ Artemis saved her' I protested.

"It was true," Ulysses explained to the guests in the hall. "When we'd needed the right wind to sail to Troy, Artemis had demanded Agamemnon's daughter as a sacrifice. He had been willing to do it. Then, at the last minute, Artemis had changed her mind, and taken the girl as a priestess instead.

"I reminded Agamemnon's ghost of this, but he just stared past me.

" 'We never saw her again,' he said sadly. 'And Clytemnestra hated me for it. I'm telling you, Ulysses. Don't trust women. Never, ever put your trust in a woman. Look what happened to me.'

" 'But Penelope wouldn't—' I faltered.

" 'Don't you believe it!' Agamemnon warned. 'You heard what Teiresias said. Even now, your house is filling up with good-looking suitors, all with their eye on your queen. And Ulysses,' he whispered, 'women are weak. She won't hold out forever. Take my advice ~ be prepared. Don't walk into a trap like I did. When you get back, you'll have to be ready with a plan to get rid of them.'

"As he spoke, he too began to fade, and the eerie moaning of the other ghosts grew louder. Suddenly there seemed to be even more of them, crowding and fluttering around us. My fear caught up with me again, and I was terrified that some monster, like the terrible gorgon, might rise out of the ground and destroy us. We started to stumble backward. Then we turned and ran for our boat, leaving the legions of the dead sinking slowly, wailing, back into the ground.

"But just as we were about to reach the ship, we became aware of another ghost in our path. It was a forlorn figure, his head hanging to one side.

" 'Elpenor!' gasped Eurylochus. It was the oarsman who'd fallen off the roof. He didn't need to drink the blood. 'My friends, help me!' he called out. 'I am not living, and I am not dead. When you hurried away from Circe's island, you forgot to bury me, and until I'm buried I cannot rest in peace!'

"We gazed in horror at his decaying flesh, his hollow eyes, and his neck, twisted and hanging slack where he had broken it.

" 'Bury me!' he cried. 'You must go back to the island and bury me!'

"We quickly embarked, cut loose the ropes, and let the River of Ocean carry us swiftly out to sea, and back the way we'd come.

"We couldn't let Elpenor suffer the life of a zombie. We had to go back to Circe's island. And it was just as well we did. When Elpenor's body had been put to rest, and we were ready to leave, the beautiful goddess took me to one side.

" 'Ulysses,' she purred, 'what amazing courage! By visiting the Land of the Dead, you've proved yourself the *bravest* of men. But let me tell you,' she added, drawing closer to me, 'there are more challenges lined up for you. And only I can tell you what they are.'

" 'My fair goddess,' I replied politely, 'Teiresias did explain to me about the sheep and oxen of the Sun.'

" 'But did he tell you about the ladies who are lying in wait?' she asked me, enigmatically. 'Ulysses, I think I may have some very useful advice for you. Just stay with me for one more night, and, well,' she said, winking slyly, 'I'll teach you all I know.'

"Well," said Ulysses to the sniggering guests, "that seemed like a fair exchange. After all, it's always better to set sail in the morning.

"So we stayed one more night, and Circe warned me about the terrible dangers that lay around the corner: the Sirens, beautiful yet evil monsters, who would try to lure us to our deaths; and Scylla, the many-headed monster, who would try to snatch men screaming from the deck.

"These horrors were yet to come. And without Circe's advice, I would certainly never have survived."

CHAPTER SIXTEEN

THE ISLAND OF THE SUN

"By the time we finally set off from Circe's island, the crew had recovered their spirits and were excited about going home. But I was full of a strange sense of foreboding," Ulysses told Alcinous and his guests. "And my instincts were right. It was to be our most dangerous journey yet."

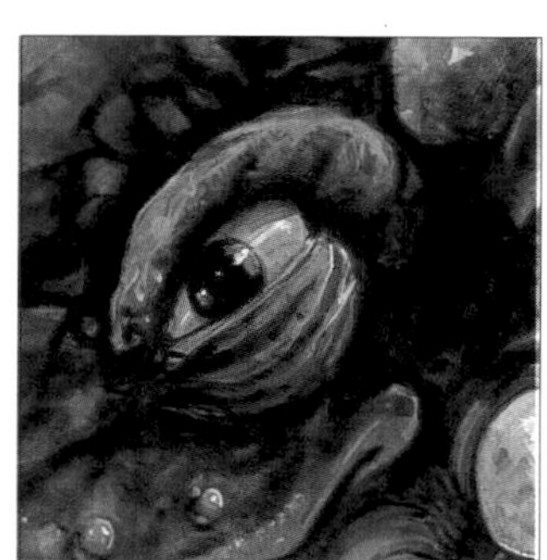

"But you *were* on your way home," said King Alcinous. "After all, Teiresias and Circe had warned you of the dangers."

"Yes," said Ulysses, "well, I knew how to get past the Sirens ~ but I hadn't even told the crew about Scylla and Charybdis. I didn't know how to. The truth was, Circe had said there was no way we'd get past Scylla without losing at least six men. I told her I was willing to fight, but she just laughed. She assured me that no mere mortal ~ not even me! ~ could fight that six-headed monster."

Ulysses sighed. "I *should* have told them," he said through gritted teeth, angry at his own cowardice. "But I wanted to get home as soon as possible. There was also the little matter of not killing those animals on the Island of the Sun. It sounded easy enough, but I had a nasty feeling I wasn't going to be able to control things. I decided it would be better to avoid the island altogether. I was sitting there, wondering what to do, when Eurylochus hurried up and tapped me on the shoulder.

" 'Sir,' he said, shaking me out of my daydream, 'what are those islands ahead? I've never seen such an eerie-looking spot, sir! Should we turn back?'

"And there they were ahead of us, the needle-sharp, jagged rocks where the Sirens live. Some say the Sirens are just mythical ~ but they're not."

All the guests in the hall had heard stories about the deadly Sirens, but none had actually seen them. People said that no one had ever sailed past them and lived to tell the tale. Yet here before them was a man who claimed he had. The guests were more amazed than ever.

"Oh yes," went on Ulysses, "they look just like beautiful women, singing on the shore. But they're evil. They call out to passing sailors, singing the most beautiful, hypnotic music in the world. It makes you go mad with desire, but when you try to get nearer, SMASH! You hit those sharp rocks ~ and that's exactly what they want. Well, I wasn't going to let that happen to me.

" 'It's too late to turn back!' I shouted to the men. 'Quick ~ we must follow Circe's instructions.' The men gathered around me while I feverishly tried to roll and soften a lump of beeswax between my palms. I pinched off a piece of wax for each man to plug his ears with. But I wanted to hear the Sirens singing, so I asked the men to tie me firmly to the mast, as Circe had advised.

"They'd just finished tying the last rope when I heard the first strains of music floating on the breeze.

"The men went about their work, but I was absolutely transfixed. That music ~ the singing ~ I can't describe it. It was like the taste of honey and sparkling wine mixed together. It was like being tickled with a feather all the way down your spine. It was as if the air had turned golden and silver. But no. . . it was even more beautiful than that. Those soft, soaring, intertwined voices. . . it was so beautiful, I just longed to, had to hear more of it. I couldn't bear the thought of sailing on past those rocks. . . the thought of never hearing that incredible sound again.

"So I tried to catch my men's attention, which wasn't easy, because they were all temporarily completely deaf. I motioned to them to untie me. I didn't care any more ~ I just wanted to stay with the Sirens for ever.

"But they knew what to do. They were such a good crew," said Ulysses, drifting off into a sad reverie for his old comrades. "I still can't believe I'll never see them again."

"What did they do?" asked the Queen.

"They tied me on tighter, of course!" replied Ulysses. "And it was just as well. As we rounded the rocks, we came to the highest, most jagged pinnacle of all. And piled up on it, like the remains of yesterday's dinner, were the bones. Hundreds of human bones, picked white by the seagulls, and speckled with slimy green moss ~ the skulls and skeletons of seafarers, like me, lured to their deaths. We'd had a narrow escape.

"Soon, the Sirens' voices faded, and there I was, tied to the mast, wondering why I'd been such an idiot. Seeing that I was back to normal, the men unplugged their ears and untied me. We sat down and congratulated ourselves on our escape. And then I saw the two rocks of Scylla and Charybdis poking out of the water like gigantic grey fingers."

"What are Scylla and Charybdis?" asked Demodocus. "Why be afraid of two rocks?"

"The rocks merely mark the spot," Ulysses replied gravely, "where thousands of men have lost their lives. A strong current forces every ship to pass between them. On one side, the rock rises straight up out of the sea. And in a cave,

halfway up, lives Scylla. Of all the monsters I've ever seen, she was the most terrifying.

"Six heads," he whispered eerily, peering from one face to another in the darkened hall, "each one on the end of a long, snaky neck. And on each head, rows and rows of long, pointed teeth, like a shark's. Circe had warned me that Scylla could dart out of her hole in half a second, and that her necks could reach anyone on deck. But, Circe said, it was better to sail close to Scylla's rock and risk losing a few men, than to go near Charybdis, the powerful whirlpool, which would suck our ship down in an instant.

" 'All hands on deck!' I cried. 'Row between the rocks, but keep close to the left-hand one, to avoid the whirlpool.'

"My comrade Eurylochus turned to me. 'Whirlpool?' he asked, looking horrified.

" 'There's nothing to worry about,' I lied to the panicking men. 'Circe told me we'll be fine as long as we keep close to the left-hand rock on the way through. All hands on deck!'

"So the men set to work, rowing us nearer to the tall, spooky grey fingers of stone. I stared up at the left one to see if I could spot Scylla crouching in her cave. But even though I peered at every inch of the rock's surface until my eyes hurt, I couldn't see any cave at all, let alone any sign of the monster.

"I began to think maybe it was our lucky day, and Scylla wasn't at home.

"Suddenly I heard a loud sucking, belching sound. I looked around. All the men were staring in horror across to the opposite side of the channel.

"The sea had opened up into a gaping, swirling vortex. Faster and deeper it spun, until we could peer down into it, and even catch a glimpse of the wet, sandy floor of the ocean

itself. It was like looking over the edge of a watery cliff. Then, just as suddenly as it had opened, the whirlpool collapsed in on itself with a resounding SLAP!, forcing a great jet of water into the sky. It surged up even higher than the rocks themselves, and showered onto the deck. The men cowered in terror.

" 'See,' I said, trying to reassure them. 'We're out of its range. Row on, and we'll make it through safely. Row on!' And the men strained at the oars, dragging us through the water, scraping close by Scylla's rock. Everyone's eyes were fixed on the bubbling whirlpool, which was beginning to boil and swirl around for a second time.

"Then I was aware of a quick snapping sound, and I heard the agonized cry of Polites, one of my best oarsmen. I spun around.

"Scylla's heads were among us, darting this way and that around the deck like serpents. Her scaly, writhing necks coiled and twisted out of a cleft high up in the rock. The heads snapped and grabbed at the men, who tried to fend them off with their oar handles, and the air was filled with an awful, strangled hissing sound. Instinctively, my hand reached for my sword. But then I remembered Circe's words: *no mere mortal can fight that six-headed monster.* There was nothing I could do.

"The first head waved above us, and clamped firmly between its rows of teeth was poor Polites, bleeding and screaming. Soon the other heads caught five more helpless oarsmen and lifted them, kicking and shrieking, until they disappeared into the rock face. We heard a disgusting crunching, slurping sound. Then nothing but the regular slap of the waves on the sides of the ship, and the whirlpool's belching.

"I looked back down into the boat. The appalled, horrified faces of the rest of the crew stared at me.

" 'Row on,' I ordered, shakily. 'Let's get out of here.'

"Grim-faced, the men rowed on determinedly until we were clear of that horrible place. And after all that, I could hardly deny them a rest. They were exhausted and traumatized, so I said we could stop for the night. And we'd found a nice little low-lying island and dragged the ship ashore before I realized where we were.

"There was something about the place that made me sure it was the Island of the Sun. It was partly the sheep and cows that were wandering around. They were just too perfect. They were strong and large, with broad foreheads and thick, glossy coats. Not a single one of them was lame or dirty. They were like gods among animals. And the light ~ everything was suffused in a golden-pink glow, like sunlight in the late evening. It was a truly beautiful place. But I was worried.

" 'Comrades,' I announced, 'You know Teiresias predicted we would come to the Island of the Sun. I think this is it, and—'

" 'Don't worry,' said Eurylochus in exasperation. 'We'll just eat our own rations. We won't touch a single sheep or cow. You can trust us!'

"But still, I made every single man promise not to kill any of the Sun's cattle, before I would sit down to supper.

"It would have been fine," lamented Ulysses. "We had plenty of rations, and no one wanted to annoy the Sun god, or any other god for that matter. But that bully Poseidon still found a way to cause trouble.

"He sent us a storm, didn't he? The whole island was lashed by gales and huge waves, and we couldn't set off. It carried on for a week. Then another week. A month after we'd arrived, it was *still* going, and we were running out of supplies. I told the men they could try to catch fish if they wanted, but they were not, under *any* circumstances, to kill the sheep or cows. And with that, I left them at our camp on the beach while I went to find somewhere to pray.

"I tramped through the dripping wet undergrowth, feeling furious, but trying to control myself. I had to pray to all the gods ~ including Poseidon ~ if it was going to work.

"After a while I came to a temple in the woods, and I knew I'd been right. It was the shrine of Apollo, the Sun god.

"I stepped inside, wiping my feet and trying to shake the worst of the rainwater off my clothes, before going up to the altar.

"I kneeled down and tried to calm my nerves. All I could hear was the hammering of the rain and the thumping of my own heart.

" 'Lord Zeus, ruler of the sky,' I began. 'And Apollo, bright god of the Sun. Gorgeous Athene of the flashing eyes! Hermes, handsome messenger, and all the wise and beautiful gods of Mount Olympus! And, er, Poseidon,' I added. 'Please, please stop this storm, and let us go home.'

"Then, I willed my message to fly up to the gods. Perhaps they would send me a sign. But nothing happened, except that an old goblet on the altar toppled over and rolled onto the floor, breaking in half.

"I don't know if that was a bad omen, but I decided to ignore it. I'd done my best. So I set off in the rain, back to the beach.

"But as I tramped down the last little stretch of grass onto the sandy shore, I smelled something that made me realize my worst fears had come true. It was a smell that would normally cheer me up, but on this occasion it made my stomach lurch. It was the warm, familiar aroma of roasting beef."

" 'NO-OOOOO!' I screamed, running down over the green grass, over the golden sand, and wrenching the blackened carcass of the cow off the spit the men had built. But it was far too late. I slumped down on the damp beach and covered my face with my hands. 'We're ruined!' I groaned. Flashing through my mind were the fateful words the Cyclops and Teiresias had used: *You will come home late. . . on an unknown ship. . . with all your comrades dead. . . trouble brewing. . . trouble brewing. . .*

" 'Better to take whatever the gods throw at us than die a lingering death from malnutrition!' said Eurylochus indignantly. 'We had to do it, or we'd have starved to death!'

Scylla's heads were among us. . .

darting this way and that around the deck like serpents

" 'Don't eat it!' I wailed, 'Don't eat it!' But they were already tucking hungrily into the perfectly roasted flesh of the cow they had killed. I was the only one who refused to eat the meat.

"Then, something really strange happened. Although there were no other cows nearby, we heard a low mooing sound. We couldn't tell where it was coming from. But it got louder and louder, until it felt as if a cow was mooing right in our ears. We hid behind some bushes, and peering out from behind them, we saw the leathery hide of the dead animal begin to move from where the men had thrown it. It got up slowly, and wobbled around, like a new-born calf, making this awful, eerie mooing noise. It had to be a bad omen, I knew that much.

"At last it went and lay down again, exactly where it had been before. When we came out from behind the bushes, some of the men convinced themselves they'd imagined it. They went ahead and helped themselves to more meat, seeming totally carefree, while I went down and sat by the waves and prayed, knowing all the time that there was no longer anything I could do."

"Soon after that, the storm died down, and we prepared the ship. We set sail, but I was hardly surprised when, as soon as we were out of sight of land, the sky grew black, and heavy raindrops began to plop onto the deck. The waves grew rough, the rain was replaced by hail, and a gale-force wind hit us from the north. We manned the oars, trying to guide the ship out of trouble, screaming instructions at each other through the blasting wind.

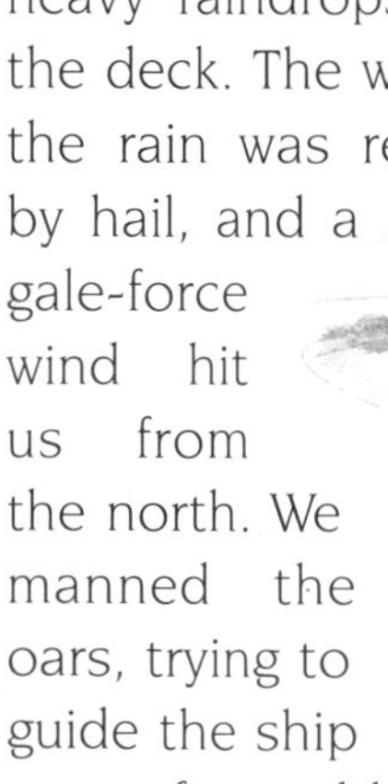

"Then, through the noise of the storm, I heard the slow, creaking sound of the mast toppling. It gathered momentum and crashed down onto the deck, hitting the helmsman on the back of the head and splitting open his skull. He fell off the front of the ship and plunged like a stone into the billowing waves. As he hit the water, a shaft of lightning crashed out of the sky and scored a direct hit. There was nothing accidental about it. The Sun god must have been furious with us.

"The boat exploded into fragments, and we were flung into the black, roaring sea. I kept afloat by clinging to a piece of wood. Every single one of the others drowned."

"For nine days I floated helplessly, trying to stay conscious, and hallucinating that I was back home with my family in Ithaca. I only stayed alive by counting the sunrises and sunsets, making myself watch the stars at night and the patterns of the clouds by day.

"When I felt two arms pull me from a shallow bay, and heard the soft whispering of a woman, I dreamed it was Penelope.

"But it was Calypso, the nymph. She rescued me, but she held me prisoner too. It was seven long years before I was able to escape to this wonderful place."

Ulysses surveyed the hall, the empty dinner plates, and all the astounded faces of the guests, and reminded himself how lucky he was to be alive.

CHAPTER SEVENTEEN

COMING HOME

Ulysses's tale was finished. There was complete silence as he looked around the shadowy hall at his audience. They stared back at him, each one wondering at the things Ulysses had seen and the horrors he had survived.

Then the gentle sound of snoring drifted from the back of the hall. Ulysses smiled. "I'm sorry to have kept you all awake," he apologized.

"It was worth it," said King Alcinous. "Ulysses, that was the best story I've ever heard. We're very lucky to have such a great hero here to entertain us. However," he yawned, rising from his throne, "it is very late. I propose we all go to bed, and tomorrow our oarsmen will take you home, carrying the most precious gifts Phaeacia can provide, in return for your excellent tale."

The next day, King Alcinous chose some expensive bronze bowls, rare jewels and beautiful rich silk clothing embroidered with silver thread as presents for Ulysses. He took them down to the ship himself and stowed them under the rowing benches, while Queen Arete sent her servants to load the ship with bread and wine for the oarsmen.

The sun was sinking in the west by the time everything was ready. Although he was itching to get going, Ulysses watched patiently as the oarsmen carried a soft rug and blanket onto the deck for him to sleep on. He turned to the crowd standing on the beach, the generous king and the wise old queen, and their beautiful daughter, Nausicaa, who had rescued him and brought him to the palace.

"My friends," he cried, "may your country be blessed, and may you live in happiness forever! Thank you for all you have done for me. And thank you, Nausicaa, for your kindness. I hope you find a wonderful husband!"

With that, the crowd erupted into cheers, Nausicaa blushed, and Ulysses stepped on board. He waved to the excited people as the oarsmen heaved on the oars and the ship began to pull slowly out of the bay. Then, exhausted after the previous evening's

performance, Ulysses climbed into his makeshift bed on the deck. And as he slept, the ship gathered speed and sliced through the dark water on its way to Ithaca.

"Where am I?" said Ulysses sleepily.

It was dawn. Ulysses was lying on his rug, under his blanket, which was damp with dew, on a strange beach. His breath formed clouds in the cool morning air. All around, a thick mist shrouded the landscape.

"Oh no! " said Ulysses angrily, sitting up. "It's happened again! I always think I'm about to make it back to Ithaca, and I always end up miles from anywhere!"

Then he saw a pile of precious bronzeware and jewels sparkling in the sunlight nearby. His gifts from King Alcinous! What was going on?

"Ulysses," came an amused voice from behind him. "You're not going to give up, I hope! Not now you're back in Ithaca."

"Athene!" Ulysses spun around. There she stood; tall and radiant, with a mocking look in her eyes, her hands on her hips, and her spear planted firmly in the sand.

"But this isn't Ithaca!" blustered Ulysses. "It doesn't look like it, anyhow. Where are the fields full of sheep? Where's Mount Neriton? How did I get here?"

"The Phaeacians dropped you off," answered the goddess simply. "You were sleeping, so they left you here. And I didn't want you waking up and storming into town, half asleep, and announcing you were back. Ulysses, those suitors would have your guts for garters! They'd kill you on the spot! So, I disguised Ithaca."

As she spoke, the mist gradually faded, and Mount Neriton slowly took shape, looming above them.

"Ithaca!" yelled Ulysses, hardly listening. "It is Ithaca! Oh Athene, I'm home! I'm home!" He grabbed large handfuls of white sand and let it trickle through his fingers.

"Penelope! Telemachus! I must see them!"

"No!" cut in Athene. "Don't you remember what Teiresias warned you about, and what the Cyclops wished on you? Ulysses, your palace is full of enemies, who are trying to win the hand of your wife. You've only just come back in time to stop her from choosing a husband. You must act fast. But if you go to the palace all alone, without preparation, they'll kill you. And that would be a waste of all your efforts to get home, wouldn't it?"

"Arrogant fools!" fumed Ulysses. "How dare they! I'll. . . I'll. . !" He stumbled upright, catching his foot in the blanket. "Where's my sword?"

"Ulysses," said the goddess patiently. "Calm down. There's a better way. You're not going to defeat them without my help, so you might as well take my advice."

Ulysses stared at the sand, looking annoyed.

"Now listen," said Athene. "I'm going to disguise you as an old beggar. Don't go to the city yet. Go and see Eumaeus, the swineherd, who's been loyal to you all this time. Stay in his hut until I tell you what to do. And don't tell anyone who you are."

She picked up her spear. "I'm going to fetch Telemachus. He's gone to Sparta to look for you, and you'll need him here if there's going to be a battle. I'll tell him to come to Eumaeus's hut as well."

"But why didn't you tell Telemachus where I was, and save him the journey?"

"He was better off away from those suitors," Athene answered. "Even now, they've sent a ship after him to try to ambush him. But don't worry," she added, seeing his worried face, "I'll make sure he comes to no harm."

Then she touched Ulysses with her spear, and shot into the sky.

Ulysses looked down. He had the body of an old man, and instead of the spotless new tunic given to him by Nausicaa, he was wearing tattered, smelly rags. He felt his face. It was wrinkled and saggy. He hoped he wouldn't have to stay like this for long. But there wasn't much he could do about it now. So, after hiding his presents in a cave, he set off for Eumaeus's pig farm.

Trudging up to Eumaeus's hut, Ulysses caught sight of the old swineherd sitting on the garden wall, making himself a pair of leather sandals. After so many years away, Ulysses longed to cry out to his old servant, "It's me! Ulysses!" But he stopped himself.

"Hello!" he shouted out instead, and was shocked to hear how old and croaky his voice was. "Any chance of a bed for the night?"

"Good day to you, sir! You look down on your luck, if you don't mind me saying so!" called out Eumaeus. Ulysses was delighted to see how polite the swineherd was, even to an old beggar.

"You're welcome to share my hut, such as it is," Eumaeus went on regretfully. "It's not much of a place, I know. Time was when I'd have sent you down to the palace for a proper welcome. My old master King Ulysses, or his son Telemachus, they would have put you up in style! But now. . ." He shook his head. "Now, you'd probably just get a good kicking. The place is full of young good-for-nothings!"

Ulysses opened his mouth to thank the swineherd for his hospitality, but Eumaeus went on, "I'm the swineherd, sir, you see. It's my job to rear pigs for the palace tables. But these days, I spend my time feeding my lady's suitors, as my master's been away for years!"

"Thank you, sir, for your kind welcome," put in Ulysses quickly. "I must say, I'm a little hungry at the moment. Any chance of, er—?"

"Of course, sir, where are my manners?" said Eumaeus, hopping off the wall in a surprisingly sprightly manner. "Do come inside for a bite to eat. I was just about to have breakfast myself. Nice day, isn't it?"

That evening, while Ulysses was tucking into his third meal of bread and pork, Eumaeus explained that Telemachus had gone on a trip to look for his father.

"Strapping young lad!" said Eumaeus. "Looks like his father, too. Anyway—"

His story was cut short by the appearance of a young man in the doorway. The evening sun shone from behind him, so Eumaeus and Ulysses could only see his silhouette. He was muscular and tall, with a mop of curly hair.

"Is that my young master?" ventured Eumaeus excitedly. "Back from abroad?" He ran to the door, grasping Telemachus's hands. "Oh sir, we thought we'd never see you again, after you slipped off in the night like that! What on earth were you thinking! You know those suitors were after you! But you're safe! The gods be thanked!"

He pulled Telemachus into the hut. "This is him!" he exclaimed to Ulysses. "My master Telemachus! And this here," he said to Telemachus, "is a friend who's staying the night. Do sit down, and I'll bring you something to eat. It's such a joy to see you ~ you hardly ever come up here to visit."

While Eumaeus bustled about preparing more food, Ulysses reached out to shake his son's hand, fighting back a lump in his throat. Telemachus's handshake was warm and strong.

"You're very welcome to Ithaca, sir," he said. "I'm afraid my father's palace isn't fit for entertaining guests right now, but it's not our policy to turn away beggars. I'll have food and clothing sent up to you here."

"Thank you," was all Ulysses could say.

Athene had given Telemachus careful instructions. He didn't know Ulysses was at the hut. But Athene had told him to go there, and to send Eumaeus to tell Penelope her son was home. She'd also made him promise not to reveal the news that Ulysses was alive.

So, after the three of them had spent the night cosily around Eumaeus's fire, Eumaeus set off for the city.

"Don't tell anyone except my mother that I'm back!" Telemachus called after the old swineherd as he tramped down the hill. "I don't want those suitors finding out yet!"

Meanwhile, Ulysses had heard Athene's voice in his ear. "Meet me outside!" she whispered. "At the back."

He found the goddess behind the hut. Raising her spear, she transformed him back into his old self: tall, handsome and well-dressed. "Go and join your son, and together you can plot an attack on the suitors," she said. "I'll be back soon." And she disappeared.

Ulysses went back into the hut. When Telemachus came back in, Ulysses was sitting on a stool. Telemachus took one astonished look at him, and fell to his knees.

"Sir, you have changed!" he gasped. "And only the immortal gods can change their

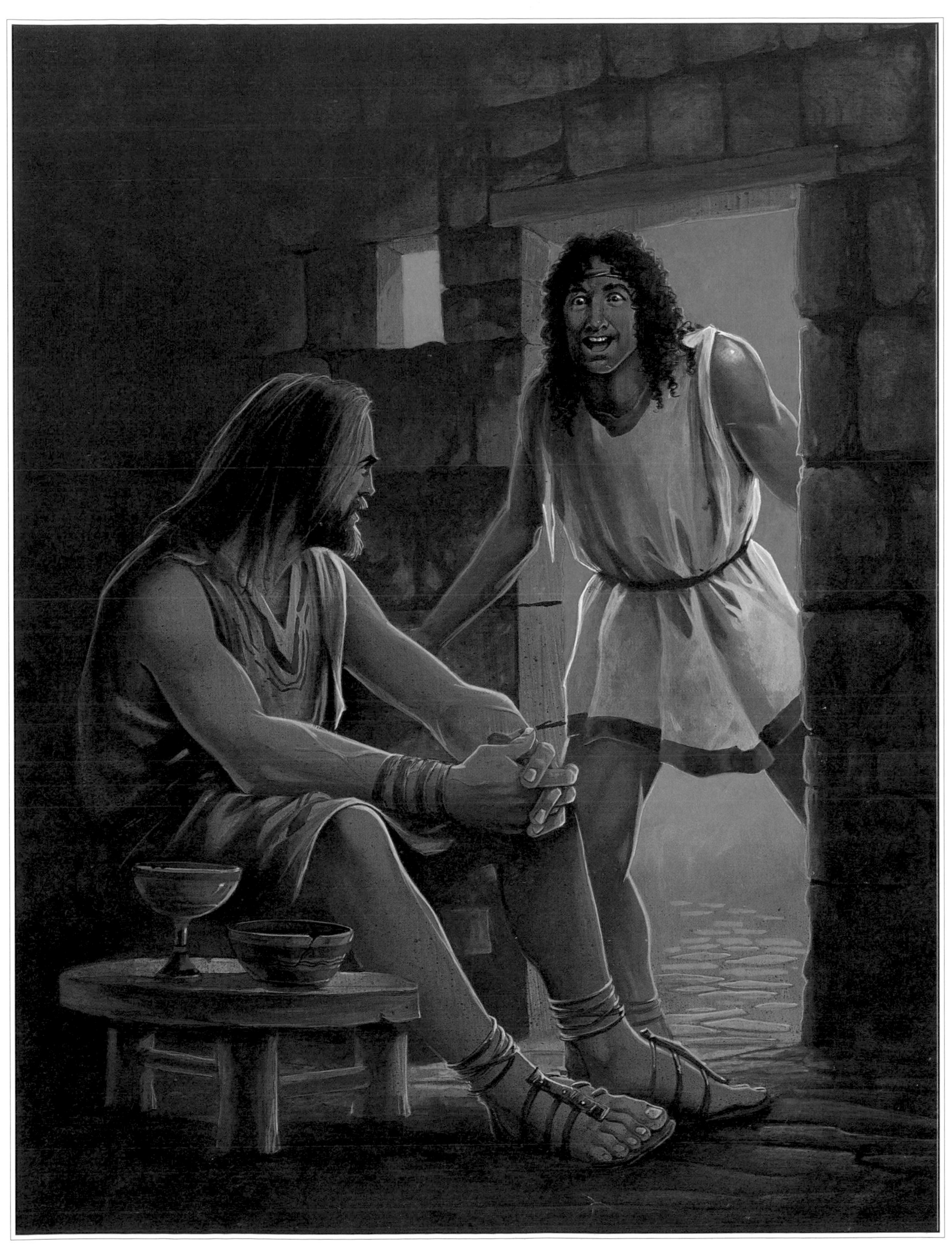

Telemachus took one astonished look at him

appearance. If you are a god, please have mercy on us!"

Ulysses took his son's hands in his. "I am not a god," he said gently, "but I am your father." He looked into his son's frightened, uncomprehending eyes.

"I'm sorry, Telemachus," he began. "I'm sorry I've been away, and you've had to grow up without me. Can you forgive me?"

"You're not my father!" shouted Telemachus, standing up. "It's a trick! No mortal, not even Ulysses, can just change his appearance whenever he feels like it!"

"I *am*," said Ulysses in exasperation. "That disguise was the work of Athene, who you know is helping us both. I am your father. After nineteen years abroad ~ and I thought about you every day ~ here I am."

Telemachus stared at him distrustfully through narrowed eyes. Ulysses had to smile at how much Telemachus resembled him ~ always cunning and thoughtful.

"What? Why are you laughing?"

"Nothing," said Ulysses. "I was just thinking that we look alike. Don't we?"

"Yes," said Telemachus cautiously.

"Telemachus," Ulysses said at last. "What's your middle name?"

"I never use it," said Telemachus, blushing. Ulysses took his son's arm, drew him closer, and whispered a single word in his ear. Aloud, he said, "I gave you that name."

"You are Ulysses," said Telemachus slowly. "Father!" he cried, and burst into tears, flinging his arms around Ulysses. They hugged each other, and then Ulysses stood back to admire again the way his son had grown up so tall, so strong and so like himself.

"But Telemachus," Ulysses continued, sounding more serious, "there's no time for tears. We must do something about those suitors. We have to get rid of them."

"How can we?" said Telemachus despairingly, sinking onto a stool. "I mean, I know you're renowned for your bravery and cunning, and I'd do my best. But there are so many of them, and only two of us."

"Exactly how many?" inquired Ulysses. He looked as if he were thinking up a plan.

"Well. . ." said Telemachus, "fifty-two from Dulichium, and twenty-four from Same. Another twenty from Zacynthus. And twelve from Ithaca itself, I think. Father, they'd slaughter you. Even you!"

"But we aren't really alone," Ulysses reminded him. "What about Athene? She is the goddess of wisdom and war. And perhaps she can persuade her father Zeus to help."

Telemachus looked miserable.

"Listen," said Ulysses, sitting next to him. "Let's try my plan ~ there's nothing else we can do. This is what I have in mind.

"You'll go down to the palace and take your place among the suitors. Ignore them if they bully you. I'll arrive disguised as a beggar, and that way I'll be able to get a good look at them and weigh up our chances.

"When I give you the signal, gather up any weapons that are lying around and lock them in the storeroom. If anyone asks, say you're worried the weapons might get dirty. But remember to leave a few for us to use. And don't tell anyone that I'm back!"

Now Telemachus's ship, which had dropped him off near the farm, had sailed into the port. The crew hadn't been told to keep quiet, so they ran ashore, crying out: "A message for the queen! Telemachus is back!"

Eumaeus, who had whispered the message to Penelope herself, realized that the suitors would soon find out. He set off back to the farm at once.

It was only a few moments before the news reached the suitors, who were sitting around yet another feast in the palace. Eurymachus stood up and banged the table.

"My friends," he announced, "we thought Telemachus had been dealt with. But Antinous's ship must have missed the little squirt. We've got to send a messenger to tell Antinous to come back at once!"

"There he is!" cried Amphinomus. "No need for a messenger!" He had spied Antinous's ship through the window. It was racing into the port, its sail flapping angrily in the wind. The suitors streamed out of the palace and down to the shore.

"Curse the little fool!" stormed Antinous, as he disembarked. "There we were, waiting around at Asteris, like a bunch of idiots, and Telemachus sails straight past us! He's got some god on his side, I'll bet!"

"So what do we do now, Antinous?" asked Eurymachus, with a hint of sarcasm.

"Shut up!" barked Antinous. "If we can't kill him at sea, we'll just have to kill him at home, won't we? When I catch him. . ."

"But Antinous. . ." said Amphinomus gingerly, "what if he has got a god on his side? Then we'll be in trouble."

Antinous glared at him.

"Let's go back inside and eat, while we think about it," suggested Eurymachus, and everyone agreed. They headed for the palace.

Penelope was waiting for them.

"Antinous!" she said, biting her lip with rage. The suitors shambled around while Antinous came guiltily to the front.

"People say, Antinous, that you are wise, charming and clever!" she bristled, "but they're wrong! What's this I hear about you plotting against Telemachus? The gods are to be thanked that you failed! It's bad enough that you all abuse our hospitality and make a nuisance of yourselves. But if you must do that, you could at least leave my son alone!" Her eyes blazed furiously at Antinous, who, for once, wasn't sure what to say.

"Your Majesty!" It was Eurymachus, in his most charming tone. "How could you think such a thing! It must be the servants gossiping. Why, if anybody hurt Telemachus, they'd soon feel the point of my spear!"

"Mine too," said Antinous, uncertainly.

Penelope shot him a withering look. Then, holding her head high, she turned and left the room, her cloak swirling behind her.

But back upstairs, she threw herself on her bed and wept. "I've lost Ulysses!" she sobbed, "and now they're going to get Telemachus too! Oh Ulysses, my love! If only you'd come home!"

CHAPTER EIGHTEEN

THE BEGGAR IN THE PALACE

As Eumaeus toiled up the hill back to his hut, he thought for a moment that there were three people standing there. Did he have another visitor?

But as he drew closer he saw that there were only two after all ~ his master Telemachus, and the old man who'd turned up the day before. Eumaeus didn't spot Athene disappearing into the clouds above. She'd turned Ulysses back into a beggar in the nick of time. If Eumaeus had recognized his old master, he'd have been so excited he'd have rushed back to the city to tell Penelope, and that would have ruined the goddess's plan.

"Hello, Eumaeus!" said Telemachus. "My ~ I mean, our, er, old friend here has decided he'd like to try begging at the palace. Could you take him along, later? I'll be leaving myself in a few minutes."

"No, my boy," panted Eumaeus. "You can't go down there ~ the news is out! The suitors know you're back, and they'll be baying for your blood by now! Take an old man's advice and stay up here, at least until they've calmed down.

"And as for you, sir," ~ he turned to Ulysses ~ "I've told you before, they're not the sort to look kindly on beggars. You stay here as well ~ goodness knows we've enough pigs to keep you fed!"

"Sorry, Eumaeus," said Telemachus, in a serious voice. "I've got to go. I can't always hide away from those bullies. I've got to face them. When I've been gone for half an hour, you are to bring our guest to the palace. And that's an order. Goodbye."

Eumaeus was shocked. "Right you are, then, sir," he mumbled, as Telemachus picked up his spear and marched off down the hill.

"Well," grumbled Eumaeus, "I can't imagine what's wrong with him." He went on shaking his head as he trudged into the hut.

Ulysses smiled to himself.

"Telemachus!"

It was one of the maids, busy cleaning the steps of the palace, who first saw Telemachus striding through the gates. She dropped her mop and ran inside. "He's here!" she yelled to the other women. "Tell the queen it's true, Telemachus is back safe and sound!"

Telemachus soon found himself surrounded by maids. "You've been sorely missed, sir!" said Eurycleia, his old nurse. "The suitors have been getting worse and worse!" chimed in Melantho, a young kitchen maid.

"WHERE have you been?"

Penelope had arrived. On her face was an expression of fury mixed with huge relief. "Why did you leave without telling me?" she shouted. Then she threw her arms around her son. "Oh, Telemachus," she sniffed into his shoulder. "I thought I'd never see you again!

The suitors are becoming uncontrollable. What are we to do?"

"Mother, it's all right, I'm safe," Telemachus murmured, hugging her tightly. Since Ulysses had sworn him to secrecy, he thought he'd better not tell her anything.

"Don't worry," he reassured her. "It'll be over soon. I promise." He hoped he was right.

When his mother had returned to her rooms, Telemachus picked up his spear and strode through the hall and across the lawn. Athene had made him seem even taller and better-looking than usual, so that the man the suitors saw pacing up to them over the grass looked like a handsome young god.

He expected snide remarks and mockery from the men who had tried to kill him. But instead, the suitors seemed to be doing their best to behave.

"Telemachus!" Eurymachus, cried, slapping him on the back. "Pleasant trip? Good to see you, old friend!"

Antinous didn't manage to be quite as polite. "Hello there!" he said, trying to twist his sneering face into a welcoming smile.

But Telemachus knew they weren't to be trusted. "I wish I could say it was as pleasant to see you," he said curtly, "but it isn't. There's just one thing I've got to say to you, and you'd better listen—"

"Suppertime!" yelled a maid, and Telemachus was almost crushed by the suitors stampeding to their places in the hall. Burning with rage and embarrassment, he dusted himself down and followed them, taking his father's old seat at the top table. He wasn't going to let them get to him.

"You were saying?" Eurymachus asked him sweetly.

"It can wait," said Telemachus.

"Who's that?" shouted Antinous an hour later, when the feast was in full swing. There was a commotion in the doorway. Eumaeus, the old swineherd, and Ulysses, disguised as a shabby beggar, were trying to come in, but Argus, Ulysses's old dog, was jumping all over his master and licking his face.

"Stupid dog," grumbled Antinous. "Eumaeus, what are you doing here? You've brought today's pork already, haven't you?

"Let them in," ordered Telemachus. Everyone stared at him. "Eumaeus, come and sit by me. And take this food and give it to our guest." He filled a plate with meat and bread and handed it to Eumaeus, who went and gave it to Ulysses.

"Thank you kindly, young sir," Ulysses croaked to Telemachus.

"That's typical!" fumed Antinous.

"And after that, if he's still hungry," said Telemachus as Eumaeus sat down, "tell him to beg a little food from our friends here,

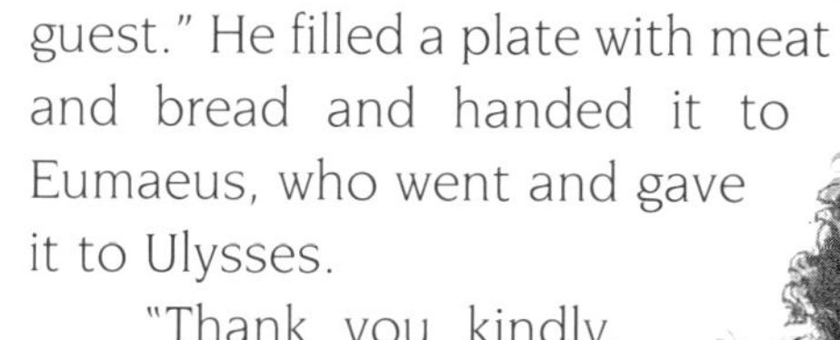

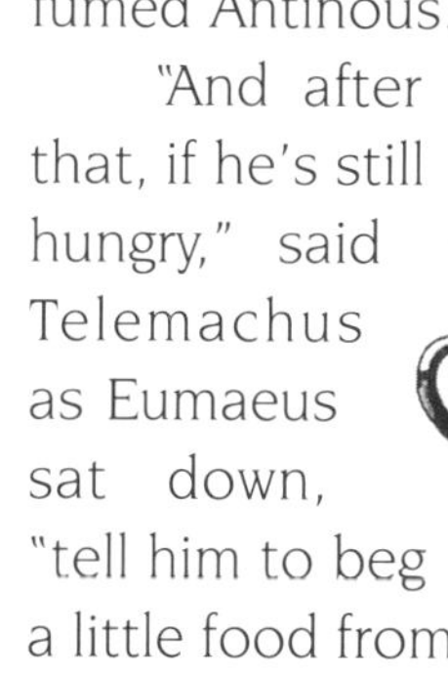

the suitors. After all, they're all noblemen," he added, keeping one eye firmly on Antinous, "and no man of quality turns away a beggar!"

Ulysses soon finished his plateful, and realized that he *was* still hungry. Perhaps Athene had something to do with it, for now he could hear her whispering in his ear, "Go on, do the rounds of the suitors and beg from them. Let's see how they treat you."

So Ulysses got up and hobbled to the nearest table. He held out his plate and pulled a pathetic, self-pitying face at Leodes, one of the younger of the suitors.

Leodes wasn't sure what to do. He knew Antinous would shout at him, but Telemachus was right. It was the correct thing to do to take pity on beggars.

And what if the beggar turned out to be a god in disguise? So he heaped some meat onto the plate. Ulysses trudged along to the next suitor. Under Telemachus's steely glare, Leocritus added a hunk of bread to the plate, giving Antinous an embarrassed shrug. He didn't want to be accused of not being a gentleman.

"This is ridiculous!" yelled Antinous, standing up and flinging back his chair. "You're all under Telemachus's thumb, aren't you? Eumaeus, why did you bring us this stinking tramp? We have enough people to feed!"

"If we have, it's because you lazy hooligans are hanging around uninvited!" blurted out Eumaeus. "Anyway, I don't have to answer to you! Telemachus is my master~ and King Ulysses, if he ever gets home."

By now, Ulysses had trudged around to Antinous's seat, and was giving him his most pitiful, long-suffering stare.

"My noble lord," he wheedled, holding out the plate. "Your looks tell me that you're *extremely* well-bred. Don't you have anything to give a poor, weary, unfortunate beggar?"

"A smelly, disgusting, good-for-nothing beggar, more like!" roared Antinous. He grabbed his footstool and lifted it over his head.

"Oh dear. I see your brains don't match your looks, after all," said Ulysses with mock sadness, and wandered off.

In a raging fury, Antinous hurled the stool at Ulysses's back. It hit him on the shoulder. Ulysses paused, then limped away.

Penelope soon heard from the servants about what Antinous had done. "The bully!" she muttered to herself. "They're all rowdy hooligans, but he's by far the worst! Eurycleia!" she called. "Eurycleia!"

The old nurse scurried into the room.

"Eurycleia, I want to meet this beggar who has been so badly treated. Ask him to come and see me."

Eurycleia passed the news on to Eumaeus, who whispered in Ulysses's ear.

"Tell her I'll see her this evening," said Ulysses. Then, remembering that he was supposed to be a beggar, he added, "Of course, I will gladly meet her majesty. Please tell her I will talk to her after supper." And Eumaeus hurried off.

At that moment, another ragged figure appeared at the doorway. It was Irus.

Irus was one of Ithaca's regular beggars. He'd been around for years. He was large and stupid, with a very deep voice. "Hey!" he boomed, spying Ulysses. "Who are you? Get off my patch!"

Eurymachus burst out laughing and pointed at the two beggars in the doorway. "You tell him, Irus!" he snorted.

"Yeah, go on, Irus!" shouted Leocritus. "Kick him out!"

Antinous got up from his place and swaggered over.

"Gentlemen!" he announced, "I think we've just found ourselves the perfect after-dinner entertainment. A fight!" The suitors all jumped up, laughing and shouting, and crowded around as Irus threw off his cloak and raised his fists. "Come on then!" he taunted.

Ulysses looked at him. Then he calmly pulled up his own ragged sleeves to reveal his bulging muscles. Irus looked shocked. He'd thought his rival was a weak old man.

"No ~ wait!" shouted Antinous gleefully. "I've got it! A prize! The winner gets a side of pork from the spit! How about it?"

"Er, I think I've changed my mind. . ." bumbled Irus, but the suitors were having none of it. They pushed him forward, and started jeering and shouting, "Go on! Hit him, Irus! Give him one from me!"

Ulysses didn't want to kill Irus. So he drew back his fist only half way, and landed a light punch on the beggar's left temple.

Irus staggered, fell to his knees with a crunch, and then keeled over into the dust. Ulysses grabbed one of the beggar's arms and dragged him outside, where he propped him up against a tree. "Sorry, Irus," he said. "I think this patch is mine."

The suitors looked pale as they made their way back to their places. Amphinomus went to get the side of pork and presented it to Ulysses. "Well done, sir," he said, avoiding Antinous's gaze. "And good luck to you."

"Thanks, but no thanks," said Ulysses. "It's mine anyway."

Amphinomus looked puzzled. "Listen, Amphinomus," said Ulysses quietly. "I knew your father, Nisus of Dulichium. He was a good man, and I think you are too, at heart. So I'm going to be frank with you."

Amphinomus stared at him.

"The gods don't look kindly on men who abuse others' hospitality, overstay their welcome and plot to murder their host."

Amphinomus's eyes nearly popped out of his head. He wondered if the beggar really was a god in disguise.

"And I can tell you, it won't be long before Ulysses is back. In fact," he said, staring into Amphinomus's face, "he's very close indeed. So watch out."

"What's going on?" yelled Eurymachus. "Now you've won a fight, you think you're the greatest, don't you? Well shut up, and go and sit in the doorway where you belong!" Then he too picked up his stool, and threw it in Ulysses's direction. It missed and hit Leodes. He grabbed the stool and flung it back.

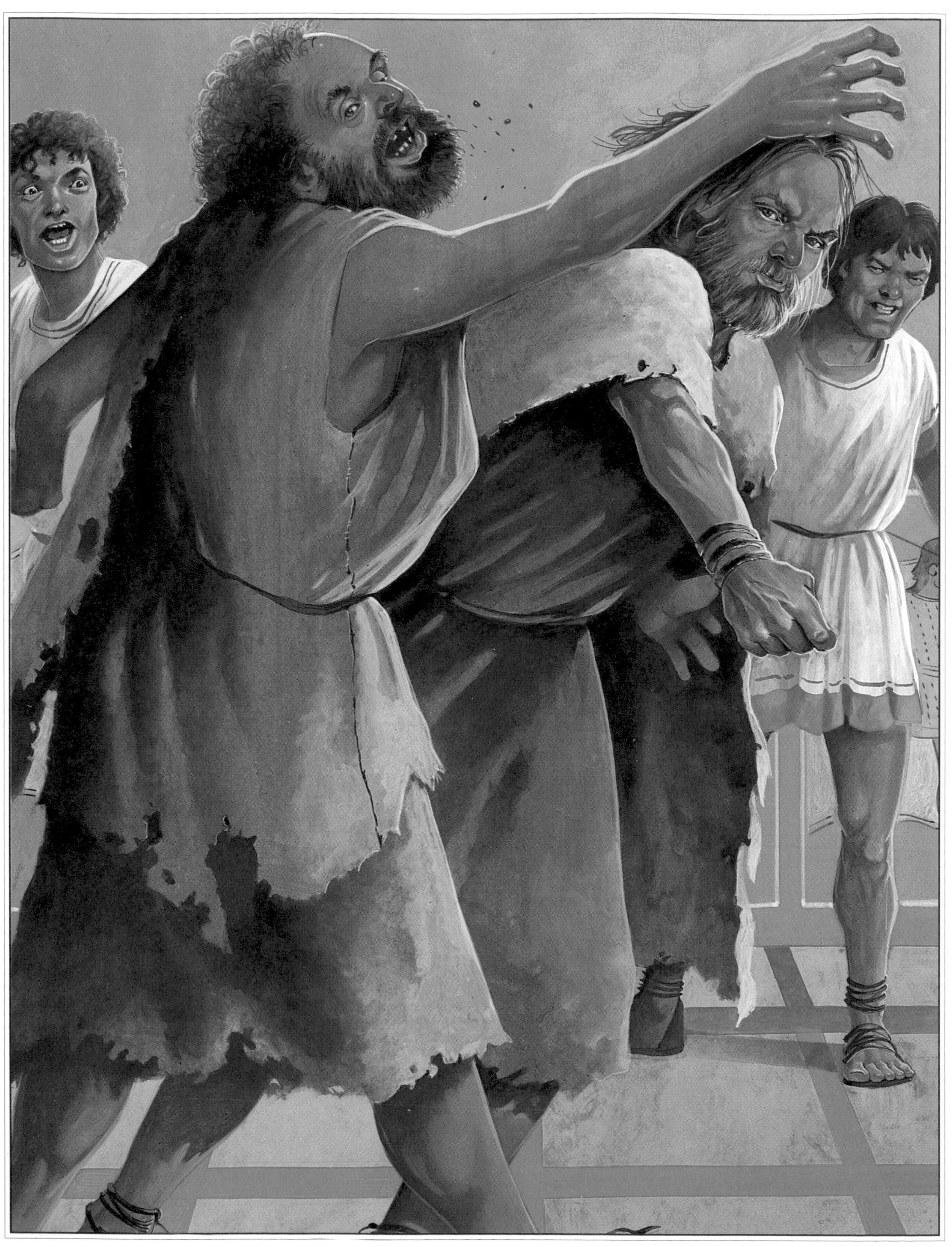

. . . and landed a light punch on the beggar's left temple

Suddenly the whole hall was in uproar, with suitors shouting and hurling food, furniture and plates at each other.

"STOP THIS AT ONCE!" bellowed Telemachus above the din. His voice was so loud that it cut through the noise and stopped the suitors in their tracks.

"I've had enough!" Telemachus roared, his eyes darting wildly. "You can all go and stay with your friends in Ithaca tonight. Get out of my palace. GET OUT!"

The suitors were so surprised that they dropped the things they were holding and started wandering sheepishly over to the door. Only Antinous tried to answer back.

"Who do you think you are?" he barked at Telemachus. "Hey! All of you! Don't take orders from him! " But the hall was emptying. Furiously, Antinous followed. On his way out, he turned around and said, "You needn't think we're going for good. We'll be back tomorrow. And we're staying until your mother gets her act together and makes a decision." With that, he stomped off.

"Well done." Ulysses squeezed his son's trembling shoulder.

"It's no use, though," Telemachus sighed, as the last suitor left. "They'll be back first thing in the morning."

"Good," said Ulysses. "I'd hate them to get away with it, after all they've put you through. But for now, you've given us a chance to hide those weapons." He scanned the hall. Tables were overturned, food was splattered across the marble walls. "The servants can tidy up. We'll lock the weapons in the storeroom."

The weapons were all locked away, except for a few which Telemachus had hidden in a wooden chest by the door. Telemachus had gone to bed, and Ulysses was sitting in the darkened hall when Penelope and the nurse, Eurycleia, came down.

"Where is everybody?" asked the queen.

"All gone, my lady," said Ulysses through the darkness. "The young master of the house has sent them packing. But I'm here to see you, as you requested."

Eurycleia lit a lamp and Ulysses's old, wrinkled face flickered into view.

"Old man," said Penelope gently. To Ulysses, she looked every bit as beautiful as she had on the day he'd left for Troy, nineteen years before. But he couldn't touch her, or tell her who he was.

"First of all, I must apologize for the rudeness of our guests," Penelope said. "I must take responsibility, as they're my suitors. But I wish they were gone!" she added, looking angrily away. "I wish my husband would come home and reclaim his throne!" Regaining her composure, she carried on, "And that's what I wanted to ask you about. You move around a lot. Have you ever. . . I mean, did you by any chance hear anything? About him? Ulysses, that is?"

"Well. . ." began Ulysses, his brain racing. "Yes ~ yes, I did."

Penelope took Ulysses's wrinkled hands in hers. "Please, please tell me all you know," she begged. "You may name your reward!"

"No reward, my lady," Ulysses replied. "I'll tell you all I can. I knew Ulysses at Troy. And there he fought like a demon, like a mighty whirlwind! And his cunning was second to none. Why, he almost won the Trojan War on his own!"

"And did he escape?" asked Penelope.

"Oh, yes. But he was doomed to wander the world, chased by murderous monsters, trapped by wicked witches, pounded by perilous sea storms ~ until he came to the land of Phaeacia."

"Phaeacia! But's that's not far from here at all!" gasped Penelope.

"And word has it that he's coming back very soon," Ulysses added.

Penelope's hand went up to her mouth. "Really?" she asked, quietly.

"Yes," said Ulysses, almost in a whisper. "In fact, he's very close."

"Oh!" Penelope looked troubled. "But how do I know you're talking about the real Ulysses? Describe him for me."

"Well," said Ulysses, "he's tall, and very handsome. And when I knew him, he had this brooch ~ pure gold, with an image of a hound catching a deer. Beautiful, it was."

"That's him!" cried Penelope. "I gave him that brooch when he left for Troy!" She started pacing the room. "I had such a strange dream. . ." she went on. "I dreamed that a huge eagle flew down and killed all the fat white geese in the courtyard. What do you think that means?" She turned to Ulysses, her face a mask of uncertainty.

"It means, my lady," Ulysses said patiently, "that Ulysses will descend on this house, and kill the suitors who have been abusing his property, harassing his wife and threatening his son."

But Penelope ignored him. She was now thinking about something completely different. "I know what I'll do," she said decisively. "My husband was a great archer. His bow is still in the storeroom. He was the only person in Ithaca strong enough to string it. For practice, he used to shoot a bronze-tipped arrow through the handles of twelve axes, all stuck in the ground in a row.

"I'm going to hold a competition," she declared. "I'm going to get that bow out, and let the suitors try to shoot through the axes, as my husband used to. If any one of them can do it, well, I'll *think* about marrying him."

Little did Penelope realize that Athene had given her this idea.

"You must do as your heart commands, my lady," said Ulysses, smiling to himself.

Penelope turned to him. "Thank you, sir, for your wise words," she said. But she was distracted. She was thinking about the competition. It was a good plan, but what if one of the suitors did succeed?

"I'm going to bed now," she said. "I'll have a mattress put down for you here in the hall. The servants will bring you some blankets." Her voice echoed as she disappeared into the darkness of the hall.

CHAPTER NINETEEN

THE FINAL CHALLENGE

Ulysses woke with the dawn. No one was about in the hall. He went outside, feeling the cold, dewy grass on his bare feet, and looked up at the pinkish sky.

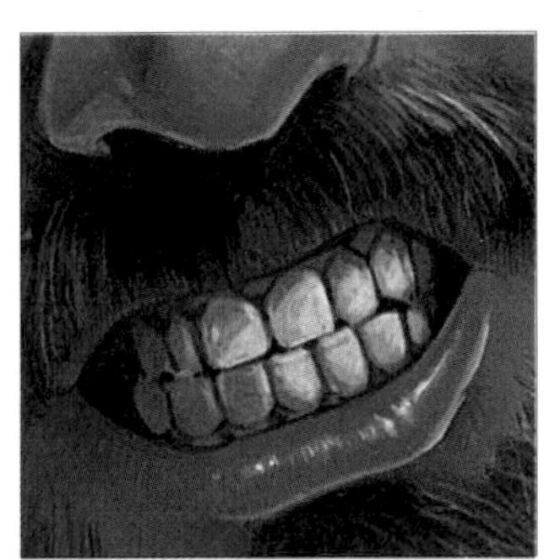

"Zeus," he whispered. "Please, send me a sign. If today is the day when I will battle with the suitors ~ send me a sign."

A rumbling sound began in the far north. It grew and grew until a huge roaring noise echoed around the whole sky, and culminated in a thunderous CRASH! right above the palace. Then, all was silent.

Ulysses hugged himself, hopping from one foot to another and clenching his fists in excitement. "Yes!" he whispered. "Yes! Today's the day!"

Telemachus was right that the suitors wouldn't be away for long. By the time he'd dressed and come downstairs, there they all were, lying around the palace drinking.

But Amphinomus wasn't happy. He couldn't help thinking about the mysterious warning the old beggar had given him the day before. What had he said about Ulysses? *He's very close indeed* ~ that was it.

Amphinomus plucked up his courage and strode over to Antinous. "Hello," he said. "Just came by to talk." He sat down beside Antinous and twiddled his thumbs.

"What do you want, Amphinomus?" snapped Antinous. "Spit it out."

"Well. . . it's about that plan t-to kill Telemachus," stuttered Amphinomus. "I mean, er, perhaps we shouldn't—"

"Oh, I see," mocked Antinous loudly, so that several other suitors looked round. "Chicken, are we? Chicken, Amphinomus?" Antinous stood up and started flapping his elbows and squawking. "Oh, count me out!" he squealed. "I'm chicken!"

"No, you don't understand," said Amphinomus hurriedly. "You see, the thing is, that old beggar. . ."

"Yes, that disgusting old cripple," snarled Antinous, "I'd forgotten about him."

"I vote we kill them both," said Eurymachus.

"Excellent idea!" said Antinous. He turned to the crowd of suitors that had gathered around him, and said, "Listen, I've got a plan. All we need to do is make sure Penelope's out of the way, surround Telemachus in the hall, and—"

"Look!" shrieked Amphinomus, pointing above their heads.

The suitors all looked up. There, only feet above them, a huge, black eagle was grappling with a terrified pigeon. The suitors could feel the wind from the eagle's beating wings as it tore viciously at the pigeon's neck with its talons. Feathers swirled down, a few of them landing on Antinous's head. Then the eagle swerved off to the left and flapped away, the pigeon hanging limply in its claws.

"Antinous!" gasped Amphinomus, hardly able to speak for trembling.

"Y-you know what that was! An omen! That eagle must have stood for Ulysses, and that pigeon. . . Antinous, that was *you!*"

"Shut up, you soppy idiot!" Antinous raged. "We can do without your pathetic, stupid omens! It was an eagle, that's all! And if you open your mouth one more time, Amphinomus, I'll—"

"Hello, boys!"

Penelope had appeared on the palace steps. Flanked by maids, she stood erect, tall and beautiful, her silver-embroidered gown gleaming in the sun. The suitors all turned around and smiled at the queen. Each of them wanted Penelope to like him best.

"You'll be pleased to hear," Penelope announced, "that I've decided to hold a competition to choose a husband. I'd like you all to assemble in the courtyard." And with that, she and her maids glided back inside.

"See," mocked Antinous as they all filed through the hall into the courtyard. "Ulysses is dead ~ he must be, or she wouldn't be doing this, would she?"

Penelope unlocked the storeroom using her set of keys, and stepped into the gloom. There seemed to be a lot more weapons in here than she remembered, but she soon found what she was looking for ~ her husband's great bow. It was hanging on the wall, covered in a thick layer of dust. She took it down carefully. It was heavy, and almost as tall as she was.

For a moment, Penelope stood in the dank, sunless storeroom, clutching the bow.

"Madam?" called a maid from outside. "Are you all right?"

"Yes," said Penelope quickly. "Yes, I am." She started picking out old axes and handing them back to the servants at the door. Then they set off for the courtyard. The door to the storeroom slowly creaked shut.

"Now then," said Penelope, as the maids piled up the axes on the grass. "This bow belonged to my dear husband. He could shoot an arrow through the handles of twelve axes, all in a row. So, gentlemen, I challenge you to do the same. If any of you can prove yourselves as strong and clever as my husband. . . " She couldn't quite bring herself to say it. "We'll see," she said, finally, then went and sat on a throne brought outside by her servants.

Standing at the edge of the crowd, Telemachus glanced at his father. "Is this all right?" he asked in an urgent whisper. "I mean, what if one of them does it?"

"They won't," said Ulysses. "Athene's behind this. Just keep a straight face, and wait for my instructions."

The suitors set to work ramming the axe handles into the ground. Then they started arguing over who should go first.

"Youngest first!" shouted Leocritus. "No, let's do it in alphabetical order!" yelled a suitor named Agelaus.

"What about the order we sit in for dinner?" asked Amphinomus. No one had any better ideas, so Leodes was first to try.

Trying to look like an experienced archer, Leodes strolled over to the bow and picked it up. The first job was to string it, as the old bowstring was worn and frayed. Trying to grip the huge bow with his knees, Leodes reached up to loop the new string over the other end. But it was just too short. To tie it on, Leodes had to bend the bow, but however hard he tried, he couldn't keep it bent and tie the string at the same time.

The suitors slapped their thighs and roared with laughter as Leodes grappled hopelessly with the bow. Eventually, after it had sprung out of his hands and hit him on the nose, he flung the bow on the grass and stormed, red-faced, back into the crowd.

"Who's next?" called Telemachus, trying not to look smug. Leocritus came forward. He was even younger and slighter than Leodes, and he was having an equally hard time with the bow, when Telemachus saw Eumacus, the swineherd, approaching the palace gates. With him was Philoetius, who looked after the cows. Each of them led several animals, ready for the evening meal.

Telemachus slipped out of the courtyard to greet them. Ulysses hobbled after him. "You'd better tie the animals up around the back,"

said Telemachus. "They're having an archery competition in there. Whoever wins might be getting married soon."

"What, my lady's going to pick one of those young layabouts!" gasped Eumaeus.

"Eumaeus," Ulysses interrupted. "And you, sir, what's your name?"

"Philoetius," said the young cowherd.

Ulysses glanced at Telemachus, then beckoned all three men over. "I want to ask you something. If Ulysses was here ~ if he arrived right now to fight those suitors ~ what would you do? Would you be on his side? Would you fight for him?"

"I would, sir," said Philoetius. "Though he left before I was born, and folk say he'll never be seen around these parts again, I know he's our rightful leader, sir."

"Of course I would, what do you take me for?" grumbled Eumaeus. "But he's not coming back, is he? We've waited and waited. I dare say he's been dead for years."

"That's where you're wrong," said Ulysses. "Here I am. It's me. Ulysses."

"What?" said Philoetius.

"No, it's not," said Eumaeus. "You're not Ulysses. You're an old man, he'd be. . . now then, how old was he when you were born, Telemachus?"

"This is my father!" Telemachus told the two farmers. "He is back. But he's in disguise. Athene disguised him as a beggar."

"Why?" said Philoetius.

"Nonsense," snorted Eumaeus, "he's pulling your leg!"

"I am Ulysses!" said Ulysses through gritted teeth.

"Prove it, then," said Philoetius boldly.

Ulysses pulled up the rags covering his legs, and showed his right thigh to Eumaeus. "Look," he said. "I got this scar chasing wild boars at my grandfather's house, didn't I?"

In disbelief, Eumaeus dropped his rope tether. The pigs started to wander off.

"And I know all about you, Eumaeus. My father Laertes rescued you when you were a boy, from a trading ship that had kidnapped you from Syrie, didn't he?"

"Ulysses. . ." said Eumaeus in a barely audible whisper, his eyes filling with tears. He gripped Philoetius's arm. "It is him! It is him! Oh, my dear lord and master, the gods be praised!" And he threw his arms around Ulysses's neck.

"There's no time to lose," said Ulysses, when Eumaeus stopped weeping. "I intend to make my move while the competition is going on. Are you really prepared to fight with me?"

"I'd give my life!" wailed Eumaeus.

"No need for that," said Ulysses kindly, "as Athene is on our side. If you follow my instructions, I'm confident of our success. Philoetius, you are to bolt all the doors, locking us inside. Tie the main gates shut with a rope, then join us in the courtyard.

"Eumaeus, I want you to get the maidservants out of the way. They must be locked safely in their quarters. Then come to the courtyard. When I ask if I can have a try with the bow, fetch it and bring it to me ~ whatever the suitors say.

"And you, Telemachus," said Ulysses at last, turning to his son, "your job is to make sure your mother is out of the way too. She must be safe in her room before the battle begins.

"Then, when I give the signal, I want you to leap up onto the steps leading from the courtyard into the hall. From there we'll begin our attack.

"And none of you breathe a word to anyone that I'm here."

While the others raced off to carry out their instructions, Ulysses and Telemachus strolled back to the courtyard. The suitors were sitting around watching Eurymachus struggle with the bow. Behind him sat Penelope, with a satisfied smile on her face.

"Oh, so there you are, Telemachus!" taunted Antinous. "Still hanging around with that smelly beggar?"

"Hello, Antinous," replied Telemachus calmly. "How's it going?"

"Ow!" shouted Eurymachus as the bow sprang from his grasp and smacked him in the forehead. "It's useless! Everyone's given it a try, but no one can even string it! It's embarrassing. What will people say when they hear what weaklings we are compared to Ulysses? We'll never live it down!"

"Excuse me," began Ulysses, stepping forward. "But could I try?"

"You?" gaped Antinous incredulously. "You? You don't really think that Penelope's going to marry *you*, do you?"

"No," said Ulysses, "I don't think that will be necessary. I just wanted to try my hand at it, that's all."

"Go on, let him try," said Eurymachus, who was bored.

"No way!" Antinous stood up. "Why doesn't that stupid tramp stop bothering us, anyway?" But underneath his rude exterior, Antinous was thinking about how easily the beggar had knocked out Irus in the fight. What if he was strong enough to handle the bow?

"Antinous!" boomed Penelope. "I'm in charge here. Let the old man try. Of course I'm not going to marry him. If he meets the challenge, I'll give him a new set of clothes."

"No, I'*m* in charge!" said Telemachus, striding over to Penelope. "And I suggest, Mother, that you go to your rooms before this gets out of hand."

Penelope looked aghast at her son for speaking to her so rudely.

"Please," Telemachus begged her under his breath. "I'm sorry. I'll explain later."

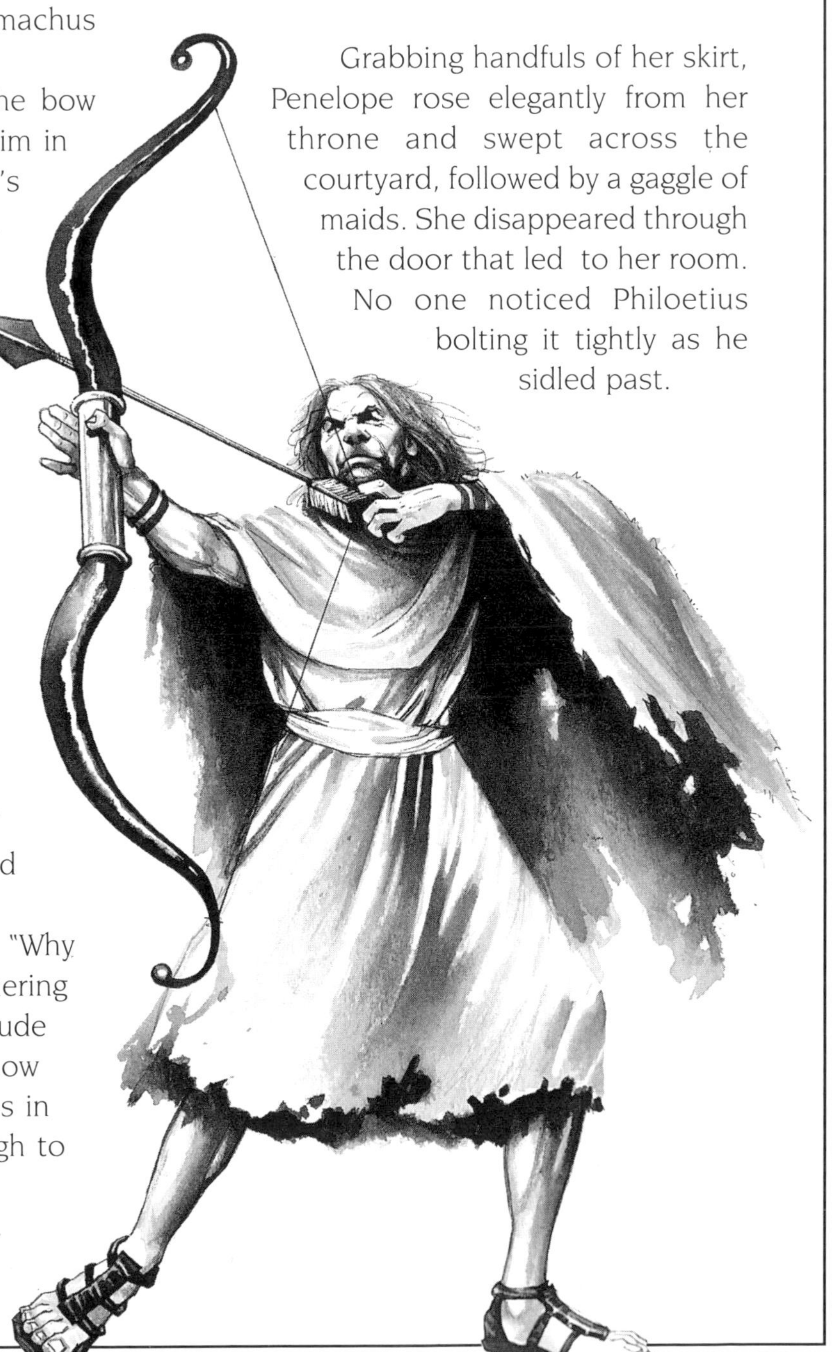

Grabbing handfuls of her skirt, Penelope rose elegantly from her throne and swept across the courtyard, followed by a gaggle of maids. She disappeared through the door that led to her room. No one noticed Philoetius bolting it tightly as he sidled past.

Meanwhile, Eumaeus had picked up the bow and arrows. The suitors jeered and spat at him as he plodded up the courtyard and handed the weapons over to his master.

In a couple of seconds, Ulysses had expertly strung his old bow and was flexing it back and forth. The suitors stared.

"Stand back," he said in his old man's croak. "Let me get a good shot."

The suitors shuffled back a few steps.

Ulysses selected an arrow. Its bronze tip gleamed in the sun as he laid it against the bow, drew back the bowstring, and aimed.

There was silence. Then a loud Twanggg! and a whooosh! as the arrow whizzed away

from the bow, and a series of satisfying splintering noises as it sliced right through the middle of the handle of every single axe in the row.

Antinous suddenly went pale. Some of the suitors were about to cheer, when they noticed that Ulysses was in the process of reloading the bow with another deadly arrow. As he did so, he glanced meaningfully at Telemachus, Eumaeus and the cowherd, Philoetius, who followed him onto the marble steps.

"What's going on?" shrieked Antinous desperately.

"Oh no!" wailed Amphinomus.

THWACK! Ulysses's second arrow had hit its target.

Antinous lay sprawling and writhing on the grass, his legs kicking violently. The arrow had torn right through his neck, pinning him to the ground. Blood spurted from the wound and soaked the grass around his head.

"Aaaaaaaeeeurggghhh!" he groaned. He wriggled, helplessly, one last time. Then he lay still.

A sea of pale, terrified faces surrounded the men on the steps.

"L-look what you've done now," said Eurymachus, trembling. "You'd better put the bow down. That was a foolish mistake."

"It wasn't a mistake," said Ulysses.

At that moment, Athene made his rags fall away and replaced them with a tunic and a gleaming breastplate. She changed his hair from wispy white back to thick, glossy black. She pumped up his muscles, smoothed away his wrinkles, and made him taller than ever.

"I'M BACK!" roared Ulysses.

"I'M BACK!"

Frantically, the suitors hunted around for any weapons they could find. But there were none in the courtyard, and the door to the hall was blocked by Ulysses. Panicking, they backed up against the locked gates, each one trying to hide behind the others.

"Don't just stand there cowering and waiting to be killed!" shouted Eurymachus. "He's going to shoot us all unless we do something! I say we fight!" He drew a small dagger, the only weapon he was carrying, and rushed at Ulysses.

WHOOSH! The third arrow shot through the air and thudded into Eurymachus's chest. He gulped and staggered back, and the dagger fell, uselessly, from his slackening hand. Finally, he crashed into the row of splintered axes and crumpled into a twitching heap.

"Telemachus," whispered Ulysses, "bring the weapons from the storeroom."

Telemachus tiptoed away as the suitors, following Eurymachus's example, began to edge forward, clutching their daggers. While he rummaged desperately in the chest where he had hidden the weapons, Telemachus heard more arrows swishing through the air, more screams and more thuds. When he hurried back, carrying helmets, spears and shields, he could see many more bodies scattered across the grass.

"Quick! I'm nearly out of arrows!" panted Ulysses as he grabbed a spear. Eumaeus and Philoetius, who had been standing on the steps wide-eyed with panic, tied on their helmets and took a spear and a shield each.

"What's going on? Father, look!" shouted Telemachus as six suitors advanced on them, each carrying a long, silver-tipped spear. "Where did they get those from?"

"The storeroom, of course!" yelled Leodes. "Very sneaky of you to hide our weapons. But you forgot to lock the door!"

At that moment the suitors flung their weapons, and a shower of spears hurtled through the air. But Athene had not deserted Ulysses. She redirected the spears away from their targets, and they clattered against the marble walls of the courtyard. "Give them the same back," Athene whispered.

The four men drew back their spears and hurled them as one into the crowd. Athene directed each spear into the heart of a suitor. The other suitors retreated in panic, and Ulysses and his comrades rushed forward to retrieve their weapons.

"Again," whispered Athene. Ulysses felt a new surge of energy suffuse his body as he drew back his spear a second time. And again, Athene sent all four weapons whistling through the air to their targets, but in the same instant, six more spears came speeding back at them.

This time, one of the suitors' weapons sliced through the flesh of Telemachus's right arm. But taking his spear again in his left hand, he hurled it with all his strength along with the others, and four more suitors fell to the ground.

"I beg you, save me!" One of the few men left alive in the courtyard hurried up to the steps. "It's me, Medon, the herald. I was your loyal servant, sir, but the suitors forced me to serve them! Please. . ."

"You served my enemies!" roared Ulysses, dizzy with bloodlust and adrenalin. Grabbing Medon by the hair, he pulled out a gleaming dagger.

"Father! No!" Telemachus wrestled with Ulysses's arm. "He's innocent! Spare him ~ and poor Phemius, our minstrel, who was forced to play for them!" Phemius, hearing his name, crawled out from behind a pile of bodies, soaked in blood. Telemachus took both men by the arm and led them into the safety of the hall.

When Telemachus came back out, clutching his bleeding arm, there was silence. Ulysses was leaning on the steps, breathlessly wiping his face with his sweaty arm. Eumaeus was standing and staring into space, shellshocked, his blood-stained spear dangling loosely in his grasp. Philoetius sat a little way off, his face in his hands. The whole courtyard was filled with dead bodies, spreadeagled on the grass, sprawled against the walls and lying broken on the steps. The sickening stench of blood filled the air.

Telemachus approached his father and tried to touch his shoulder. Ulysses looked away from him and sat down heavily on the step. "Find my wife," he mumbled.

Telemachus unbolted the door and sprinted up the steps to Penelope's chambers. As he threw open the door, Penelope and her maids screamed.

Penelope stood up and came over to him, her face a terrified mask. She touched the blood on his arm. "What's been going on? Telemachus?"

"My father is home," said Telemachus, wiping his lip. "There's. . . well, there's been a battle. I think you should come downstairs and see him."

When the crowd of women filed out of the doorway into the bright sunlight of the courtyard, they gasped in horror at the terrible sight. Then, seeing Ulysses, they began to shout and cheer, and eagerly surrounded him, asking him questions and trying to touch him. Only Penelope stood alone on the other side of the courtyard, staring quietly at the man in the middle of the crowd.

"This isn't a time for celebration!" said Ulysses at last. His voice was stern. "These men fell victims to the hand of the gods, and must be buried. Carry out the bodies and clean up the courtyard!" The servants drew back from him in awe, and turned to their gruesome work.

Ulysses gazed at Penelope. She stared back. Neither of them spoke.

"Mother. . ." began Telemachus. "Aren't you going to greet my father?"

"Telemachus," she said painfully, holding out her hand to her son. "My heart is numb. I don't know what to say to him."

"It is your husband," said Telemachus kindly. "Don't you want to be alone with him?" Ulysses stared at them anxiously.

"If it is him," said Penelope at last, swallowing hard, "then he'll survive a night alone outside my bedroom, as a test of his love. Tell Eurycleia to move my bed out of the room for him."

"No!" roared Ulysses suddenly. "How can that bed be moved? I built that bedroom myself around a tall olive tree, and made its trunk into one of the bedposts!"

"Ulysses. . ." said Penelope faintly. Now she knew it was him. Her eyes filled with tears. "My husband. . ." Her legs gave way and she crumpled onto the steps as Ulysses bounded forward and threw his arms around her. "My love!" he whispered. The servants and Telemachus crept away into the hall, leaving Ulysses and Penelope alone.

"This way!" called Hermes, the messenger of the gods, clutching his golden wand. Groaning and wailing, weeping and moaning, the ghosts of the suitors floated after him, past the River of Ocean, through the region of dreams, and down into the depths of Hades, dwelling-place of the dead.

"Who's there?" barked Persephone, the Queen of the Underworld, as they approached. "It is Antinous!" groaned the soul of Antinous as it fluttered in through the gates, its face already green with decay, "and my comrades, victims of the brave warrior Ulysses, who has killed us all! Oh, if only I'd listened to Amphinomus. . ."

"He's done it! Ulysses has done it!" The soul of Agamemnon clenched its fists jubilantly. "Well done, Ulysses! I knew he'd come up with the goods! Tell us what happened, then!"

And so the ghosts of Antinous and the others told the dead how Ulysses had returned as a beggar to his own palace, how he had tried to warn the suitors, and how he had fought with Athene's help in the battle that had ended their lives. The soul of Agamemnon twirled around with delight. "Good old Ulysses! He's lost none of his cunning!" it grinned.

"But our families will avenge us!" wailed Antinous's soul. "And Ulysses himself will be down here with us before you know it!"

Outside the royal palace in Ithaca, the families of the dead were gathering. "Come out and show yourself, murderer!" they cried. "Ulysses, you coward! Come out and fight!"

Suddenly, the sky was filled with a pink glow. A figure appeared before them, descending slowly, eyes flashing, a long, shining spear in her grasp. The families shrank back, shading their eyes and gaping in amazement.

"People of Ithaca, Same, Dulichium and Zacynthus!" Athene boomed, her voice echoing around the city. "Justice, not murder, has been done in this city."

The families gazed at the goddess in awe, as the people of Ithaca streamed out of their houses and crowded around the palace to stare at the incredible sight of the goddess hovering in midair in front of the palace.

"There is only one rightful ruler of Ithaca!" she cried, "and he is no coward. He has done battle with monsters and murderers, witches and whirlpools, giants and the looming shadow of death itself, and he has survived to fight the insolent wretches who would have stolen his wife and destroyed his kingdom. Are these the fools you came to defend? They deserved to die; the gods ordained it. Do you wish to fight the murderer?"

She glowed more brightly and terrifyingly than ever. "I am the murderer!" she roared. "Are you going to fight me?"

There was silence. Everyone hoped someone else would dare to speak to the goddess of wisdom and war. But no one did.

"Good," boomed Athene. "Then I suggest you bow down before your king, Ulysses, who has returned after nineteen years, to rule this land as wisely and as well as any god." With that, she shot up into the clouds like a firework.

When Ulysses and Penelope came out of the courtyard gates to find out what was happening, they saw hundreds of people, the people of their country, kneeling before them on the soft, grassy slope that led down from the palace.

Penelope came to the front of the steps, leading her husband by the hand.

"Citizens of Ithaca!" she cried out. "Rise up and greet your king!"

Gradually, falteringly, the people began to stand. The bright light that had accompanied Athene was gone, replaced by normal sunshine. The people took their hands away from their eyes.

Ulysses stepped forward and cleared his throat.

"I have an apology to make," he began. A murmur of surprise spread through the crowd. People strained forward to hear what he had to say.

"Those young men didn't deserve such a terrible end. I did try to warn them ~ but they were stubborn. I am sorry that some of you have lost your sons and brothers. They brought their fate on themselves, but their punishment was far worse than was fitting. It was an act of the gods ~ and that means we must give them a proper burial."

Some of the suitors' relations were weeping quietly. Others hung their heads. Nisus of Dulichium, the father of Amphinomus, came forward.

"Friends, we must accept this apology," he said. "Retaliation won't get us anywhere. Athene was right. We must respect our rightful king." The families of the suitors nodded sadly.

"Now that I am home," continued Ulysses, "I hope we Ithacans can stand together, and put all these horrors behind us. The Trojan War is won. Your rightful king has returned. Peace and prosperity will rule again in Ithaca!"

Now the people let out a huge cheer. "But," shouted Ulysses, raising his hand to quieten them, "if ever I have to leave Ithaca again, while I'm away, power will rest with my wife, Penelope, and my son, Telemachus ~ your future king."

At that moment, Telemachus stepped out of the courtyard gates, blinking in the sunshine. An even bigger roar went up, and the people surged forward and lifted him off his feet, shouting his name and waving and cheering. And in this way, the whole population of the city swarmed down the hill and onto the shore.

There, they knelt to give thanks to the gods. And when the suitors had been buried, they held a huge feast and made sacrifices to Zeus, Hermes, Hera, Apollo, and even to Poseidon ~ and most of all to beautiful Athene, whose wisdom and guidance had brought their leader safely home.

WHO'S WHO IN THE STORIES

Achilles (a-*kill*-eez) Son of Peleus and Thetis. One of the Greek leaders and their best soldier at Troy. Withdraws from the fighting after an argument with Agamemnon, but returns after his friend, Patroclus, is killed while pretending to be him. Kills Hector, and is killed by Paris.

Aegisthus (a-*gis*-thus) Lover of Agamemnon's wife Clytemnestra, and murderer of Agamemnon.

Aeolus (ee-*ole*-us) King of Aeolia and ruler of the winds. He gives Ulysses a bag of winds to help him on his journey.

Agamemnon (ag-a-*mem*-non) King of Mycenae and brother of Menelaus. Commander of the Greek armies. Killed on his return from Troy by his wife Clytemnestra and her lover Aegisthus. Ulysses meets him again when he visits The Land of the Dead.

Agelaus (a-ge-*lay*-us) One of Penelope's suitors.

Ajax (*age*-ax) Greek soldier known for his strength.

Alcinous (al-*sin*-o-us) King of Phaeacia who helps Ulysses get home.

Amphinomus (am-*fin*-o-mus) One of Penelope's suitors.

Andromache (an-*drom*-a-kee) Hector's wife.

Anticleia (an-ti-*clay*-a) Ulysses's mother and wife of Laertes. She dies of grief while Ulysses is away. Ulysses meets her again in The Land of the Dead.

Antinous (an-*tin*-o-us) Leader of Penelope's suitors.

Aphrodite (aff-ro-*dy*-tee) Goddess of love. Daughter of Zeus. Very beautiful. She helps to bring about the Trojan War by promising Paris that he can marry Helen if he picks her as the fairest of the goddesses. Supports the Trojan side in the war.

Apollo (a-*poll*-o) God of the Sun, healing, music and the arts. Son of Zeus and brother of Artemis. Sends a plague on the Greek army after they steal Chryseis. Supports the Trojan side in the war.

Arete (a-*ret*-ay) Queen of Phaeacia, wife of Alcinous and mother of Nausicaa.

Argus (*ar*-gus) Ulysses's dog.

Artemis (*ar*-tem-iss) Goddess of hunting. Daughter of Zeus and sister of Apollo. Demands sacrifice of Iphigenia, but relents at the last minute.

Athene (a-*thee*-nee) Goddess of wisdom and war, daughter of Zeus and step-daughter of Hera. Supports the Greek side in the Trojan War.

Astyanax (as-*tee*-a-nax) Hector's baby son.

Automedon (or-*tom*-a-don) Achilles's chariot-driver.

Balius (*bal*-ee-us) *see* **Xanthus**

Briseis (briss-*ay*-iss) Achilles's servant girl, taken by Agamemnon to replace his own girl, Chryseis. This leads to an argument between the two men and Achilles's withdrawal from the fighting.

Calchas (*kal*-cass) A soothsayer (someone who can see into the future) who accompanies the Greek army to Troy.

Calypso (ka-*lip*-so) Nymph (a being who is half goddess, half human) who holds Ulysses prisoner for seven years on her remote island, Ogygia, until Zeus orders her to release him.

Cassandra (kass-*an*-dra) Daughter of Priam and Hecuba, and sister of Hector, Paris and Polydorus. Has psychic powers but is usually ignored.

Charybdis (ka-*rib*-dis) A deadly whirlpool.

Chiron (*kee*-ron) A centaur (half man and half horse), renowned for his wisdom. He taught Achilles and other Greek heroes.

Chryseis (kriss-*ay*-iss) Daughter of Chryses. She is stolen by Agamemnon to be his servant girl, but returned later to appease Apollo.

Chryses (*kry*-seez) Priest at one of Apollo's temples. Father of Chryseis.

Circe (*sir*-see) Minor goddess and powerful sorceress who turns some of Ulysses's men into pigs and then entraps him for a year.

Clytemnestra (kly-tum-*nes*-tra) The wife of Agamemnon and mother of Iphigenia, she kills Agamemnon on his return from the Trojan War.

Cyclops (*sy*-klops) Plural: **Cyclopes** (*sy*-klo-peez) A type of giant with one eye. Ulysses enrages the sea god Poseidon by blinding the Cyclops Polyphemus, who is Poseidon's son.

Demeter (de-*may*-tuh) Goddess of children and crops.

Demodocus (de-*mod*-o-kus) A bard (singing poet) at the court of King Alcinous in Phaeacia.

Diomedes (dy-o-*mee*-deez) One of the Greek leaders.
Echeneus (e-ke-*nay*-us) Wise old lord at the court of King Alcinous in Phaeacia.
Elpenor (el-*pen*-or) Young member of Ulysses's crew who dies by falling off the roof of Circe's cottage. Ulysses meets him again in The Land of the Dead.
Eris (*air*-iss) Goddess of spite. She helps to cause the Trojan War by bringing the golden apple to the wedding of Peleus and Thetis, in order to cause trouble because she hasn't been invited.
Eugenie (yoo-*jee*-nee) Friend of Nausicaa, the Phaeacian princess.
Eumaeus (yoo-*may*-us) Ulysses's faithful swineherd in Ithaca.
Eurycleia (yoo-ri-*clay*-a) Penelope's chief lady-in-waiting.
Eurylochus (yoo-*ril*-o-kus) Ulysses's most senior crew member.
Eurymachus (yoo-*rim*-a-kus) One of Penelope's suitors.
Hector (*hek*-tuh) Leader of Trojan army. Kills Achilles's friend, Patroclus, and is killed by Achilles.
Hecuba (*hek*-yoo-ba) Queen of Troy, wife of Priam, and mother of Hector, Paris, Polydorus and Cassandra.
Helen (*hell*-un) Wife of Menelaus and lover of Paris. The most beautiful woman in the world. She had many admirers, including Ulysses, before her marriage. Menelaus starts the Trojan War after Helen runs away to Troy with Paris, who has been visiting Menelaus's kingdom. At the end of the war, her husband takes her back.
Hephaestus (heff-*eest*-us) Blacksmith of the gods. Makes splendid shield, sword and helmet for Achilles.
Hera (*hee*-ra) Queen of the gods and wife of Zeus. She is very jealous of Zeus's dealings with other women and goddesses. Supports the Greek side in the war.
Hermes (*her*-meez) Son of Zeus and messenger of the gods, he also leads dying people down into the Land of the Dead.
Hesione (hess-*eye*-on-ee) Sister of Priam, captured by the Greeks.
Idaius (id-*ay*-us) Priam's wagon driver on his journey to the Greek camp to ask Achilles for Hector's body.
Ino (*ee*-no) A minor sea goddess.
Iphigenia (if-ij-a-*nee*-a) Daughter of Agamemnon and Clytemnestra. Almost sacrificed to Artemis by her father in order to make the wind blow so that the Greek ships can set sail, but saved at the last minute and sent to be a priestess at one of Artemis's temples.
Irus (*eye*-rus) An Ithacan beggar.
Laertes (lay-*er*-teez) Ulysses's father and husband of Anticleia. King of Ithaca before Ulysses.
Leocritus (lay-*o*-crit-us) One of Penelope's suitors.
Leodes (lay-*oh*-deez) One of Penelope's suitors.
Lotus-eaters (*lo*-tuss eaters) People who live on the fruit of the lotus plant, which makes them forget about everything except wanting to eat more of the fruit.
Lycomedes (ly-*com*-a-deez) King of Skyros, the island where Thetis hides Achilles from the Greeks.
Medon (*med*-on) Herald (servant who makes announcements) at Ulysses's palace.
Melantho (me-*lan*-tho) Maid at Ulysses's palace in Ithaca.
Menelaus (me-ne-*lay*-us) King of Sparta, brother of Agamemnon, husband of Helen and one of the Greek leaders in the Trojan War. He declares war on Troy when Helen runs away with Paris.
Mentes (*men*-teez) Name assumed by Athene when she first visits Telemachus.
Mentor (*men*-tor) A friend of Ulysses, and the name assumed by Athene when she goes with Telemachus to look for Ulysses.
Nausicaa (no-*zik*-ay-a) Princess of Phaeacia, daughter of King Alcinous and Queen Arete. She finds Ulysses after he is washed up on the Phaeacian shore, and invites him to her palace.
Nereus (*nee*-ryoos) A sea god, father of Thetis.
Nestor (*nes*-tor) King of Pylos, and one of the Greek leaders in the Trojan War.
Nisus (*nee*-sus) Father of Amphinomus (who is one of Penelope's suitors).
Noemon (no-*ay*-mon) Young Ithacan who lends Telemachus a ship.
Nymphs (*nimfs*) Demigoddesses, (only one parent is a god or goddess), spirits of water, trees and mountains.
Palamedes (pa-la-*mee*-deez) Greek soldier. Goes to Ithaca to track down Ulysses and tricks him into agreeing to join the army bound for Troy.
Pandarus (*pan*-da-rus) Trojan soldier. Spurred on by Athene, he fires an arrow at Menelaus, thus breaking a truce and causing the war to continue.

Paris (*pa*-riss) Son of Priam and Hecuba. Brother of Hector, Polydorus and Cassandra. The gods predicted at his birth that he would bring destruction to Troy, so his parents abandoned him on Mount Ida, where he was rescued by shepherds. Ordered by Zeus to choose the fairest of the three goddesses Hera, Athene and Aphrodite, he picks Aphrodite. In return she promises him the most beautiful woman in the world as his wife. He returns to Troy and is welcomed by his parents. On a visit to Greece he falls in love and runs away with Menelaus's wife, Helen (the most beautiful woman in the world). This leads to the Trojan War, which eventually causes the destruction of Troy. Paris is not particularly brave during the war and is killed at the end when the Greeks invade the city.

Patroclus (pa-*tro*-klus) Greek soldier, comrade and best friend of Achilles. Goes into battle instead of Achilles, and is killed by Hector.

Peisistratus (pay-*zis*-tra-tus) Son of King Nestor. He accompanies Telemachus to Sparta on his search for Ulysses.

Peleus (*pee*-lyoos) King of Phthia, husband of Thetis, and father of Achilles.

Penelope (pe-*nell*-o-pee) Queen of Ithaca, wife of Ulysses and mother of Telemachus. When her husband does not return from the Trojan War, she is besieged by admirers, or suitors, who want to marry her because they will then gain possession of the royal palace. She avoids having to marry by saying she has a piece of weaving to finish first. She weaves all day and then unpicks her work at night, so it is never finished. Her trick is found out, and she is about to give in when Ulysses returns at the last minute.

Persephone (per-*seff*-o-nee) Goddess of death and guardian of The Land of the Dead.

Phemius (*fee*-mi-us) Bard (singing poet) at Ulysses's palace in Ithaca.

Philoetius (fill-oh-*ee*-shus) Faithful Ithacan cowherd who helps Ulysses fight the suitors.

Polites (po-*lit*-eez) Member of Ulysses's crew.

Polydorus (poll-ee-*dor*-us) Youngest son of Priam and Hecuba. Killed by Achilles.

Polyphemus (poll-ee-*fee*-muss) The name of the Cyclops whom Ulysses meets and tricks.

Poseidon (poss-*eye*-don) Bad-tempered god of the Sea, brother of Zeus and father of Polyphemus, the Cyclops. He hates Ulysses for injuring his son, and causes trouble for him during his journey.

Priam (*pry*-am) King of Troy, husband of Hecuba, and father of Hector, Paris, Polydorus and Cassandra.

Proteus (*proh*-ti-us) The Old Man of the Sea, a minor sea god.

Scylla (*sill*-a) A man-eating monster with six heads who consumes some of Ulysses's crew members.

Sinon (*sy*-non) Greek soldier. Pretends to be a deserter when the Greek army sails away from Troy, and tricks the Trojans into bringing the wooden horse into Troy.

Sirens (*sy*-runs) Monsters with the faces of beautiful women. They live on a rocky island and lure men to their doom with their singing.

Sleep God of Sleep.

Suitors (*soot*-ers) The young men who take over Ulysses's palace while he is away, hoping to woo and marry his wife Penelope.

Teiresias (ty-*ree*-zi-as) A soothsayer (fortune-teller) whom Ulysses meets in The Land of the Dead.

Telemachus (te-*lem*-a-kus) Son of Ulysses and Penelope, grandson of Laertes and Anticleia, and future King of Ithaca. He is only a baby when his father leaves for the Trojan War, and is finally reunited with Ulysses nineteen years later.

Thetis (*thay*-tiss) A goddess and sea nymph. Wife of Peleus and mother of Achilles. Tries to make her son immortal when he is a baby by dipping him into the River Styx, but forgets to immerse the heel that she's holding him by.

Ulysses (yoo-*liss*-ees), (also known as Odysseus) (o-*dee*-si-us), King of Ithaca, son of Laertes and Anticleia, husband of Penelope, father of Telemachus. He at first tries to avoid joining the Greek army by pretending to be insane, but this fails. Becomes a great leader at Troy, renowned for his cleverness and cunning. Has the idea for the wooden horse which leads to the destruction of Troy and the Greek victory. It takes him many years to get home from the war and he has numerous mishaps and adventures along the way. On his return to Ithaca he has to defeat all of Penelope's suitors, who have taken over his palace in his absence.

Xanthus and Balius (*zan*-thus and *bal*-ee-us) Achilles's golden horses.

Zeus (zyoos) King of the gods and father of the human race. Ruler of the sky. Married to his sister, Hera. Rules from Mount Olympus and often gets involved in human affairs. All-powerful.

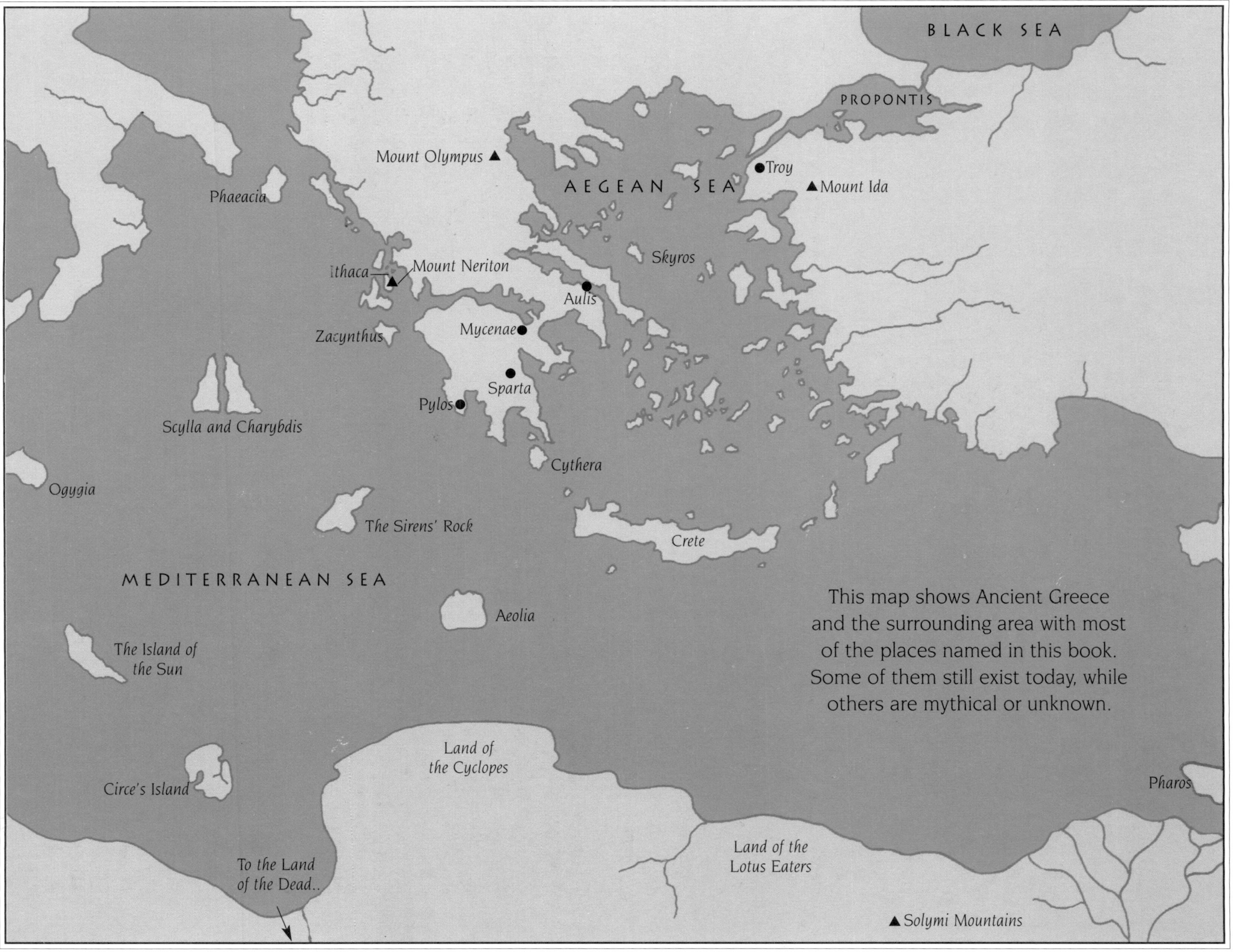
BLACK SEA
PROPONTIS
Mount Olympus
Troy
AEGEAN SEA
Mount Ida
Phaeacia
Skyros
Ithaca
Mount Neriton
Aulis
Mycenae
Zacynthus
Sparta
Pylos
Scylla and Charybdis
Cythera
Ogygia
The Sirens' Rock
Crete
MEDITERRANEAN SEA
Aeolia
This map shows Ancient Greece and the surrounding area with most of the places named in this book. Some of them still exist today, while others are mythical or unknown.
The Island of the Sun
Land of the Cyclopes
Circe's Island
Pharos
Land of the Lotus Eaters
To the Land of the Dead..
Solymi Mountains

WHERE THE STORIES COME FROM

The stories in this book are based mainly on two long, Ancient Greek poems known as *The Iliad* and *The Odyssey*. *The Iliad* tells the story of the last year of the Trojan War, while *The Odyssey* recounts the epic struggle of the hero Odysseus (or Ulysses) to get back home to Ithaca after the war in Troy ends. The Greeks believed the author of these poems was a man called Homer.

Not everyone now agrees that the same person was responsible for both poems, though some think Homer worked on *The Iliad* when he was a young man and *The Odyssey* in old age. Many experts think the poems may have been changed and added to by different poets over the years.

WHO WAS HOMER?

Nobody is sure who Homer really was. He lived at a time when no written records were kept, so there is no account of his life, and his poems were not written down until much later. Seven different Greek cities claim to be the place of his birth. However, most experts now agree that Homer probably lived about 2,700 years ago, in the 8th century BC. He may have come from the island of Chios, or from a Greek colony on the coast of Asia Minor, known as Ionia. It is likely that he recited or sang his poems while playing the lyre, in much the same way as the blind bard Demodocus in *The Odyssey* tells his story about the Trojan War (see page 101). Tradition maintains that Homer was also blind.

Bards were professional poets who learned poems by ear and passed them on to other bards. In this way the ancient legends were handed down from one generation to the next. Even in much later periods, after the poems had been written down, Greek schoolboys had to learn long passages of Homer's poems by heart.

WHO WAS ODYSSEUS?

The stories that Homer told in *The Odyssey* were probably based on tales of voyages made by seamen who explored the Mediterranean coast. It is not known if the character of Odysseus was based on a real person. In the poems, Odysseus is renowned for his luck, cunning, craftiness and quick thinking.

THE LEGEND OF TROY

The legends of the great city of Troy are probably based on a real city which existed many thousands of years ago. Historians think that there was also a real-life Trojan war, in roughly the 12th century BC. So, even if Homer was alive as long ago as 700 or 800 BC, he was writing about events that happened long before his lifetime.

The real city of Troy was situated across the Aegean sea from Greece, in what is now part of Turkey. It is marked on the map on page 159 of this book. You can still visit the area today, and see the ruins of Troy, which have been excavated and preserved.

First published in 1998 by Usborne Publishing Ltd, Usborne House, 83-85 Saffron Hill, London EC1N 8RT, England.
www.usborne.com. First published in America in 1999.